DARKNESS IN HER REACH

CLARE C. MARSHALL

BOOK FOUR
THE SPARKSTONE SAGA

Darkness In Her Reach
Book Four of the Sparkstone Saga
Text Copyright © 2019 Clare C. Marshall
Cover Illustration © Bramasta Aji
Cover Design © David Farrell & Clare C. Marshall
Editing by Leigh Teetzel

FAERY INK PRESS
faeryinkpress.com
Calgary, Alberta
clare@faeryinkpress.com

Other books by Clare C. Marshall:

The Violet Fox Series:
The Violet Fox
The Silver Spear
The Emerald Cloth
The Midnight Tablet

The Sparkstone Saga:
Stars In Her Eyes
Dreams In Her Head
Hunger In Her Bones
Darkness In Her Reach
Voices In Her Song

Other Titles:
Within
Gear and Sea

PART ONE

Tonight, I watched my love die, by the traitor's hand.
I have been trying to get through.
If you are reading this—this is the beginning of the end.

-an excerpt from Sunni's Journal. Verse 4212.

PROLOGUE

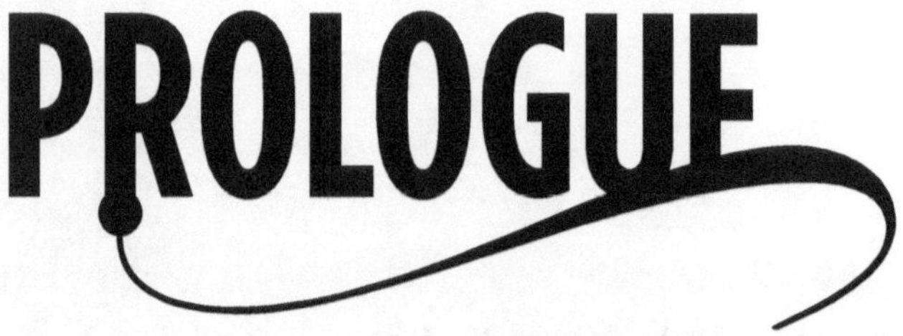

With the large, underground hanger beneath the Sparkstone University Library finally clear, Jadore ventures down the steps and into the dark sanctuary. She swiftly removes the sunglasses from her face and rests them in her nest of black hair. At least down here, her light-sensitive eyes aren't as bothered by the Terran sun. Jadore inhales the lingering smell of old books, an earthy scent she identifies with, and is transported back to her ignorant days in the swamp, when she was surrounded by males, and the urge to reproduce silenced all other thought. She had not been half as beautiful then, yet her influence was strong.

The starcraft hanger had been built to house the Sparkstone Project. Put two pilakee on the Council, allow them to rule with their ludicrous species' drive to collect all knowledge, and what results is a hanger posing as an underground library. Books are for primitives and scientists—not for rulers like Jadore. Rulers use their cunning to blackmail and poison the pilakee and elect more pliable replacements.

She stops at the bottom of the incline, her pointed shoes at the edge of the green glow bathing the room. Squinting, she reaches for her sunglasses, but thinks better of it. She must train herself to be stronger. Relying on primitive technology is for weaklings. The light sources appear artificial, though staring too long at the tall ceiling strains her eyes and her neck. She doesn't remember them in the original schematics, although Councillor F'aqu'wein is a daquin, and their species *does* prefer green lighting, possibly for ridiculous spiritual reasons.

"Who installed those green lights?" Jadore's anger echoes in the space.

No response. The familiar buzz of workers had quieted. She's waited an entire month for this area to be ready since the *incident*. Stray shelves lay toppled to her left and right. Jadore tastes the air with her long, forked tongue. The foul stench of the hafelglob workers lingers, hours old. The lazy liars had assured her that the space was ready for the portal—perhaps they think they can fool her, and do only the minimum to satisfy her demands?

Just because the books have been removed and disposed of doesn't mean there's nothing left to do. On the contrary. Work has just begun. In the distance, an unfinished circular structure stands erect, casting a long shadow in the haunting green light. Surrounding it is a series of dark-coloured consoles, meant to be manned even at this hour. A single steel horseshoe-shaped portal, twenty feet tall—that was what she had come to this planet for. That's where the Hunger was meant to sit. It's where she's meant to step through, and spread the Collective's influence—*Jadore's* influence. An inelegant realization of Campbell's explanation in his treatise, planned out by the Council, and made real under Jadore's hand.

She'd be the first one to step through. Campbell or no Campbell, all that lies beyond is hers for the taking. The Council won't be able to stop her. Not once she reaches phase four.

Jadore grits her teeth. Furious at the hafelglob workers' lack of regard for her twenty-four-hour work schedule, Jadore marches toward the unfinished portal. Abandoned tomes lay haphazardly in her path. Walking on two legs instead of relying on four and a tail is still cumbersome at times—she nearly trips on the mess. So not every book had been removed after all. Had *anyone* bothered to finish their jobs?

A lone hafelglob in human form inputs commands at the console, occasionally looking up to the towering portal, sighing and shaking his head. The creature has picked up too many human mannerisms. So has she.

Ohz's abandoned dark robe rests over the back of a chair; on the hood is a white symbol that looks like an *a*. Who authorized the creation of that? Possibly another Councillor F'aqu'wein move. He often indulges the hafelglob's flair for the dramatic to gain their favour. As if the Collective needs more expenses.

"Where are all the workers?" she demands, adjusting her suit jacket.

Ohz lifts his gaze to her, and turns swiftly to give an apologetic report. "Gone back to their apartments. They heard the Hunger had been—"

"I'm not interested in excuses." She narrows her eyes. They ache. The hafelglob would say nothing if she put her sunglasses back on, but she leaves them off. "The outlined rules dictate that there must be at least three of you working on-site at any given hour. Are there two others here with you?"

"No, Mistress." He sounds more dismissive than remorseful. "Ohz carries the torch for his brothers. Just needed some rest. Have been calibrating."

"The punishment for disobeying a primary working order is suspension of planet-side privileges."

"Yes, Mistress." He glances up at the portal. "Has Mistress seen it this far built?"

Jadore exhales impatiently. "No. I have been waiting for you to clear out the space before stepping down here. I don't have time to oversee every move you blobs make."

"Understandable, Mistress." The hafelglob hunches his shoulders beneath the weight of her insults and slinks around the console, as if that will save him from her wrath. "Does the incompetence and flesh weakness of my brothers and the... uh...recent setbacks..." At least he doesn't openly mention the Hunger's destruction. Thinking about her defeat, Jadore could feel that pathetic creature's flames licking her skin again. It took three whole jars of her cream to restore her beauty to a satisfactory state. She will need more soon, and if the Collective is unable to provide allowance for it because of her failure, she will take matters into her own hands.

She will personally harvest Misty Carter's DNA. No—harvest enough to extract the talent that allowed her to wield such power, and then watch her burn. Yes. That would be fitting. Thank goodness the Collective granted her the power of foresight.

Ohz continues his stammering excuse for a question. "...does this mean the project is no longer on schedule?"

"We are still on schedule." A lie, perhaps, but confidence is an ingredient in beauty, something that must be applied as regularly as her cream. "Tell your brothers to get back here. Now. The Hunger is no longer part of the Sparkstone agenda, and the machine must be altered to accommodate a new power source."

"But that could take—"

Her venomous glare arrests his retort.

"Very...well, Mistress." He wrings his hands like an anxious mouse. "What sort of power source?"

Jadore sweeps her gaze across the vastness of the space. There's enough room here for some sort of solar construct, but this is an underground facility. It will have to be a separate machine with enough power to run an interplanetary—and with any luck, an interdimensional—portal. Humans from off-campus have already poked around about Sparkstone's power usage. Yet another facet of human society the Collective had to isolate and infiltrate to ease suspicion of their activities here. She needs a victory to win back the Council's trust. Constructing another Hunger would take at least a decade. That's too long—she'll be dead by then. She doesn't want to die on this planet. She has to live long enough to return to the swamps and pass on her perfect genes to the next generation—that is, once her task here on Earth is complete.

"Campbell refuses to lend us his skills for the time being, and I cannot coerce something that moves beyond my influence to move with me," Jadore says, more to herself than to the curious hafelglob.

"Mistress...if Ohz can make a suggestion?"

"I suppose." No one else had bothered to make a show of loyalty lately.

"The Crosskey's talents have ripened to a considerable level."

The Crosskey. There's been too much of that moniker as of late. It leaves a bad taste in Jadore's mouth. Like foul water, filled with iron. Campbell would bear down on her if she attacked Ingrid directly. She'd already taken a great risk in the music trailer since he could phase in and out of reality, appear at any moment.

"Could debilitate Crosskey's father again to convince her. Was very effective, Mistress."

True. "She'll be expecting that." They were already monitoring Ingrid's family and close friends. All of them, ideal targets. Yet all of them, not at Sparkstone. More immediate action is needed.

"So how will the Mistress encourage the Crosskey to help with project?"

Ingrid has had plenty of encouragement. In fact, she needs anything *but*. An insidious idea takes root and curls around Jadore's augmented brain. The Collective's greatest achievement, according to her. So why not look to the second-greatest accomplishment to solve this unfortunate predicament?

"Tell Agailya to stop by my office," she says, looking up to the portal. "Effective immediately, the vitaphage dissemination project is now under my control."

CHAPTER 1

Wil looks nervous. I don't need to be a mind reader like him to know his thoughts. He should not have come. None of us should be here.

Crammed in the cafeteria like cattle, some of the students at Sparkstone University are more aware of our fates than others. Gone are the rows of tables, the smell of tantalizing drugged food, and the grand piano on the stage before us. A black cloth banner hangs above the stage, flaunting a stark white symbol in the shape of mirrored *u*'s with a vertical line skewering them together. The oppressive smell of newly pressed fabric infiltrates my nose, stronger than the stench of the hundreds of students surrounding me and my friends.

Beside me, Misty crosses her arms and clutches the too-long sleeves of her dark, woollen sweater. She doesn't like crowds. "I feel like they're going to kill us. All of us."

The same thought had occurred to me. But here at Sparkstone, nothing is as it seems. Many of the students have budding superpowers. Those who control the university, an alien group called the Collective, want to harvest our abilities and use them for their own scientific, nefarious purposes.

Jia sweeps her hair around her left shoulder, attempting to cover the disfiguring, lightning-shaped scars down her face. "Then why leave the windows intact? It's not properly sealed. They can't gas us."

Misty sends a furtive glance to the only way out other than the crowded set of doors. "I could blast through."

"I guess glass shards in the face are a small price to pay for immediate escape," I say.

I can barely believe we're having this conversation. Or that we've given the scenario this much thought.

"The best way out is still teleportation," Misty says, raising her perfect eyebrows at me.

Teleportation is my superpower. One I'm just learning to control. I've used it successfully a handful of times now, but on nearly every occasion, I've lost large chunks of time, arriving hours or even days later. And then there was the time I transported into the event horizon of a black hole. That was not fun.

"Yeah, let me know if you need to get into outer space really fast," I reply.

Misty wrinkles her nose. "No thanks."

"I'll hide us if we need it," Jia says quietly.

It won't do a lot of good, Wil replies telepathically. *The crowd will still feel us moving.*

Jia purses her lips and refuses to acknowledge his presence. After what happened, I don't blame her. She saved his life when we were fighting the Hunger, earning her disfiguring facial scars from Jadore's lightning powers. She's carried a torch for him for a while now, though I can't imagine how she feels now.

That's not the worst of it. Jia has confessed her feelings to Wil, more than once. Yet every time, he's erased her mind of the event to spare them both the embarrassment of rejection. Only Misty and I know the truth, and we have no idea how to tell Jia—or if she'd even want to know.

"You could hide all of us," Misty says to Jia.

"It's too many."

"You cloaked a ship once."

"That was before."

"And what's different now?"

As they argue about Jia's invisibility power, I search for Ethan. Last night, after the demonstration in the quad, we'd exchanged barely more than longing looks before I was surrounded by the eager faces of our peers and their pressing questions: *How can I develop my superpowers? Did you really take those pictures? Can I share those on my Instagram?*

By the time Wil, Jia, Misty, and I had appeased the crowd, Ethan had disappeared. I'd texted, but no response. On one hand, I can't blame him. He'd just discovered the real reason I've withheld my time and my company from him. He is the kind of person that needs space to process things.

On the other hand, I'd barely gotten any sleep as fear gripped my imagination, playing out the worst-of-the-worst scenarios: Jadore breaking into my room and attacking me with her crackling lightning powers. Agailya waking me in bed to tell me how Ethan has died in service of her twisted science experiment. Ethan himself, leaning over me, whispering that he cannot possibly be with me because I've lied too many times. A shiver rips through me, exacerbated as more people crowd into the cafeteria around us.

The stage is no longer empty. Jadore and Agailya are deep in conversation. Agailya wears a belted white skirt and a flowing light blue blouse—but all I can see is the lab coat she wore when she was torturing poor Tilly, a girl from our tutorial group, on the mother ship. Her facial expression is the same as it was that day, when I witnessed her experiment go terribly awry: stoic, patient, and burdened. Jadore is more animated. Her fist slams into her open palm and she points at the door. Her sunglasses, which hide her black alien eyes, seem larger than usual today. She grips a cane in one hand—it's not just for her cover story as a blind professor. A hidden blade waits within to flick out and catch you with its poison. The more I concentrate, the more my nose fills with the scent of her illicit cream—the substance that keeps her looking human. Deeply earthy, the kind of green that swirls into brown-black and drills into the core of a landfill if you lose yourself in the colour. A cough erupts from me. The synesthesia is not as useful a superpower as teleportation and it's at least ten times more annoying.

Four empty chairs line the wall behind them. By the exit, two security guards stand listlessly—definitely hafelglob in disguise. It's hard to discern through the sea of students, but I don't immediately spot other professors, maintenance workers, or other security guards. Two cameras rotate steadily above the exit, searching for insurgents.

Packing us all in a room and leaving only four members of the Collective to manage us?

"Do you know what they're up to?" I ask Wil.

He frowns. "I sense they have nothing to hide here."

Before I can question him further, Jadore takes centre stage. Agailya slips into a seat behind her, tense and stiff. Hands behind her back and without a microphone, Jadore projects her voice over the din of students. "Quiet."

Our voices are vacuumed from us with the one word. Jadore's lips curl into a twisted smile, as if she is Ursula the Sea Witch. "Good. You are here for an important announcement. I am making this on behalf of Mr. Dean, who is still away from campus on business.

"Last night, it came to our attention that some of you held an impromptu demonstration—masquerading as a vigil—as you are under the impression that the university staff has done you wrong. Some of you believe in a conspiracy, and today, we hope to set the record straight on our activities here at Sparkstone."

My heart pounds against my rib cage. Misty balls her fists; I can smell the smoke of her fire in one, and feel the ice from the other. Jia wraps her hand around my forearm, readying her invisibility. Wil, ever-calm, stares unblinking at Jadore.

"You are right," she says simply. "We have attempted to hide our true purpose here. Understand this was for your benefit as well as ours. We could not risk an intelligence breach, not during the most delicate stages of our project. Now that the risk has passed, however, the university board has deemed it time to share the true nature of Sparkstone University."

Impossible. I rub my ears, unwilling to believe them.

"Aliens are real," Jadore says, "and they walk among us."

My throat tightens. Jadore's lips move and I hear the words— yet the air feels thick, dream-like.

"They wear skins like ours. They could be in this crowd now. Pretending to be your friend. They are not your friend."

I look around desperately for Sunni. That's how I know if I'm in a dream. She's always there, telling me to open a door, or materialize objects I've lost.

Sunni is nowhere to be seen.

This is not a dream.

Jadore continues. "We are a facility dedicated to scientific advancement and international security. We are a collective of officials, working for a united world body, with one purpose: protecting Earth against the alien threat that's not just outside the solar system—but here, on our soil."

It's true. But it's also a lie. I'm holding Jia's hand now and she squeezes back, both of us unable to meet the other's gaze, knowing we would find only our mirrored horror.

"That brings me to why you're here. The real purpose of Sparkstone University—and our sister schools—is to collect the greatest up-and-coming minds from around the globe, and train you. Test you. Stretch you to your limits to see if you can handle joining our fight. This is not just a physical fight. Intellectual, creative, technical—we welcome all talents. It is pure talent in one area that is the surest sign of superhuman ability. Superpowers.

"Yes, we have brought you here because most—if not all of you—have that potential within you."

The students are already buzzing. But why can't they see *she* is the real threat? Jadore, stern but pleased with their captivation, raises her hand and my peers fall silent. Agailya stands then, her voice loud and pure as a songbird compared to Jadore's husky droning. "We're here to answer your questions. All of them," she assures us. "We know you've all seen strange activity around the campus. We didn't mean to frighten anyone. No one has been seriously injured. We have excellent facilities here and access to advanced medical technology that would put your country—our country—to shame."

Jia hides her scarred face. The Collective offered to heal her. She declined.

Questions from thirsty students bombard the stage.

"What kind of powers do I have?"

"Where are the aliens now?"

"How can I manifest my superpower?"

"You said the aliens can disguise themselves? So how will we know who's an alien, and who isn't?"

This question, piercing the rest with its loud ferocity, comes from directly behind me. I get a face-full of beard as I glance over my shoulder. The guy is tall, burly, and reeks of cologne, triggering a cacophony of greens embedded with mahogany red.

"An excellent question," Jadore says, smiling. Her teeth are unnaturally white. "You may remember, when you first arrived, the doors extracted blood samples?"

Everyone nods, remembering the chill of that particular invasion of privacy.

"That was done to ensure you are human. However…" Jadore gestures to the cafeteria doors. "Bring it."

By the cafeteria exit, there's a flurry of activity. Then, the crowd parts in a direct line for the stage.

One of the guards reluctantly leads a second guard, one I hadn't counted initially, up onto the stage. His wrists are chained to his neck. He glances furtively over the crowd; I see real fear in his eyes. It's Ohz. The hafelglob in disguise that took interest in me—the first one to call me Crosskey. Not an ally, per se, but as he's led onto the stage, I can't help but feel some sympathy for him.

"This man appears normal," Jadore says. She reluctantly squeezes his forearm and then wipes her fingers on her pant leg.

"Fleshy. Real. Would it surprise you to learn its true form?"

She violently pulls down his sleeve and exposes the band all hafelglob wear around their wrist. It's the same wristband me and my friends wear, though not on purpose. We'd put them on when we'd tried to rescue Sunni, when I'd first arrived in this miserable place. Unfortunately, we haven't figured out how to remove them. For the hafelglob, the bands seem to keep them human and give them an array of powers, like invisibility and limited-range teleportation, from the surface to the mother ship orbiting Earth. We don't understand the breadth of functions the bands offer, nor could Wil figure out how to operate them as the hafelglob have. They can create full-body environmental suits and Wil tinkered with them so they can emit a camera-disrupting pulse, when we need the privacy. But that's it. I've gotten used to the band, as it's become more of a physical reminder of our imprisonment here at Sparkstone.

Jadore fiddles with Ohz's wristband, and without warning, the human image of Ohz is replaced by a writhing, beige tentacle monster. His mouth, which takes up most of his eyeless, faceless body, opens fiercely to reveal the many rows of spiralling, sharp teeth as he gurgles his protest.

Everyone screams.

Jadore smiles. This is a normal day for her.

And for us.

Some students wriggle through the tight crowd, desperate to reach the doors, yet when Jadore sees the panic she's wrought, she fiddles with the band and *slurrrrp,* Ohz's chained human form replaces the tentacled mass. His large eyes survey the crowd, as if searching for a familiar face, yet he doesn't try to escape or protest his "imprisonment."

Jadore shouts over the terrified students, regaining control. "This creature's species is highly evolved, despite its grotesque appearance. It possesses an adaptive shapeshifting ability. Mildly psionic." She coughs, backing away. "And, unfortunately for those in the front, pungent body odor."

The students closest to the stage laugh nervously, which dispels some of the tension.

"You'll notice they all wear wristbands." She holds up Ohz's hand with the barest of touches. "That is our way of controlling them. All aliens in our charge have them and they cannot be removed by conventional means. If you see someone in human form wearing one of these wristbands, stay clear. They cannot hurt you, as we have measures in place to prevent them from harming anyone, yet it is best to remain cautious. Yes, it is dangerous to keep these creatures on campus. But it is an acceptable risk while we study their shapeshifting abilities."

Misty and I exchange glances. She pulls her sleeves down further, and Wil, Jia, and I all cross our arms to hide our identical wristbands. This is bad. Very, very bad. We are not the enemy. It'll be hard to convince our peers otherwise, after Jadore's visceral demonstration.

"Why not keep them in a cage?" It's the guy behind me again, and I cringe. He's loud, a human drum on my sensitive ears.

"We are not barbarians," Jadore replies acidically, as if she's offended by the notion. "Every experiment, every test, we follow a very strict ethical code. If the aliens kidnapped you, they'd put you in a cage. But we are better than them. And we have to show them that. Compassion—and passion—is what makes us human. That is what makes us strong."

Many of my peers nod. Even I find myself nodding, until I snap out of it. The old "humanity is our strongest quality" sentiment is meaningless in a vast universe populated with sentient beings.

Behind Ohz and Jadore, a flicker of resentment breaks Agailya's mask of stoicism. I recall her passionate speech about the phage dooming her race, and the odd calm of her mantra in the face of a suffering, sentient being, Tilly Newman, trapped in her experiment: *They will endure.*

"Despite what you may have heard, we are only trying to protect you and develop what you were born with. There is no conspiracy. No secret agenda. No one has died here." Jadore scoffs at the thought. "If you wish to leave, we won't stop you. Notify the registrar's office and pack your things. A bus is waiting outside to take you to Edmonton where you can arrange transport home. But know there are no second chances. You commit to finding your true calling today—or you return to your friends and family, and apply your talents elsewhere."

This strikes the core of our shared fears. If we decide to leave, we lose the money we've put into our education. We face shame from our families and friends. Our futures, if we have them at all, are in jeopardy.

"And if we decide to go…" asks one student timidly, "does that mean we can't…tell anyone about what's really going on here?"

Jadore looks amused by the question. "Tell whomever you like, whatever you like. Why would we stop you?"

Why indeed. The knots in my stomach ache. The whole aliens-invading-Canada thing is too fantastical to be true to outsiders, and even if people are willing to believe, no doubt the ever-watching Collective will stamp out any tale that blazes out of control. If they let us go at all.

"We will be coming around to all dorms to perform a second

blood test," Jadore continues. "Those who fail to submit within twenty-four hours...well, we will assume the worst of you, and you will be dealt with."

They're closing in, Wil says telepathically.

Just when I feel like I'm about to be sick, another voice rings through the crowd. It's our new friend Elisha, from the *Don't Read Zine,* the ill-fated zine dedicated to investigating the unusual activity around the school. "And what about Tilly Newman?"

"Ah yes. The registrar's office has received a number of complaints—even threats—about the 'disappearance' of several students." Jadore gestures to Agailya, who takes the question. She gives Ohz a wide berth as she glides to the edge of the stage.

"Some students, such as Tilly Newman, left abruptly, it is true. They are alive and well. Some have transferred to other schools. Some have been given special assignments."

"That's a lie. We've seen the pictures!"

The outcry isn't mine, but it echoes my thoughts. To make such a blatant, public accusation without a plan would invite Jadore's wrath—which we know firsthand.

"Pictures can be doctored. How do you know the person who showed it to you isn't working for the enemy?"

Wil shifts beside me. *This is bad.*

"You think?" I whisper. My face burns. The stares of students who only last night supported us completely now turn sour.

"If you wish to discuss this further, I can answer specific questions in my office. My doors are open to all of you, of course." Jadore's tone is flat; empathy does not come naturally to her.

Agailya picks up her slack. "Mine will be open as well."

We just did this last night, to a smaller crowd in the cold

Albertan air. But when an authority figure becomes vulnerable in the name of "truth," of course it's more legitimate. Even with a blood test—collected and controlled by the enemy—it will be difficult to convince others that we are their real allies.

As Jadore spreads more propaganda, I turn and squeeze through the crowd, heading for the exit. I can't listen to this any longer. While the Collective makes their move, we have to be planning our next step, and I can't do that trapped in a cafeteria surrounded by alien invaders.

No one stops me, not even the bored hafelglob in disguise standing beside the doors. They give me the once-over as I push the door open with my body weight. Even the horrible *screech* and subsequent *errrr* of the door as I exit arouses no pause from Jadore, or anyone else. They don't care I've left. Because I can never truly leave.

Unless I can master my teleportation powers.

But when I do, they'll hunt me down, scoop me up to the mother ship, and dissect me for my powers. That's what they did with Sunni, Tilly, and all the others.

The sounds of voices and footsteps break the eerie silence of the hallway and give way to two students. One I know well. Ethan has lost his pale, sickly look, born again as a handsome, confident, if not somewhat wary young man. He's with a young woman our age. They exchange short words, looking up and down the corridors as if lost.

Ethan's gaze passes over me, lingers, and then drifts to the ceiling.

Something about this holds me in place, my breath an unwilling prisoner in my throat. I don't know what to say. To run up and wrap my arms around him—it's all I want to do in this moment—feels too intimate after last night. What if I'm too weird now? From our last exchange, I know he still likes me...but what if that's not enough?

The girl I've never seen before. I've only ever seen Ethan hang out with Kimberly, another artist. As Ethan works mainly in isolation on his paintings and drawings, he rarely leaves his dorm or his studio. The girl's round face is cheery and her laugh at Ethan's apparent confusion infectious and deep. She looks like she's just been to the salon; she brushes a dark strand of long, recently highlighted hair behind her ear. Silver earrings dangle, nearly as long as her hair, and gleam expensively, even in the poor LED lighting. Her rich London accent peaks my interest. "You *said* it was in this building."

"It is. That's it." He points behind me, as if I'm not there.

"Right then. Good." She grins at him, her eyes bright and hazel, and her lashes enviably long. She notices me then and evaluates me carefully. I probably seem like a weirdo, just standing there silently, watching them, but she is as equally out of place to me. She moves tentatively through the hall, looking back every second at Ethan like a concerned, ill-fated Orpheus.

"We heard there's an assembly in the cafeteria." When I don't move out of their way, she gives me an awkward smile that doesn't reach her hazel eyes, glances at Ethan again, and gestures for the door. "I guess we can just go in."

He smiles and nods agreeably, and without giving me a second glance, goes to follow her.

I can't take it anymore. "Ethan."

As if jolted from a dream, he meets my confused gaze with one of his own. "Yes?"

"I got...caught up last night, after the demonstration. I texted you."

"Uh." Ethan smiles awkwardly—just like his new friend. "I guess I didn't get it."

Right. Probably the Collective, interfering with our phone reception, just like everything else.

"We should get in there," the girl says, more urgently this time.

"Sorry, I don't think we've met before," I say, raising an eyebrow.

"Oh. I'm just visiting here, from London," she says, beaming. "I'm Mira."

I'm about to say the polite thing—*nice to meet you, now get out of Sparkstone*—when Ethan adds nonchalantly, "She's my girlfriend."

I blush. "Yeah, yes I guess I am. I'm—" I hold out my hand for Mira to shake, but both Ethan and Mira are giving me confused, horrified looks.

"I meant, *Mira* is my girlfriend," Ethan says. "Who are *you*?"

CHAPTER 2

The doors open and students flood the hallway, pouring over and between us like a river in a rocky stream.

"What do you mean? I'm Ingrid." I jab a finger into my sternum.

Ethan tried to warn me. Losing childhood memories. Losing time. Agailya's experiment has gone too far. Now, to punish me and my friends for speaking out against the Collective and telling the *real* truth about Sparkstone, she's taken away the one good thing that's happened to me.

He shrugs apologetically. "I had an accident a while ago. I have trouble making new memories."

"We've known each other for months now."

"I've gone for months before without lapsing. Apparently. Not that I can remember, really."

"Then what is the last thing you *do* remember?"

"I..." His eyes squeeze shut in pain.

"Ethan?" Mira is there again, consoling him. "I shouldn't have gotten you out of bed. C'mon, I'll show you the way back to your dorm."

I change tracks, desperate to keep him by my side. "I know

they did this to you. I promise I'll fix this."

"They?" Mira asks, curling her fingers around Ethan's arm.

Ethan never mentioned having a girlfriend from back home. He wouldn't have pursued me if he did. He isn't that kind of guy. Amnesia or no amnesia, I want to believe that if I were in Ethan's position, I'd remember strong romantic feelings, especially if I were staring them in the face.

This leads me to a conclusion: Mira is the enemy. No way she's human. Showing up like this, inserting herself into Ethan's life so conveniently? What kind of alien is she, beneath that façade?

"You know who *they* is," I say darkly. I refuse to put on airs in front of her. I'm onto her.

"Um...all right." Mira gives Ethan a *that girl is crazy* look. It's convincing. She's studied human behaviour well. "Seems like we missed the assembly. I'll get you back to your dorm and then I'll head for our tutorial."

"No, it's fine." Ethan seems distracted. "I'm going for a walk."

"I'll go with you. Give you a tour," I say. Like he did for me, my first day. Anything to jog his memory. Perhaps his past is locked up inside his brain and all it needs is a good jostle to let it loose.

He smiles and I die a little. "That's a kind offer, but I think I should go alone."

Of course. My chest tightens. I just claimed to be his girlfriend and he has no memory of me. Or anything that happened last night. He doesn't know I have superpowers. He doesn't know that Misty nearly torched his room and destroyed one of his paintings. How did he not wake up this morning with questions about *that*?

"Okay." I can't afford to scare him off. I can't lose hope—not now, not ever. I take out my phone. "Can I make sure that you have my number? Just in case you have questions about your missing memories?"

A flicker of sorrow sweeps his face. "Sure."

Mira keeps a close eye on the two of us as Ethan slides his phone from his pocket and we browse his contacts. My concerns burn fiercely: When did Mira arrive? Why did Ethan recognize her, and not me? Why would Agailya give him a fake girlfriend? Is his amnesia part of the experiment, or a side effect? My hands shake but his are steady—he is an artist, after all.

I'm in his contacts all right, just as *Ingrid*. "Doesn't seem like we've texted much," Ethan says, browsing our messaging history.

My heart sinks into my stomach. Nearly every text has been deleted, leaving only the barest, mundane ones: "See you after tutorial" and "Are you around today?"

No evidence that we were in a romantic relationship—or that we had feelings for each other.

"Check your photos," I say, desperate.

Mira sighs. "Look, Ingrid, I know you—"

"No photos," he says, returning the device to his pocket. "Guess my phone lost its memories too."

"Mine didn't." Not that I had much. But by the time I load the app and begin scrolling, Mira and Ethan are antsy, anxious to move on from this awkward interaction. I hate this too. I hate that I have to prove myself. After ten images, I can't find any of Ethan. This is not a battle I can win, not this way. The Collective is always one step ahead. "It's fine. Just...message me—"

Jia and Misty approach us casually. "Sorry about your room," Misty says to Ethan.

He frowns. "My room?"

"Yeah. When I—" Her confident joke or allusion fades when she sees my face. "When I was...there...the other night?"

"How many girlfriends do you have, Ethan?" Mira asks, her playful tone belied by concern.

"Whoa. Not where I was going with that." Misty looks uncomfortable now. "We're going outside. Coming, Ingrid?"

"Seems like I came at the right time," Mira says, clasping his hand and pulling him down the hall from where they came.

"What's his problem? Did you guys...?" Misty raises her eyebrows, allowing the question to hang in the air.

"I think Agailya did something to him," I say under my breath. Saying it out loud makes it more real. "He doesn't know who I am. Who we...are."

Jia's eyes widen. "So he doesn't remember when...?"

"Doesn't seem like it."

"If the Collective can erase our memories," Misty says, sparing a glance at Jia, "then why are we still fine? Why Ethan?"

She's got a point. If this is a power the Collective has always possessed, they wouldn't be trying so hard to keep secrets from the students. Which makes my conviction stronger. "It's a targeted attack on me. On us. They're experimenting on us like we're animals. They don't care we're sentient. We have to do something about it. "

"I agree," Misty says. "Which is why we have the meeting. Like *you* suggested last night."

The meeting can't come fast enough. I have to do something *now*.

Jadore finally exits the cafeteria, walking aid teetering back and forth on the tile. Small groups of students linger in the hallway, and they meet her with fresh enthusiasm, praise, and questions about aliens and superpowers. Jadore was never popular, and now a smile creeps across her face. She's eating this up.

I can't stand it. She doesn't deserve this. Not after what she's done.

I tear forward, blocking her path. "You hurt Ethan."

Like the snake she is, she lifts her head, and parts her lips. There are fangs beneath the fake human teeth, I know it. "Ingrid Stanley. Are you accusing me of something?"

I half expect to hear Wil's voice in my head, urging me to back down, but there's only fear and anger—my own. "Your experiments on him corrupted his mind. He's not the same anymore. All in the name of your *science*."

"*My* science?" Jadore says evenly. "You don't believe in the power of scientific process? Or are you having boyfriend troubles?" She moves her head from left to right, as if to gather support from the older students on the periphery who have clearly taken her side. "I suggest you speak with Ms. Agailya. She deals with student well-being."

"I will." She's not innocent in this either.

"Oh," Jadore adds, as she turns to leave, "be sure to be in your dorm tomorrow afternoon to submit for your blood test, Ingrid Stanley."

The unsaid threat ripples through my chest. *Submit to us, or be labelled as the enemy.*

She attempts to maneuver around me and bodychecks my shoulder in the process. Out of habit, I mutter an apology, which only embarrasses me more. She's not really blind. She did it on purpose. The students who showered her with questions and praise give me dirty looks as Jadore navigates the hallway with ease.

One foot steps in front of the other, but I can't move. All I want to do is go after her, rip off her glasses, and expose her for the alien threat she is. But Jia's on one side, and Misty's on the other, and without even realizing it, I've been struggling against them, numb to all physical sensation except the heavy feeling of hopelessness keeping me in this physical realm.

"Stop, just stop," Misty says. She lowers her voice, even as the students filter out of the hallway. "I wanna kill her too, but we can't compete with her this way."

"What other ways do we have?" I ask.

"Lots." She sighs. "Look, let's go back to the dorm, get the rest of Jia's snacks, find Wil, and meet up with Greg, Elisha, and Lynn. We can fight their propaganda with our own."

Greg and Lynn operate the *Don't Read Zine* with Elisha. Unfortunately, it's their criticisms of the school that attracted the Collective's attention and got Tilly Newman captured and killed.

"Where is Wil?" I ask.

Jia shakes her head carefully. "He ran out."

Jadore nearly had him before. With his mind manipulation ability and technical talents, I don't doubt he is target number one for the real alien threat.

"He knows where we're meeting. He can manage," Misty says, because we all need to hear it. "Right?"

Jia turns from us, unable to even look at us while we talk about him. Joseph G. Campbell admitted to me some time ago that, at some point, Wil will die. I tried to keep this from Jia, but when I let it slip in a moment of crisis, she nearly died rescuing him. My worry for Wil conflicts with my sense of injustice for what he did to Jia, and the anxiety I feel about not telling her—not knowing *how* to tell her.

"Misty's right," I say, forcing fear from my voice. "The three of us can manage without Wil. We have some allies. That's where we should start."

"I'll get the supplies," Jia says, and without waiting for us, she starts down the hallway, darting nimbly between the remaining lingering students. They don't acknowledge her, even when she grazes their shoulders during her swift exit. They treat her like a stiff breeze.

"Wil's ignored us all," Misty says, without waiting for me to bring it up. "But whatever is up with him, we can't let it get in the way of our ultimate goal."

Some of what she says rings true. "You mean, getting rid of...?" Even though she's gone, I can't say Jadore's name aloud. Not here, anyway.

Misty gets it. "Yeah."

I can't let it go. "Jia saved Wil's life. That has to mean something to him, though."

"Good deeds don't mean anything to people who can manipulate minds." Her gaze darts around the hallway, as if the walls have ears. They probably do. She heads towards the exit. "I'll make sure she doesn't get lost in her own world."

We'd made a resistance, and even though it was small, it was something. We'd talked to so many promising leads last night at the demonstration vigil—but after the assembly this morning, who knows how many will actually show up to the planned meeting. Some of them will want to know our reaction to Jadore's flashy speech. After all, we said there were aliens *first*.

We told everyone last night to meet today in Greg's room in the basement of Raylene House, the now unofficial headquarters of the Sparkstone Resistance.

At least, that is what I am calling it. I'm sure the others won't be so romantic about it. I shouldn't be either. There is too much at stake. But it keeps me sane.

I remember Joseph G. Campbell's words. I have been chosen. My special connection to him is going to help us win.

While Jia and Misty gather our precious food for the meeting, I head for Raylene House. My face is already numb from the bracing breeze of Northern Alberta. No major snowfall yet—thankfully—though I might as well be travelling through the Northwest Passage as I gather my cardigan closer to my chest and forge through the cold early November air.

I'm about halfway through my five-minute trek when I see a group of seven in the distance. They're the only other living souls on the quad. No one wants to linger long out here. The group make their way with purpose towards me, and their approach feels deliberate. I step off the path and give them a wide berth. The way they're marching—two by two—is oddly hypnotic. I don't need that right now.

As they get closer, I meet eyes with their leader—oh no. It's the loudmouth with the beard from the assembly. He has papers tucked under his arm. I look away and pretend I haven't already seen him.

"Hey!"

I feel him pointing at me. I keep walking.

"Hey, wait a minute, just want to talk!"

Their footfalls cease, and I'm pulled in by the obligation to be polite and engage. I stop and face them. They expand to block my way forward, standing like soldiers in a row, with the bearded guy before them—their commander. I search for companionship among the followers. Two of them look like women. They give me grim, friendly smiles, the kind that say, *it'll be better if you just submit and don't make a fuss.*

"Yes?" I say. "I'm late for my study group."

The bearded guy smiles and hands me a flyer. I don't want it, but it's in my hand now anyway. "Just letting everyone know about the Student Watch. Used to be the Student Action Brigade, but you could say we've rebranded. Now that we know the truth about aliens, we have to be on our guard, right? So we're doing our best to help out and we're looking for volunteers to join us."

"Volunteers?" Nothing about this school is voluntary. I hold out the flyer. "I'm not really interested, sorry."

"Keep that," he says. There's an edge to his tone. "We'll be taking over curfew patrol, spot checks on the dorms, that kind of thing. With the Review coming up, we want everyone to be sharp."

Review? Taking over curfew patrol? "Who made this group?"

"I'm running it," he replies.

"And...who are you?"

"I'm Shane," he says, as if I should know. "We have Mr. Dean's full support, as well as the staff's."

Sure. I know what that means. I fold up the flyer, hoping there's a recycling bin nearby. "Okay. Thanks. I have to go now."

I take a step forward. The members of the Brigade don't budge. It's then I note their attire. All of them in black windbreakers. Different shades of black—they're not entirely uniform, and one has a yellow stripe, another skews greyer—but enough to disturb me all the more. For a group that has only "rebranded" after hearing the assembly, they're scarily organized.

I attempt to maneuver around the group, but the person on the end shifts to block my path. Uh, okay. In any non-Sparkstone situation, I would be freaking out even more right now. A group of mostly men, preventing me from going about my business? No. Thank. You.

I can leave, I think impulsively. They don't know what power I possess. I can go to the moon if I want and they're stuck here. They don't know what it really means to have power.

They have to make up for it in numbers. And windbreakers.

They can't really do anything to me.

Emboldened, I whirl on the leader. "What do you think is happening here?"

He gives me a strange look. "I *know* there are aliens here and we have to protect ourselves. Don't you think?"

The band around my wrist feels tighter. My long-sleeved cardigan covers my wrists, yet I feel more exposed than ever. If they see my wristband, I'm toast. "I think you should leave me alone. Now."

"Why? We haven't done anything to you. You got something to hide?" He looks to the group for support. They nod accordingly. He looks perturbed as it finally dawns on him. "Hey, aren't you the girl who talked sass to Professor Jadore?"

Took him long enough. I'm sure I'm not the only one who has confronted Jadore, but my silence betrays me this time.

"Yeah. You are. You can go, if you're headed for your dorm. For the blood test."

I frown. "Jadore said the blood test is tomorrow."

"Today and tomorrow. Best if you just stay in your dorm.

It'll make it easier if you get this done for us. We have a lot of people to get through."

My resolve falters. It's easy to acquiesce when he makes it sound like I'd be doing him a favour. "Like I said, I have a study group right now. And I'm not the one you should be worried about."

"I'll worry less when the test results are posted. That's how we'll know who to trust."

Posted? I missed way more of the assembly than I thought. "Right. Well. I look forward to seeing your name on there too."

He snorts. "Yeah. With 'human' next to it. Like the rest of us."

The others share a chortle, as if this is an inside joke. They don't appear alien. Most of the aliens I've encountered have an otherworldly quality, like Ms. Agailya, or an I-Don't-Fit-In-This-Body quality, like Ohz. No, they're definitely human.

Which makes this all the more troubling.

Quickly, I see this isn't a fight I can win alone. I don't know if they've taken Jadore's words to heart, or if they're aliens who got good at pretending, or if this is a test laid out by the Collective. It doesn't matter. I'm not going to change their minds with words.

"You think her sass warrants demerits?" he asks his group.

Demerits? What is this, high school? A military academy? "Look, I have somewhere to be."

"You said that, but you keep..."

His retort falls flat on my ears as movement catches my wandering, desperate gaze. It's Wil, and he's beelining for me. He approaches from behind the group, and he's seemingly unburdened by their territorial stance on the quad. Wil navigates around them and plants himself next to me. Maybe he felt me here, exuding panic, and has come to my rescue.

His calm, stoic gaze takes in the seven of them before turning deliberately to me. "There you are. We're going to be late for the study group."

"Ah," says Shane enthusiastically to Wil, as if a second person, a man at that, confirming my destination has suddenly made it more real. "Just wanted to let you know, we're the—"

Wil tilts his head, squints, and then says, "Leave."

Shane's eyes bug out. His pupils shrink. He blinks. They're normal again. "Never mind. Let's go."

He turns and trudges down the path, away from us. His friends give Wil and I funny looks, but they follow their leader. Some of them call his name, asking about the demerits, if they should issue them at Ms. Agailya's office, if I should be written up—there's no intelligible response from Shane.

Wil is already dragging me in the opposite direction.

"You can't just mind-control people in public!" I whisper-hiss as I wrench my arm from his grip. "Especially students."

"The game has changed," Wil says tersely. His gaze darts around the quad. "The Collective knows who I am. Which is why I have to leave."

"Now? In broad daylight? How do you plan on doing that?"

He gives me a look. I don't need his telepathy to see what he means.

"Uh, no. I'm not getting you out of here. Remember all those times when I lost time, or teleported to the mother ship?"

"It doesn't matter where or when you take me—as long as it's far."

"And what if I can't make it back here?"

"Why would you *want* to come back?"

My breath catches. "Because the last time I tried to escape, Jadore nearly killed my father."

"We don't get out of here without some sacrifices, Ingrid."

"Oh, so my family is an okay price for your freedom? No. Not teleporting you anywhere, not before we get the Collective out of our solar system."

He looks indignant. "That is going to take a while."

I remember Joseph G. Campbell's visit—from six months in the future. Five months, now. When we're still fighting the Collective. I can't see us lasting this week, let alone five months. "If you leave, they'll just hunt you down. Same with all of us. We have to mount a resistance here, now, and strike at their heart, before something truly terrible happens."

"More terrible than students dying, painfully, at their hands? That's why I can't stay. I'm next. I'm too hot a target. My skills are more useful on the outside."

"Then tell me your plan."

He shakes his head. "Just in case they harvest me, in case they have another like me on their side—it's best I keep it in here." He taps his bald scalp.

"Sure, because that worked out so well last time."

He looks annoyed. He broke one of our cardinal rules—don't write anything down—the same rule Sunni broke. Instead of a journal, Wil recorded videos on a USB that he meant to send to the outside world. He also tricked my mind into thinking I was paralyzed and stuffed me in a locker to prevent me from stopping him.

"That wasn't my finest moment," he says quietly, feeling me relive the experience.

"Don't ever do that to me, or any of us, again. You do that and you're no better than the Collective."

He scoffs and shuffles down the path, looking back at me in disbelief. "You keep walking that high road, refusing to get your feet muddy. You know where it leads?"

"So taking away control of my own body, you think the ends justify the means there? Do you even know what that's like, to not be in control? Or are you so detached from what it means to be a feeling, caring person that we're all just pawns for you to manipulate?"

I've touched a nerve. He points a finger, curls it, and leans in close. He doesn't mean to be menacing, yet the intensity in his eyes delivers a different message. "If I can't separate myself from the rest of the screaming masses, I'll go insane."

"Stay here. We can help you through this."

"No." He backs away, and any crack in his steely façade seals itself before my eyes. "You're taking this too personally. You're only going to make it worse by making such public attacks. The Collective have changed their strategy—but that's all. The experiment is still the same. Develop and harvest the students' superpowers."

"And I care about saving our fellow students and getting out of here."

"Sure. That all?"

I back away. I can't argue with someone who can see into my mind, pick apart my secret desires, and spit them back in my face. "If you cared, you'd come with me to the meeting and use your powers to help us."

"The meetings won't make a difference."

"You don't know that."

"I'm not going to waste our time arguing. Do what you think

is right. You always do." He starts down the path again, towards the town of Sparkstone proper.

I have one more card to play. He can see my cards before I place them on the table, but out of respect, he slows his stride, allowing me the chance to persuade him with my voice.

"If you leave, you're going to die."

"We're all going to die." Yet the reply hangs loosely in the air—he's sensed the truth behind my words. Campbell told me that Wil would die before the five months were done. I attempt to build a wall in my mind, but it doesn't work like that.

His shoulders sag. "Campbell might be lying."

"Why would he?"

"If my fate is set in stone," he says, "then you have to let me go. Let me try my way, on my own, away from the rest of you, so you don't get hurt."

There's nothing left for me to say—he's right. I can't make him stay. He's already decided he's leaving, and if the future has already happened, as Campbell would say, then he's already set in motion the course of events that will get him killed. All we can do is minimize the damage. Considering what he's already done to Jia, maybe it's best we part ways.

Sensing my feelings on the matter, he nods, and continues down the path alone.

CHAPTER 3

I rap on the basement door of Greg's dorm in Raylene House. Jia answers the door before I can get a second knock in. Her eyebrows twitch upward as she recognizes me and glances both ways down the hallway. "You didn't find Wil?"

I don't know what to tell her. "He's not coming."

She looks disappointed, but not surprised. She steps aside so I can come in. Everyone is already here. Greg, Elisha, and Lynn sit at the crafting table, deep in conversation with Misty as she paces behind them. I've never known her to stay still for long. Relieved at my arrival, she throws up her hands. "What took you so long?"

"Wil isn't coming," Jia says, closing the door behind me.

"It's fine," Misty says. "We don't need him. We've already removed the camera from the lights and turned off our phones, just in case."

"Isn't he the one who can *read minds*?" Greg asks. He hunches over the table, wearing his usual unimpressed look and a faded tropical, half-unbuttoned shirt. When he slams a hand in frustration on the table, he startles Lynn, who curses at him under her breath. She's petite, half Greg's size, and wears her frizzy curls up in a messy bun, highlighting her many freckles. Lynn exchanges a look with Elisha, who is the most done-up of the three of them with her ironed dark blazer and white shirt, thick square lenses, and bright lipstick. Elisha rolls her eyes and points a silent, warning finger at Greg. He seems to know what this means, as he throws up his hands in silent defeat, takes a deep breath, and then slumps back in his chair.

The silence lasts all of two seconds before his eyes bug out at me. "Go *find* him!"

"No," Jia and Misty say simultaneously.

I bristle and feel a quiet warmness towards my friends. I don't like taking orders from people, especially Greg. Though we haven't known each other long, he doesn't seem hateful, just a curmudgeon without a filter. "He made it clear to me that he doesn't want to participate. He's going into hiding to protect us." I help myself to some tea from a pot perched on a tall dresser. It's lukewarm but it quiets my aching stomach.

"Then this is it?" Greg demands. "We're the resistance?"

"We can work with this," Elisha says confidently. "Four of us managed to run *Don't Read Zine* without any help. And before that, in high school, I ran newspaper club and a crafting corner. We don't need numbers or a ton of people with superpowers. Just hard workers."

"A couple more warm bodies wouldn't hurt," Lynn adds quietly, her gaze darting about the room, as if expecting surprise visitors to float in from any corner.

Greg nods, stroking his chin absently at both of them. "I just wish my superpowers would hurry up and manifest so we can get out of this dreary basement and back to the real world."

Misty purses her lips. I can tell she wants to issue a stern retort to *that* wishful thinking. No way the Collective would let us leave alive. How Wil plans to get out without my help is beyond me—but as much as it pains me to admit it, it's not my top concern. "We should keep this meeting brief. Jadore will be sending her student lackeys around to test our blood soon." I fill them in quickly about the Brigade, minus the part where Wil mind-controlled them in public. That, I'll tell Jia and Misty privately—later.

Well. Maybe just Misty. Jia hovers near the door, as if she has somewhere else to be. It could be the poor basement lighting, but her hand seems half-there, blending perfectly with the plain walls. She could easily slip out, track Wil down. I have to make sure that doesn't happen. I won't let him alter her mind again, especially since he believes it's for the greater good.

"None of us are aliens, right? Even though the three of you wear those same wristbands as that gross tentacle monster?" Greg says.

"The wristbands are alien technology. We can't remove 'em," Misty replies sourly, as she pulls down her sleeve to show it off to Lynn, Elisha, and Greg. They squint as they examine the metallic, nondescript band.

"Wil tried, and failed," Jia adds quietly.

Greg seems to accept this explanation. "So good, you're not aliens. Then what do we have to worry about? They already have our blood samples—the door took them when we all arrived here. So why would they need another sample?"

"That's the real question," I reply. "It has to do with our powers. They only want them if they're developed to a certain point. It must be to track our progress."

"My progress is zero," Elisha says.

Greg shrugs. "Yeah. Mine too."

Lynn glances nervously between the two of them and then adds, "Same."

"It's not like we can call a lawyer or the police or outside help either. My phone hasn't worked for days," Elisha says.

"My phone deleted all of my photos," Greg laments, taking it out of his pocket and scrolling absently.

So the Collective didn't just target my phone and Ethan's phone. The Collective is cracking down on everyone. Still, I know in my heart Jadore and Agailya have it out for me and my friends personally, after all the trouble we've caused. I take a deep breath. "Okay. We're here to figure out our next move. We know the Collective wants our blood. They've tampered with our phones. Probably to prevent us from getting outside help, to access information, or to erase what little evidence we have." Ethan's face flashes before my eyes and a sob wells up inside me. I swallow it, for now. "They've told everyone that we are an elite group of superheroes, chosen to protect Earth from an alien invasion. Why would this be the next step? Why tell us this now, and not when we all got here? What do they have to gain from this—knowing that their objective is to develop and harvest our superpowers for their own twisted scientific gain?"

"It's probably a response to the protest, or to those who saw the Hunger in the quad," Jia says hoarsely. She's still leaning against the door, staring into the middle distance. "That's a lot of explaining to do to many witnesses."

"The why matters less than what we need to do about it," Misty adds, crossing her arms over her black jacket defensively. "We need a plan to prevent those Brigade jerks or secret aliens from getting into our rooms and taking our blood."

Lynn and Jia nod enthusiastically.

"How are you going to stop them? By blasting them?" Greg says.

Misty shrugs. "Maybe, if they annoy me." She throws me a look. She's not being serious; she's just annoyed and frustrated with the lack of options and body autonomy.

"Then they'll just take you away," Greg says. "Some use you'll be then."

An idea blooms within me. Now I'm pacing, talking as I work it out. "Of course. Misty. The Collective already knows you and Jia have developed powers. They treated Jia. They could have harvested her then—but they didn't. They listen in, watch us, keep tallies on our families. They could waltz in here at any moment and take all of us. They should have done that after the protest we staged in the cafeteria, or the vigil a few days ago. That would have been the cleanest solution, right? Remove the dissenters. But they didn't do that."

"I thought we already theorized why that hasn't happened," Misty says slowly. She's referring to my relationship with Joseph G. Campbell, the time-travelling, seemingly omnipotent alien who is apparently tethered to me.

I nod. "Maybe that's part of it. But he doesn't control when he appears. So, instead of disappearing troublesome or powerful students, like they have done in the past, now the Collective is weaving a more complex cover story."

Elisha senses my train of thought and rises slowly to her feet. "You're right. Why not imprison students who make trouble? Do they not have the capacity? The resources? They built all of this. Clearly they have an immense network to keep this a secret from humanity as a whole. Yet when we, the caged rats, become aware of the experiment, they don't stop. They don't shy away or deny the existence of aliens. They change the game. They evolve the experiment."

Goosebumps ripple over my arms. Those were Wil's words too.

"So...why is this more important than the immediate threat of them taking our blood and our freedoms?" Misty asks. "We need a concrete plan, Ingrid. Not theory and strategy. Say what you need to say so we can get on with it."

I stand still, glancing at each person individually, feeling ill. "They're constructing a narrative where they are the saviors. They're telling the students that they are the good guys. So that anyone who resists, doubts, or takes drastic action against them—suddenly they're aliens. They're the enemy and worthy of persecution."

As the words settle upon us, Greg leaps to his feet. "So?"

"So," Jia says, launching herself from the wall. "If we form an active resistance against the Collective while they are a force for good, protecting the Earth...we're suddenly not just facing a group of aliens. We're facing our own human peers. As Ingrid said, Shane mentioned they are posting the results of the blood tests publicly. So everyone will know who is an alien and who isn't—even if it's completely false."

"Are people really that...gullible?" Lynn asks.

"Yes," Misty, Jia, Greg, and Elisha say at once.

My head is spinning. The tea doesn't help. I haven't had a real meal since the night of the Hunger attack. I feel weak and tired and I have to pretend I'm fine. We have barely anything left from Jia's stash and I don't want to—can't—ask for extra food. I have to be strong, like my friends, and see this through.

"If this is their move," I continue on, pacing again as the idea takes shape in my mind, "then our next move is obvious. We have to strike against that narrative. We have to prove that the Collective is here to hurt humanity. And since Jadore is the figurehead, we have to target her. If we can reveal that she's an alien in front of the whole school, the students will doubt the narrative. They can't believe that Jadore is fighting against an alien invasion if she *is* an alien—not easily, not right away. If we can get her to remove her human skin in an assembly, then we can prove that we're the ones telling the truth."

"Remove her human skin? Gross," Greg says. "Is that how it works?"

"She uses some kind of cream to keep her human appearance. It doesn't work on the eyes, though, that's why she pretends she's blind," Jia explains. "I could steal the cream."

"We could follow her, get video," Elisha suggests.

"Yes, but that's not enough," Misty says. "What if she has a backup supply of cream? What if the Collective disrupts our phones? You know Jadore had the audacity to try and explain why all our phones have been on the fritz? She said they were just trying to block alien forces from spying on us. Can you believe that?" Misty starts pacing again. We're in a kind of slow dance in this open dorm room. We lock eyes—she's more excited than I am now about the prospect of exposing Jadore's lies. "It has to be live. We have to knock off her glasses, somehow turn her skin green and scaly, and get her to use her powers."

"Tall order," Lynn mutters.

Jia looks uncomfortable. "Even if that was somehow possible, it sounds like one—or more of us—would have to provoke her. Publicly."

She's right. We have to prove the Collective doesn't have

humanity's best interests at heart, and what better way to do that than to have its spokesperson attack a sympathetic student? I push away the icky voice debating the morality of our strategy. "Fine, I volunteer. Jadore has it in for all of us, but I've publicly opposed her before. I might be able to goad her into an attack."

Lynn and Elisha are noticeably relieved that it doesn't have to be them. "And if she doesn't fall for it?" Misty asks.

Maybe she'll kill me—or she'll try. "I don't want to be stuck here any longer than I have to. Whatever it takes, we have to expose the Collective before they kill us all."

The words are easy to say, but they sit heavily on the journalism team. Tilly's disappearance was the final straw for them. They were fighting in the dark before we turned on the lights and exposed the monster. Yet they haven't seen the true power of the Collective like Misty and Jia and I have. They're scared, we're scared, and I don't want them to see the horrors that we have.

Greg plops back down in the chair. I see the gears in his head turning. "So we reveal Jadore is an alien. Then what?"

"Then the students revolt," Misty says, like this is the natural conclusion. I nod in agreement.

"Uh. No." Greg leans back in his chair. "They won't."

"Yeah. They will. They'll realize Jadore's been lying this whole time!" Misty looks to me for support.

I jump in. "They'll have to believe us and take action once they realize Jadore is part of the Collective and the aliens are here to take—"

"No, no, no!" The front chair legs hit the floor again and he pushes his face dramatically into the table. He gestures to Lynn and Elisha. "Little help here?"

Lynn sighs. "What Greg means is, people don't just revolt when they learn their life is a lie. Not...everyone, anyway. A few might take up arms. But that's us. We are the few. Not only is the Collective's message more powerful and enticing than ours—*you have powers, you are special, you are all the chosen one*—but it's kinda true. Some of us do have powers. They chose us to come here."

"Yeah. To kill us and take those powers," I say.

"Sure," Elisha says, nodding along with Lynn. "But once they learn that Jadore *is* part of the alien threat...people aren't just going to flock to our side. People are going to be confused. What's worse is, if the Collective is empowering—*literally* aiding, speeding up the development of superpowers in a bunch of teens and early twenty-somethings—that's basically like giving armed nukes to kids. When they find out they aren't as special as they thought, that the Collective has been using them, sure. They might turn on the alien threat. But they also might just set off those nukes."

I part my lips to argue. We'll handle it, I want to say. We've been doing this longer. But Lynn and Greg and Elisha are right. The truth won't set us free. It won't inspire the hearts and minds of our fellow students. It'll shatter their precious reality.

"What if," I say, "we reveal Jadore is an alien in public. But then we take her hostage. Leave the Collective's infrastructure in place long enough to handle the...nukes...while we negotiate with the Collective."

"Is Jadore that important within their hierarchy?" Elisha asks.

"She's pulling a lot of strings from what we've seen," Misty says. "I think she's in charge of the whole school. Maybe more. She's power-hungry."

Lynn doesn't look convinced. "Does the Collective negotiate or do they just take what they want?"

"If they realize we've mobilized enough to be a threat…they'll have to listen to us," I say, with more confidence than I feel. "We have to do something. I'm not going to put my head down."

Greg lifts his head from the desk and gives me a sarcastic look. "For your information, this helps me think."

Lynn smiles patiently and exchanges a glance with Elisha. "We'll make a list of people who are powered. And figure out who the potential nukes are."

"I can help with that," Jia says. She approaches the table slowly now, far more engaged and ready to take action. Whatever I'd noticed with her arm before, it's totally normal now. Maybe it's my starved body, playing tricks on my mind. "I can stalk them easily enough."

"Creepy and cool," Greg says, "because that is *not* the job I want."

"Good, because you can help me learn more about Shane and these Brigade members, so we know who not to trust," Misty says. "See if we can disrupt the blood collection or at least figure out what they're doing with it. If we can prevent the Collective from telling how far along we are in our power development, we can buy everyone some more time."

Greg twists his face and doesn't argue. "Sounds reasonable."

Elisha writes confidently and swiftly with a bold ballpoint on unlined paper in code. She knows our rules. Don't write information down that can be easily deciphered. "And Ingrid? What is your assignment?"

Everyone looks to me. My fingers dig into my shirt. I've known what my assignment is since I suggested outing Jadore as an alien. To say it out loud and acknowledge that I'm going to have to confront it—I'd rather face Ethan again than undertake my seemingly impossible task.

"We don't know when the next assembly will be. It could be tomorrow or next week. We need to be ready as soon as possible to handle the fallout." I clear my throat. "When we reveal Jadore as an alien, I'll have to grab her fast. And we have to get away quickly. To do so, I need my powers to be...reliable." I blush. I don't like admitting my weaknesses. "My power is teleportation. But it's not very...developed. Or reliable. I need a lot of practice."

The journalism team look uncomfortable once again. "If I had to choose between death and unreliable teleportation," Greg says, "I'd choose the teleportation."

Lynn and Elisha nod at me, looking distressed. It makes me feel so much worse. Yes, I could get them out of this place—maybe. But at the cost of their families and everyone who loves them, and who knows how much time might pass? Or where we might end up?

"I know it would be easier, better if I could just whisk you all away. But I won't put anyone's life at risk before I have it completely under control," I say. "In a pinch—it works, yes, but the cost is too high to remove any of you from the school right now. Sorry. I'll practice, on my own, so I can be ready for when the time comes."

"Of course," Lynn says sympathetically. Elisha and Greg mutter similar words of understanding, but I feel like I've let them down. Misty gives me a grim smile. I glance at Jia. Her eyebrows knit together, and I wonder if she realizes that I refused to help Wil hide or escape.

"So. We have a plan," Elisha says, satisfied.

As she recounts our meeting to the team, Misty approaches me and lowers her voice.

"I guess you probably don't need any help with your... assignment," she says, crossing her arms. It's not really a question, but it's her way of asking.

"I think I have to do this myself. But I'll...let you know," I reply, averting my gaze to the floor. Our powers are so personalized, I don't see how Misty could help me. Even if I wanted it, help isn't what I need. I need answers. Answers about Ethan's missing memories, about Wil's fate, and most importantly, about the Collective's next move.

CHAPTER 4

Misty shakes me awake the next morning.

"Jesus. You sleep like a log. Get up. Now."

My body sits up, as if pulled by an invisible puppet master. I'm barely awake. The air is heavy. Hazy. I smell gasoline. "Sunni?" Sunlight streams in from the window beside the bed. This could be a dream.

Misty stands over me, alarmed. She's already dressed. It's just the two of us in the room. The mass of blankets on the floor mattress has been neatly folded—Jia's already up and about. "No. This is real. Look out the window."

She moves aside and I swing my legs over the side of the bed. The window is open—outside noises, smells infiltrate the stale dorm room where the three of us have been sleeping for the past several weeks. Standing, I brace myself on the nightstand as I take the few careful steps to the sill. I can't shake the weight of my sleep. I don't think I dreamt—for once.

Staring down at the campus below, I see the row of black buses—no logos, no identification—lining the narrow road between Rita House and Rogers Hall. Their roar is a steady lull and the pungent gasoline smell suddenly makes sense. One puts its lights on, pulls out, and does an awkward U-turn on the flat plain beyond the road and drives away. The other buses inch forward. I pull the window shut, stifling a cough. My acute senses can't handle this right now.

"What are all these buses doing here?" My mind goes to the darkest place. "Are we being...rounded up? Taken to...camps?"

"This *is* the camp. No, everyone has been getting off the bus. All morning."

Brigade members control the crowd, directing them to Rogers Hall and Rita House. I can't identify their faces, but most of the newcomers appear older. There's even an elderly couple holding hands as they make their way to Rogers Hall. None of them have large suitcases—just purses and smaller overnight bags hanging loosely on their shoulders and carry-ons rolling loudly on the pristine sidewalks and pavement.

If Wil were here, he'd be able to tell us what's happening. But it's up to the three of us. Well—two of us. I search the room. "Where's Jia?"

"Dunno. Gone when I got up." Misty flails her arms about the room, as if hoping to find her invisible. "Unless she's hiding."

I think back to her half-invisible hand in Greg's room and a sinking feeling swirls in my stomach. I don't allow it to settle. I check my phone. No new texts from her. Not that our phones are especially reliable.

"Have you gone down there?" I ask Misty.

"Hell no," she replies. "I only woke up twenty minutes before you, and then these buses all came. You were sleep-talking again, by the way."

"Sorry. Did I say anything intelligible?"

"Not that I could tell."

I sigh. "We should go investigate."

Misty nods. "I'll try Jia."

Her painted nails fly across her screen as she texts Jia, while I throw on a fresh pair of jeans, my favourite boots, and my nicest blouse. I don't normally wear jeans, but a skirt would be too heavy for today. I need to be able to run. My hair—frizzy, unkempt, and far too long—gets braided off to one side so I can try to forget about it. I look like a warrior queen after a long night of partying. I feel like an exhausted foot solider in a war that never ends.

"Finally," Misty says into the phone. "Where are you?"

I grab the room key and my phone and open the door. Misty squints, listening intently, and hurries out of the dorm. I quickly lock the door and follow her down the hallway.

"That can't be right." Misty shoots me a worried look. "Are you sure?" Another beat. "Okay, we'll meet you." She ends the conversation and slides the phone into her jeans.

I've seen Misty in a lot of states. Angry. Sad. Afraid. But rarely does she look uncertain.

"You're not going to believe this," she says as we near the stairs, "but *the parents* are here."

She's right. I don't believe her. The words barely register at first, as she says them with such unattached surprise. We're halfway down to the main level before I can think of a response that isn't *I don't believe you* or *What are you talking about?* "All... of the parents?"

"Apparently. Though..." She trails off as we enter the lobby and beeline past the guard at the desk. When we bust open the doors, she's smiling. "Jia just said parents. She didn't say legal guardians. Or you know, extended family. Maybe I'm in the clear."

Misty was raised by her jet-setting uncle after her father went to jail for murdering her mother. That's partly why Misty had the opportunity to pick up so many languages—her other superpower. Her sarcastic jovial attitude fades as the two of us face a sea of adults, buses, and Brigade members. Last I checked, Sparkstone University had over twelve hundred students. Assuming each student has two parental units, that means two thousand people are descending upon the campus...give or take a few hundred.

I gasp as I feel Jia materialize behind me. There's no sound, just the strange, primal instinct of knowing no one is behind you being turned on its head. She's not there, and then suddenly, she is. Hopefully everyone is too busy to notice her sudden blip into view.

"Sorry," she says quietly, as we turn to face her. "I was out for a run when all this started. I snuck into Agailya's office when I saw parents coming off buses. People are reporting there first. Agailya's staff are taking their names and logging them electronically. Some are being assigned rooms, others have been told to bunk with their kids." Her gaze darts around the crowd nervously. "I hope my parents aren't here. They would know, right? Of course they'd know. But would they bring my birth mother too?"

While Jia has talked endlessly about her sister Paige, whom she loves and protects fiercely, she has only recently opened up about growing up as the adopted Asian child of two Caucasian parents. Jia had been adopted at birth by the Fields and grew up on their rural Alberta farm. A few years later, they had Paige. Her parents did their best to expose Jia to her Chinese heritage by taking her to cultural events in Calgary and Edmonton, sending her briefly to a Mandarin-only school, and hiring private tutors to give her Mandarin lessons, but it was tough with them living so far from the cities.

"Do your parents know who she is?" Misty asks.

"They met her a few times, when she was pregnant. The adoption was private. As far as I know, she went back to China. Apparently she was very young when she had me."

"What will you do if she shows up?" I ask.

Jia just shakes her head in disbelief. "Be happy to meet her? I've had a lot of questions for her over the years. Mostly I just..." She covers her scars and then clasps her hands behind her back. "I don't want anyone I know to come. To see me...as I am. Maybe I should go."

She begins to flicker out of existence. I grab her hand before she can completely disappear. I feel that awkward pull of her invisible world, and for a moment, I experience a deep inner peace. No wonder Jia wants to disappear. The surprise of my gesture keeps her grounded in our visible world.

"If you need to go later, I can't stop you. But if your parents are here...we need to keep them safe," I say. Jia has always been the voice of reason and, often, our conscience. Seeing her this distressed makes me nervous. I don't know exactly how we are going to protect our parents from the evil invading aliens, only that we need to keep a level head for whatever they've got up their sleeve.

Jia purses her lips. "Stronger together. I know. I will make them invisible the moment they are threatened."

"All of them?" Misty gestures to the sea of adults.

Jia doesn't reply. The three of us sink into a desperate silence as we wait for a familiar face to jump out at us. Other students are coming out of the dorms too, racing for the buses, their gazes hopeful. I keenly search for Ethan. Nope. Not even Mira. It's pretty early for Ethan, I suppose. He is a night owl. I spot Kimberly, though. Despite the circles under her eyes, she's alert. I wave her down.

"Why are you bringing her over?" Misty says bitterly.

I haven't spoken to her since Ethan's memories have disappeared. Kimberly excitedly weaves through the chaos of parents and students, her colourful cardigan billowing behind her as she approaches at top speed.

"Did you guys hear?" she asks.

"Yeah," I reply. "Are your parents...?"

"Haven't seen them yet!" She glances around, checking. "I mean, kinda far for them to come...and I think my dad's on business in India, so doubtful he'd be here." Laughing nervously, she looks between the three of us. I want to laugh with her, to alleviate the awkwardness, but all of my feelings have drowned in the pit in my stomach. "How about you guys?"

I sweep the crowd—ensuring that all the faces are a blur. "Don't see them. Kimberly...have you seen Ethan?"

I feel Misty's side-eye, but she doesn't comment.

"Yeah. Last night. I asked him if he was coming in to the studio. He said no. Some girl named Mira is here from England, and he's been spending a lot of time with her." Her eyes widen. "Oh. Yeah. I don't know if you knew—"

"Yeah, I know." Looks like word has spread about his memory loss. And his supposed girlfriend.

"I don't know what's wrong with him. He has issues. We're friends, but he can be really distant sometimes. It was a really—"

She catches the gaze of a man and a woman standing eagerly a few feet away. "Mom! Dad! I thought you were in Mumbai..." Waving a quick goodbye to us, she bounces towards them, speaking half in English and half in Hindi, and launches into their arms.

"I wonder if Wil's family is here," Jia whispers.

I face her, wondering when the right time to have *that* conversation will be. "We need to find a way to warn Wil's parents. All of our families."

"About the Collective's true intentions? Will they believe us?" Misty throws up her hands. "They told everyone we have the potential to have superpowers. Who knows what they'll tell the parents."

"They may have brought them here to kill them," Jia says. Her eyes are red. This isn't the first time she's had this thought.

Another bus roars by. I cough as the gas fumes mix with the air. "It seems like a lot of work to bring them all here just to kill them. How does this fit into their narrative as the Good Guy Protectors?"

"They didn't deal with Hildie in the best way. Maybe now they're making up for it," Misty said.

"But to bring every parent, every guardian here, for each student? Seems...inefficient."

"So does making a bunch of universities all over the world just to trap some teenagers and zap their superpowers. Why not beam them all up to the mother ship and keep them in cages?"

I can't argue with that. "Okay. Once we find our families, we'll all meet back here, take them up to the dorm room, and—"

"No."

I frown at Jia's objection, but she's staring past me, and then she's running by me and Misty, weaving desperately through the crowd. Misty and I hurry after her.

A Caucasian man and woman in their late fifties spot Jia and laugh heartily as they take her in their arms. Next to them, a teenager, maybe sixteen with platinum blonde hair, bright pink lipstick, and bright blue eyes, squeals as Jia tackles her next. The girl wraps her arms around Jia, madly happy as she returns the fierce hug.

"Why are you crying? Stop it! Mum! Jia's *crying...*" She looks up at the older woman, who is nearly in tears herself.

"What are you doing here?" Jia manages to get out through her sobs.

Finally, the teenager—Paige—gently escapes Jia's hug and holds her at arms length. "We were invited. Surprise, I guess?"

"Yeah. It's...it's a surprise." Jia glances over her shoulder at us. Misty and I hadn't meant to share in her touching reunion. Jia hasn't let go of Paige. Her head rests on her sister's shoulder, and although tears run down her face, she's smiling.

Jia's mother notices Misty and I awkwardly standing a foot away. "I'm Noreen Fields. Jia's mum. And this is Seymour. Her dad." She sticks out her hand to Misty. "You must be Misty!" she says warmly.

"I am." Misty numbly takes it as her and I share an awkward glance.

Noreen turns to me. "And you're Ingrid?"

"Yes," is all I can manage, as I too shake her hand. It's firm and calloused. "Nice to meet you."

"Likewise. Jia has told us all about her friends," Noreen replies.

"Mum!" Jia says, trying to playfully dismiss her with a wave.

She smiles. "Well, she's told us enough. We—" Noreen is about to launch into a story when her gaze narrows in on Jia's face.

Oh no.

Noreen grabs Jia's chin and angles her face to expose the lightning scars. "What happened? What is this?"

Jia recoils and begins stammering some excuse.

"Noreen, don't embarrass her," Seymour begins, though he too looks concerned.

"Does it hurt?" Paige asks.

Misty and I jump to her rescue. "It's not what—" Misty begins, as I say, "It's prosthetics."

Both Misty and Jia look at me with alarm. I hadn't meant to speak that loudly. It was just the first plausible explanation that came to mind.

Noreen squints at Jia again. "It looks so real..."

"It's okay, Mum," Jia says, and then hugs her. "I'm testing them out. Part of another student's project. For...theatre."

"That's nice of you," her mother says, holding Jia close, her worry somewhat subsided.

When she finally releases Jia, Jia shoots me a look. I mouth *sorry*. I clear my throat to change the subject. "Long bus ride?"

Paige shrugs. "Yeah. Took me out of school for this."

Jia squeezes her younger sister tighter again. "I'm going to put you back on that bus soon."

Making a face, Paige tries to wrestle out of Jia's grip but Jia begins tickling her younger sister.

What seems like the final bus parks at the curb. The crowd has thinned, but it's still busy. Misty gestures with her thumb. "I see my uncle. Better go say hello."

She gestures to the field, to a beanstalk of a man: dark hair with speckles of grey, a day-old beard, and deep-set, penetrating eyes—Misty's eyes. His suit looks expensive and clean and it doesn't match his weathered shoes. His hands are shoved in his pockets and he's intensely focused on Misty with a kind of distant respect.

Noreen, Seymour, and Paige say polite goodbyes and I smile as Misty hurries away. Jia asks Paige about high school, and Paige lights up as she recounts her school year so far. I nod and offer quips in the right places, but this isn't my place. When the conversation lulls, I excuse myself to find my own parents. Jia meets my gaze and nods reassuringly. She'll be fine. Or perhaps, she's saying that *I'll* be fine.

I wander the crowd. It was a lifetime ago that we showed up late to Sparkstone University, Agailya insisting that school started nearly a month before—but who starts university in August? Real universities have summer terms. Real alien invasions masquerading as universities start school early, and keep people contained and quiet, no matter the cost.

So why bring hundreds and hundreds of people here from all over the world at great expense and risk exposing what's really going on?

If I turn and sprint across the quad, I might be able to get away and hide. If the Collective can't find me, they can't hurt me.

The thought is juvenile and fleeting, like a bird taking to the sky in high winds. Is that what Wil believes—if the enemy can't find him, they can't hurt him?

I spot my parents then. Mum wears a blue blouse with dark jeans beneath her winter coat, while Dad sports a long-sleeved green sweater with his dress pants. He must have been dragged from work. They both look travel-weary, but relieved to have arrived. If only they knew the truth, they would be as worried as I am.

But, they're here. That's something.

They've located a Brigade student, and they're following him with their gaze. They're debating whether to approach him for help. Nope. Can't let that happen.

"Mum! Dad!"

My voice, carried by love over the crowd, turns their heads, and their faces light up with joy. I sidestep other reunions and hurry to their waiting arms, seeing nothing else.

"You look surprised to see us!" Mum says as I embrace her in a tight hug.

"I am!" I reply before I can stop myself.

Dad hugs the two of us. "You didn't know we were coming for the Open House?"

Open House? My confusion is lost to a deeper concern as I nestle against them. What if they aren't my parents? Could they be hafelglob in disguise? My gut says no. Hafelglob are strangely uncomfortable in the human form, and to me have a distinct scent of body odor and garbage that is absent in the quad. There are too many parents and loved ones here, expressing genuine emotions, to be aliens in disguise.

"You shouldn't be here," I whisper to them.

They look concerned. "We came all this—"

"I know. We're going to figure out a way to get you out."

I remember Wil's words. Just teleport. Use your power. Gripping them both by the arms, I try to centre myself and drudge up a happy thought. Ethan? That thought is sullied now with despair. My parents? They're here with me—but why has the Collective brought them here, is it to kill them? I squeeze my eyes shut. I'm too heavy. I have no hope. Only fear for their lives. I can't whisk them away, even if I thought that was the best course of action.

"I promise I'll tell you everything. Let's just—"

"Ingrid Stanley?"

The words freeze in my throat. I don't have to turn around to know who has interrupted my reunion, but I do anyway, because every second my back is turned towards Jadore is an opportunity for her to attack.

She's dressed in a black dress suit with a bright green top. Her hair, as usual, is slicked back in a tight ponytail that goes halfway down her back. I frown—it was definitely shorter yesterday. What gene manipulation has she undergone to look absolutely perfect after our battle in the quad, just a few evenings ago? Was it just her cream? Apparently, the Collective made Jia a similar offer to take away her scars. I can only imagine what they asked for in return for Jia to turn it down.

"I'm Professor Sistrine Jadore," Jadore says, adjusting her sunglasses. A thin ruse to cover up her alien eyes and sensitivity to light. She extends a manicured hand in my parents' general direction. "Acting president for the university. I heard Ingrid talking to someone, I assumed they're her parents."

My mum moves towards Jadore's hand and reciprocates the gesture. "I'm Margaret. This is Craig."

"Oh. You sound lovely." Jadore smiles slyly and turns her head towards me. She knows exactly where we all are—she doesn't bother to pretend in front of me. "Ingrid. Where is Wil?"

I don't reply immediately, which looks and feels suspicious, even though I can be honest with her this time. "I don't know."

She raises two brows—they appear thicker than yesterday.

"That is unfortunate. You are sure you don't know?"

Behind Jadore, a middle-aged African-American man and woman edge closer to us. They are dressed in fine fall coats and each carrying a travel bag. The man is the spitting image of Wil, except with thicker glasses and a head full of hair. The woman smiles politely at me. She has Wil's intelligent eyes. I feel like I'm being evaluated for a surprise pop quiz.

His parents look at me expectantly. Waiting.

"I don't know," I say again. If our parents weren't hovering over this conversation, I would have stormed away. "Why don't you know where he is?"

Jadore smiles thinly at my insolence. "Members of the Student Watch saw you with him yesterday."

I can see why the Student Watch "rebranded" from the Student Action Brigade. The Collective wouldn't want the students taking *real* action. Better to use neutral wording for something inherently sinister. "I really don't know where he is. I assume he's around."

"He's not answering his phone," his mother says. "He always answers."

"I'm sorry. I don't know." I see why Jadore brought them before me now.

"But you—" Jadore holds her forked tongue, as if remembering my parents were also in our company. "Ingrid, you are responsible for Mr. McBride and Mrs. McBride until Wil shows up. Excuse me." Without further airs, she turns and heads down the road, towards MacLeod Hall.

Wil's parents are just as baffled as me and mine. They came all the way from Boston to middle-of-nowhere Northern Alberta, just to be snubbed by the acting leader of the university they're paying thousands of dollars for their son to attend. Although erasing people's minds is abhorrent, I wonder why Wil doesn't bother to erase his existence from his parents' memories. It would have saved them a trip—and this current worry.

"You don't need to entertain us," Mr. McBride says politely. "Wil is a freshman, but he's nearly an adult. He can make his own decisions."

"We should call him again," Mrs. McBride adds, taking her cell phone from her jacket pocket. As she tries to reach Wil, my parents, eager to bridge the awkwardness, proceed with introductions and pleasantries with Wil's father. His name is Antoine and his wife is Leah.

"Wil doesn't tell us much about his social life or what activities are going on at the university," Antoine says. "He's always been extremely devoted to his work. Are you also studying computer engineering? Or math?"

"No, but Wil and I are in the same tutorial. That's how we met. There are a couple of us that hang out together." I feel hollow. Wil should be here. Jia and her family are heading for the dorms. Misty and her uncle have disappeared.

"I left another voicemail," Leah says, pocketing her phone. Her exasperation is beginning to show. "I told him what room we're staying in. I'd like to freshen up before tonight. Professor Jadore set us up in a very nice room. The least the school could do, after all the planes we took to get here."

"All right, they don't want to hear about that," Antoine says good-naturedly. "Very nice to meet you, Ingrid, was it?"

"Yes. I'll let you know if I see Wil," I reply.

My parents say their goodbyes as Antoine and Leah head towards Rogers Hall.

"They seem nice," Mum says. "Too bad your friend Wil isn't here to greet them. I don't know what I'd do if you hadn't been here."

"I'm sure Wil'll turn up," I say noncommittedly.

"Jadore? Was that that woman's name? Why would she think you knew where Wil was? Is he...?" Mum smiles as she trails off.

"No, we're just friends." I look around. Some of the buses are starting to pull away and most of the students and parents have gone into Rogers Hall or one of the many other dorms. For the most part, Sparkstone University has cultivated a traditional, conservative atmosphere when it comes to the sleeping arrangements. I'm in Rita House, with Misty and Jia. Raylene House is the other girls' dorm, though it has co-ed floors. Morris House and Hynes House are the two boys' dorms. Both Wil and Ethan are in Morris House. The dorms are clustered around Rogers Hall, while down the road is MacLeod Hall, where we would meet for our tutorials. Beyond that is the library with the secret underground warehouse, and the town of Sparkstone proper. Sparkstone has basic amenities, though we trust none of them at this point. Everything is run by the Collective, and all the Collective wants is to cultivate and steal our powers.

I feel exposed out here in the quad, and while the open-fielded campus is one of the safer spots to have a conversation, I won't feel completely safe until my parents are in my dorm. "Follow me."

Mum and Dad pick up their bags and follow me towards Rita House. Mum continues her line of questioning. "That was odd for Professor Jadore to just leave us with Antoine and Leah. She was extremely rude to you, Ingrid. Why would she speak to you like that?"

Because she's a literal dictator. "I don't like her and she doesn't like me, and we've decided to no longer hide it."

"Why don't you like her?" Dad asks.

"She's...difficult." That's putting it mildly. "And she's not really blind. For the record."

"Yeah, she walked right up to you. I guess she could have asked someone where you were." Dad is already second-guessing himself.

"We should file a complaint with the university's HR department. There's no need for that kind of behaviour, not towards a bright student," Mum says.

I almost laugh. Sparkstone University, with an HR department? Right. "I'll handle it, Mum."

She glances around the buildings. "Which way is Rogers Hall? We were told on the bus to check in there to be assigned a room. Apparently we're just staying the night."

"They were very insistent on the bus about checking in," Dad added. "They only told us about fifty times."

"Yeah. Well..." No way am I taking them to see Jadore, Agailya, or any Collective member. "Maybe later. There's a lot we need to catch up on!" I put on my best smile. It hurts. My throat is a prison for my sobs. "This way. Is that all you brought?" Dad has a small duffel bag and Mum has her large, stylish purse.

"Yes. They didn't give us much time to pack," Mum replies. The two of them follow me on the path to Rita House. "I got a phone call saying that we were invited yesterday morning to an Open House today and tomorrow. I said, 'I never knew anything about an Open House.' To which the woman on the other end said, 'Everything is in the email newsletter.' And I said, 'I am not subscribed to an email newsletter, why wouldn't you send physical mail about that, or better yet, why wouldn't my daughter, a student at the school, tell her mother?' In my head, I thought that I wouldn't want to go anyway. If it were in Calgary, or even in Edmonton, we'd make an effort, but to come all the way up here..."

"Oh, nope, I'll get the door for you." I wrap my hand firmly around the handle and pull it forcefully open. Nothing takes my blood. That would be a more efficient way to take my blood, instead of sending their Brigade goons, I think bitterly. Mum and Dad smile at me as they enter Rita House. At least this prevents the door from sampling my parents' blood. What if that was the whole reason they brought all the parents here? Just for a blood sample? No, again, that is absurdly inefficient.

Mum takes an intermission with her story as we pass the security desk. Three guards are there now, all hafelglob in human form from their demeanour and rude stares. One sits lazily in a plush chair while the others lean against the desk. They don't talk. When they catch my don't-try-me stare, they look away. Perhaps they know who I am—and what my more powerful friends can do to them if they cross me.

"Just up the stairs. Third floor," I say to my parents, letting them go ahead of me as I give the security guards the once-over.

"Crosskey," says the one in the chair in greeting, nodding his head.

My gaze narrows as I try to hide my surprise. Only one hafelglob in disguise calls me by that name. Ohz. Yet this isn't Ohz. This is a new guard I haven't met before. His human form appears Caucasian, perhaps Italian, though the accent is similar to Ohz's, in that it sounds vaguely like someone is gargling water while sounding Eastern European.

"Is Ohz all right?" I ask, aware that my parents are nearly to the second set of stairs and out of sight.

The three guards nod. "Kind of the Crosskey to be concerned for him."

Ohz has a reverence for me that I don't understand nor reciprocate. He is part of the Collective, though he seems sympathetic to my plight. I've barely seen him in the last month. Something must be keeping him busy—or away from me. "Tell him...I said hello."

"We will," say the three in unison, with creepily friendly smiles. It's then I notice a white symbol stitched into the collar of their jackets. It looks like an *a*, though it's so small, it's hard to say for sure.

"Ookay." I back away slowly towards the stairs. I hear my parents above—they must be on the third floor by now. I put a tentative, clammy hand on the banister. Jadore certainly didn't hold back at the assembly yesterday as she tortured Ohz in front of the entire school. Perhaps the hafelglob could be my allies? It's a disturbing thought. They smell like garbage and body odor no matter what they look like. If I had anything left to vomit, I might feel nauseous.

Recognizing the repulsion in my face, they laugh, and I snap out of my thoughts. I race up the stairs. "Wait, Mum, Dad, don't go too far."

I nearly run into three students coming down the stairs. By the time I make it to the top, I'm flustered, but not out of breath. Mum and Dad are waiting patiently before the doors on the landing. I let us in, sighing, trying to put the disgusting security guards from my mind. "My room is just down here. We can put your bags there and relax a little."

"I don't need to relax," Dad says good-naturedly. "A bathroom break, maybe. But I'm fine. It's nice of the school to invite us here. Even at short notice."

"And it's nice to see *you*. Even though you rarely call anymore." Mum puts her arm around me as we walk down the hallway towards my dorm.

"Sorry, Mum. Cell coverage here has been spotty." I lean against her. How am I going to tell her the truth about this place? What if other students are blabbing to their parents about how the school is training them to be secret superheroes? Unless the Collective wants that. But I can't see how that furthers their agenda.

"What's wrong? You seem tired. Are you eating enough?" Mum asks, holding me closer. "I think you've lost weight!"

"Don't stay up all night studying for exams. A little bit every night goes a long way," Dad chimes in.

"I could be eating more," I admit. "Just...busy. I'll tell you about it when..."

At the end of the hall is a door that leads to a separate set of stairs, which take you up to the fourth floor. I trail off as Ethan Millar barges through that door. His determined steps falter as he sees me with my parents. I pull away from my mother instantly.

He tilts his head and gives me a little smile. "Hi. Can you tell me which building this is again? I think I wandered into the wrong one."

My stomach sinks. From his tone, I can tell he doesn't know who I am. Again. "Ethan. You're in Rita House. The girls' dorm."

He purses his lips in embarrassment as he glances between Mum and Dad. "Ah. Of course. I should have known that, I feel."

"Didn't we already have this conversation with this guy?" Dad asks me.

My eyes widen as I realize he's right. When I first arrived in my temporary dorm, Agailya showed me to my room. Ethan had wandered into my room while searching for Agailya. That was how we met.

Ethan looks confused. Seems like he doesn't remember that either. "Sorry, have we met before?"

"Yes, I believe so," Dad replies. "Though it was months ago."

Laughing politely, Ethan starts to edge away from us. "Well, I'm not so good with faces these days."

"Ethan, wait," I say. I can't let him get away, even if he doesn't know who I am. I point at myself. "Ingrid. That's my name. These are my parents, Margaret and Craig. Are your parents coming today too? The school is bringing everyone here. Don't know if you heard that."

He brightens, seemingly relieved I've introduced myself. Again. "Ah. Yeah. Mira was telling me about that. I got a message from my parents. They're coming, but their flight's been held up in Toronto. Guess they're having a storm there."

"I see." I wonder how many other overseas students are waiting on parents stuck in airports. Maybe they're the lucky ones. "You're welcome to hang out with me and my friends if you're lacking company. Or parents. If you need parents for... whatever activities the school has planned." My face heats. The words out of my mouth are so dumb and desperate.

Ethan doesn't seem to think so, however. "Oh. Well, I may take you up on that. I was going to head back to my dorm room, though, I"—he hesitates, trying to remember—"I think... You know, I don't entirely remember why I was going there. I had this idea for a painting... Anyway, it doesn't matter. I should probably find the right building. I have a feeling if I'm caught in the girls' dorm—"

"*There* you are!"

It takes every bit of composure to hide my disappointment. I turn around as Mira marches down the hallway towards us. She's wearing dark leggings and a bright, short skirt, and a white blouse. She's got colourful earrings, perfect makeup, and powerful, floral perfume. Of course she looks great. She's grinning with relief at Ethan, ignoring me and my parents completely. "Did you get lost again?"

"Yeah," Ethan says sheepishly. His face softens as he smiles and it hurts to look at him, knowing he used to look that way at me.

"Silly. This is the girls' dorm. I'll take you back to the boys'," Mira says. She takes his hand, and finally acknowledges me with a polite but firm nod. "Hello, Ingrid."

"Hi." My voice cracks. "Your parents here yet?"

Her eyebrows knit together. "Oh. No. My aunt hasn't arrived yet. She's stuck on the runway at Heathrow, last I heard. I'm sure she'll be here very late tonight, if she isn't rebooked on a different flight."

"That's too bad," Mum says politely. "I can't imagine getting off an international flight and then having to take another, what, four-hour bus ride from Edmonton?"

Mira stares at my mother blankly, as if she hadn't expected her to join the conversation. "Yes. Perhaps Sparkstone will charter a plane from Edmonton. Or London."

"That sounds incredibly...generous," Dad remarks.

"Too bad Sparkstone won't charter a plane for my parents,"

Ethan mutters. "I haven't seem them in...it feels like a really, really long time."

"You remember them?" I ask.

Mira's grip on Ethan tightens. She doesn't hurry him and she doesn't interrupt, yet there's a shift in her perfume. The floral smell wilts in my nose.

"Yeah. I do," Ethan replies earnestly. "Their faces are...fuzzy... but...well, it's more of a feeling than an image-memory. Sounds silly, doesn't it?"

"I don't think it's silly." I take a bold step towards him.

Ethan's face reddens. He stares at the floor. Here we are, trying to have an intimate conversation about his memory condition in front of my parents, who are real and true strangers. Unlike me, a false stranger, waiting to be remembered.

"They'll be here soon," Mira promises him, rubbing his arm. "Probably the same time as my aunt. I think they're on the same flight."

"I thought you said your aunt was stuck in Heathrow?" Ethan says.

"Yes," Mira says. "Like your parents."

"No, mine are in Toronto."

"Oh." Mira looks confused, and then brushes it off. "They'll be here when they get here. Nothing we can do about that now. Except go back to your dorm, Ethan."

"Yeah, but it's cramped in there. Filled with half-finished canvases. There's an art studio, right?"

"Yes. It's Lewis Art Building," I say before Mira has the chance. "It's just down the road. All the buildings look the same, but it's written on a plaque outside."

"Thanks." Ethan gives me a genuine smile. "Nice to meet

you," he says to my parents, and steals a last glance at me as Mira drags him down the corridor, speaking to him in harsh whispers. She is always around him. If I could just have him to myself for one moment, maybe I could ask him to the music room, to try and recreate our second kiss, or for a walk in the field, to recreate our first.

"Is your room around here?" Dad asks, snapping me out of my thoughts.

"Yeah. Here." I take out the key and walk towards the door.

"Good," Dad says, relieved. "We haven't used the bathroom since our pitstop in Edmonton, and with all the water we were drinking..."

Mum hovers over me as I unlock the door. "If boys aren't allowed in the girls' dorm, why would she be allowed to take him to the boys' dorm?" Mum stage-whispers to me. "Does he have mental difficulties? Is she his helper?"

"No, Mum. That's his girlfriend."

"You don't seem very happy about that."

"I'm not," I reply.

"She seems bossy," Mum says helpfully, checking over her shoulder to ensure that Ethan and Mira had gone. The hallways were quiet and empty, save some thumping and mild activity on the floors below. "Let the boy have his space! Can you imagine babying your boyfriend like that? It's not healthy."

"I know, Mum. It's really weird."

"Well, at least you know what he's like now. If he likes being coddled, then he's not the boy for you."

Normally I'd have some kind of retort ready for that, but my wit is grappled by my hurt feelings. That isn't how Ethan is. When we first met, he was vibrant and outgoing and quirky and romantic. Now he's under Mira's thumb, and seemingly content to be that way.

I finish with the door and hold it open as Mum and Dad enter with their luggage. They linger in the entrance, blocking my way as they survey the room.

"Oh. Whoops. Sorry for the mess." I've gotten so used to having Misty and Jia stay in my room—and alternating rooms as we saw fit—that I haven't noticed the pigsty it has become. Unmade bed with fitted sheet half-off, a second queen-sized mattress we'd dragged from Misty's room on the floor, and our combined dirty laundry litters most of the free walking space.

"Uh. Excuse me." I push between the two of them, fumble across the floor mattress with my shoes still on, tangling myself in the sheets and the previously folded blankets, to open the window. It doesn't smell terrible to me in here, but it seems the right thing to do, given the situation. "Just set your bags on this mattress here, on the floor."

"Ookay," Dad says, and does so, before entering the bathroom. I make a face, hoping it's not too dirty in there.

Mum meets my gaze, makes a similar face, and then laughs. "What is going on in here?"

"My friends and I are having sleepovers," I reply. It feels nice to tell the truth, even if it's a sugar-coated one.

"Well, where are we supposed to stay?" Mum asks. "This is why we should just report to the registrar's office like they told us."

"No!" Sighing, I take off my shoes and hurry by her once more to shut the door. "Sit down. On the bed. There's a lot I need to tell you."

"Wait for your father. Then I have to go too." She reluctantly does what I tell her and clutches her purse as she settles it in her lap. "Maybe I can help you tidy this up a bit."

"My friends and I can do it later. Misty and Jia are their names."

"Jia. Is that Chinese?"

"Yes."

The toilet flushes and after the sink runs, Dad emerges from the bathroom and Mum hurries in.

"Yep, pretty nice bus they sent us up on," Dad says, settling himself on the bed as we wait for Mum. "All the snacks and bottled water you could drink. For free! Your mother packed us snacks but I guess we availed ourselves a bit too much of the water."

Thank goodness for that. We drink the water from the sink, even though I was paranoid about it at first. Jia and I had talked about stealing kettles from the kitchen, though we haven't followed through on that yet.

"So they told you this was an Open House?" I say.

"Yeah," Dad replies. "Like your mother was saying. They call us up out of the blue just yesterday and tell us we are obliged to come here. Ridiculous, I say. Fortunately, since my work is having IT issues right now, I can't get anything done anyway, so I figured I might as well come. I mean, I'm excited to see what you're doing here. What our hard-earned money is paying for you to do."

My stomach turns. "Right." Just another thing to add to the list: after stopping the systematic alien invasion, refund all Sparkstone University tuition. That should be easy!

I pull out my phone and compose a coded text to Misty and Jia, telling them to come to my room ASAP. They're probably busy with their families so I hope they check their phones, assuming the message gets through. We need to stick together, all of us. We need a plan to deal with whatever the Collective is throwing at us. I glance at the light. The Collective has cameras everywhere. I stealthily activate the silent audio disruption pulse in my wristband. That should buy us about ten to fifteen minutes.

I blow out a big sigh as the toilet flushes again, the sink runs, and Mum exits the bathroom. "Why don't we clean up this room now while we wait for dinner?"

"What do you mean? Did they promise you food?" I ask suspiciously.

"Of course. This is an all-expenses paid trip!" Dad exclaims brightly.

I wring my hands. I can't keep going like this. "Mum. Dad. There's something I have to tell you. It's really important. Mum, you need to sit down."

"Okay, but watch your tone." She sits next to Dad.

I pace before them. I've thought about this moment a lot over the last few months, yet in my hypotheticals, I'd somehow managed to escape Sparkstone and I'm telling them frantically over tea in my childhood home. Telling them everything here, in this messy dorm room, feels rushed. Wrong.

"There's something very wrong going on here." I take a deep breath. "I highly doubt there's a real Open House here, Dad. Your money has been going into the bank accounts of murderers."

Mum pales. "Did someone die, Ingrid?"

"Not just one person, Mum. Let me finish. It's complicated." I check my phone quickly. No reply from Jia, which I expected, but a coded message from Misty: *Coming soon.* I can't wait for them. Misty and Jia will have to tell their families the truth in their own way. "The school is a sham. It's part of a massive cover-up by aliens."

Dad makes a face, but doesn't comment. Mum looks sincerely distressed.

"And yes, yes, just wait, I know how that sounds," I continue. I take another deep breath. Slow and steady, easy does it. "Aliens are real. That's a big one to swallow. I can prove it. Kind of. There are a bunch of different species and together they make up the Collective. The Collective controls the school. Their mission, as far as we have been able to determine, is to gather up the smartest teens and young adults and extract their DNA. Why? Well...because some of us—perhaps all of us, in time— have superpowers. Yes, including me. Okay. Now you can ask questions."

"What superpowers do you think you have, Ingrid?" Dad asks. He now shares Mum's distress.

"Wait a minute," Mum says, putting a quieting hand on Dad. "I don't follow. There are aliens in Alberta? Why would they be here? There's nothing here."

"Yes, why wouldn't they attack a more populated area?" Dad adds.

"Because they are trying to quietly kill us and take our superpowers. Mine is teleportation. And I'd show you but...I'm not very good at it."

"I would like to see it anyway," Dad says earnestly.

"I'll show you...in a bit. Tonight, maybe, when it's dark and there are fewer people."

"Did we accidently send you to a magic school? Is that what you're saying?" Mum asks. Her knuckles are white from gripping her purse too tightly.

I smile. "A little. Except way more dangerous. Haven't you noticed how strange it is, that they brought all the parents, all the families, up here? Why would they do that? There can't be any Open House. There aren't real classes anymore."

"No more classes? So the school is wasting our money. On... invasion expenses. And murder."

"Who was murdered, Ingrid? Do we—?" Mum asks.

A sharp knock at the door startles me. I check my phone again. Still nothing from Jia, and nothing new from Misty. My heart is pounding. My slippery palms can barely hold onto my phone. If it's Agailya or Jadore, I think I'll be sick. Will they punish me for telling my parents the truth? They already put my Dad at death's door once. No doubt they'd do it again.

I put a finger to my lips as I tiptoe to the door and eye the peephole. I bite down on my lip hard to keep from making further noise. It's Shane, and two others from the Brigade. They're even wearing their stupid jackets.

He knocks again. Harder this time. "Open up, Ingrid. Time for the blood test."

My hand hovers above the doorknob as I silently shake my head. I look to my parents, my eyes bugged out of their sockets, willing them with a power I don't have to be quiet. Mum narrows her gaze and shrugs in question. There is no way I'm letting the Brigade in here to take my blood—or my parents'. The Collective has done that enough already.

"C'mon. I know you're in there. I heard you." He bangs on the door again, and I bite down on my knuckle as I brace myself on the wall next to the door. "If you don't submit for testing, we're going to assume you're an alien imposter. You'll be detained for questioning."

Mum and Dad share equal looks of horror and confusion, yet they don't move. All colour drains from my mother's face.

The knocking keeps coming. "Ingrid. Ingrid Stanley!"

I'm on the floor now, with my head between my knees. I can't teleport. I'm trapped by my own fear. I've never teleported another person before. Would that even work? How much time would I lose? Where can I even go? I teleported with the Hunger, but that was different. It wasn't solid and it had me in its grasp, ready to devour me.

I hear the two others talking in low tones to Shane. Then, a pair of footsteps from down the hallway. One heavy and fast, and the other, softer but equally sure. They're coming right for our door.

"Hey. I'm Shane. With the Student Watch. What's your name?"

"Misty," says Misty's voice smugly.

The sound of a pen hitting a clipboard punctuate Shane's noises of consideration. "Misty...Misty...oh. I see. Last name Carter. Almost slipped by me there, but fortunately we have your preferred first name on this list. Looks like no one has gotten to you yet. Might as well do you now. Just roll up your—"

"Excuse me," says a deeper, authoritative voice. "Who are you?"

Quietly, I move to the peephole again. Misty is with her uncle in the hallway. Shane and the two other Brigade members have their backs to the door so I can just barely see.

"I'm Shane. With the Student Watch. We're here to collect Misty Carter's blood sample for today."

I can hear the disgust in her uncle's voice. "Unhygienic conditions, impromptu blood screening? No. She's not doing that."

"She has to," Shane says. His jovial tone is undercut by his impatience. "Don't know if you've heard, but we're in the middle of a crisis here."

"Yes," says Misty's uncle calmly. "The crisis will be a lawsuit against you, your student group, and the school if you continue to insist on illegal blood tests."

"We're not looking for trouble. Only cooperation," Shane says.

"Not from us. Who is the professor in charge of your organization? I'd like you to take me to her immediately."

Silence. Then, Shane, fiddling with his clipboard, heaving a sigh. "Right this way."

"I'm just going to get some stuff," Misty calls after them as they hurry down the hall.

I move out of the way of the door as Misty quickly opens and shuts it. She's equally startled by my proximity.

"What was that?" her and I ask at the same time.

Misty goes first, rolling her eyes. "My uncle is going to give Agailya or Jadore or whoever a tongue-thrashing. As if that will do any good."

"You're not worried about letting him go by himself?" I ask.

Misty twists her lips. "Well I am *now*. No, no, it's fine. I'll catch up with them." She walks further into the room and then notices my parents. She hesitates at first, and then extends a hand. "Hey. I'm Misty."

They introduce themselves. "Sorry about Shane," I say, pursing my lips.

She heaves a sigh and grumbles. "I should have punched him in the face, or worse, but my uncle would have made a big deal out of it. Don't they already have our blood, anyway?"

"Do you have superpowers too, Misty?" Mum asks.

Misty side-eyes me. "Uh...?"

Mum laughs. "Sorry. Just something Ingrid told us just now."

"Really," Misty says dryly. "Well, I just came by to make sure you knew about the reception for the parents tonight. A real *assembly of people*." She raises her eyebrows in suggestion.

She's right. We might not get another chance to abduct Jadore. Yet it's all the more risky to do so now, with our loved ones in their clutches.

"Thanks," I say. "I'll be there."

"We'll all be there," Mum adds.

"You don't have to go," I say. "You can just stay here."

Mum makes a face. "I don't think so. I think it's best we get our own room. Or leave entirely."

Misty nods. "I'll leave that up to you. See you later?"

I see her out and shut the door.

"Well," Dad says, wandering back to the bed. "Jesus."

"Yeah," I agree.

The three of us digest the last fifteen minutes in silence for a while, until Mum says, "We can't stay here."

"If I don't stay, they'll hurt you." Them being here is just another reminder of the Collective's power over us.

"They're already hurting you."

"Leaving doesn't solve the problem," I reply. "I have to fight them."

"This seems like an awfully big fight for one person," Mum says.

"I have friends."

"Didn't you say you can teleport?" Dad asks. There's still some disbelief in his voice.

I walk over to both of them. "Yeah. But...not very well. It's unpredictable."

"Maybe you should start from the beginning," Mum says.

My stomach does flip-flops. "Does this mean you... believe me?"

They exchange looks. There is no concern in their eyes, only affection.

"Of course we do," Mum says. She wraps her arms around me. "We're your parents. We are always on your side."

For once in my life, I am not enthused about dressing up for a party.

I shove myself into the dress. I certainly don't feel as vibrant as the summer-sky blues and the orange-red flowers around the bust and trim, but I need to inspire confidence somehow. I fiddle with the off-the-shoulder elastic. Every time I raise my arm, the stupid thing rides up past my shoulder. I'm going to be playing with that all night.

Undoing the braid, I let my long red hair fall loose around my shoulders and evaluate the look. My wristband is as conspicuous as the dress. Unfortunately, there's no way to remove it that we've been able to find, and since Wil isn't here to do further tinkering, Misty, Jia, and I are stuck with them. I hide my hands behind my back. There. Now I just have to do that all night and no one will suspect a thing.

I blow out a sigh. No, I'll wear a jacket. That's the sensible solution.

I open the bathroom door. Misty and Jia are nearly finished getting ready. Misty rushes by me to use the mirror to perfect her makeup. She looks stunning in her long, lacey-sleeved black dress. She's gone bold with her eye look: long lashes, dark eyeshadow, and cat-eye lid liner. She glances at me through her reflection with her deep blue eyes and I give her a thumbs up. She returns the smile.

"You'd think we're all looking for hot dates, the way we're dressed," Misty remarks, leaning over the sink to give her lashes another coat of mascara.

Jia smooths out her pristinely white dress pants and fixes her flowered, orange-yellow blouse. "I suppose we never know what's going to happen."

I move out of the way as she stands in the bathroom doorway on her tiptoes to evaluate the visibility of her lightning scars.

"How are you holding up?" I ask her.

"I'm fine," she says, perhaps too quickly as she brushes her long, dark hair over her scarred cheek. "Paige and Mum and Dad are waiting for me in my room. I shouldn't keep them."

"I thought we were going in together," Misty says, sliding the lid of her mascara shut. She throws it haphazardly out of the bathroom, onto my bed.

"We can go in together. With my family. When we're all ready," Jia replies coolly. "Where are your parents, Ingrid?"

"In the public bathroom, on the second floor. Getting ready." I hope they're still there.

"I told my uncle to go ahead," Misty says. She steps out of the bathroom and flops on the bed. She's wearing her same old worn black boots. "He'll be fine, and if he's not, I'll make sure whoever messes with him pays the price."

As Misty finds Jia an appropriate lipstick colour and offers her cover-up suggestions, I realize that if we were regular university students, we'd be having a similar discussion while getting ready for a night on the town. We'd probably be on our second drink by now, warm and fuzzy and giddy for adventure. Ethan would be here too, I'd be sure of it, and Kimberly and Sunni, and we'd let the music carry us away at the hottest clubs in town until the early hours of the morning and our weary bodies force us back to our beds.

I grab my daintiest purse and place my phone inside. No dancing tonight. Instead, a different kind of rebellion.

"Why bring them all the way here?" Jia asks. She pins her hair to one side to cover her scars. "What can the Collective do here that they can't do in the real world?"

The question casts a quietness over us, and while each of us has a false start, we can't come up with a good enough answer. The Collective has influence over our families. They demonstrated that well enough when my father had a so-called accident—and when I took care of Ethan for Agailya, a miraculous treatment saved my father's life.

"Assuming we're here because our superpowers are tied to our DNA, maybe they plan to harvest our parents as well?" Misty suggests.

Jia raises her eyebrows. "Except for those who aren't biologically related to their parents."

"Paige is almost old enough to go to university," I said darkly. "Maybe they're looking at her. Nature versus nurture."

Jia pales. "I won't let that happen."

I think on it some more as Misty and Jia put on their shoes, retrieve their phones, and choose appropriate purses. "Maybe there's no practical reason. It could be a message to us. Specifically, the three of us. They have the upper hand, and they can take the lives of those we love whenever we fall out of line."

Misty shrugs. "That's a lot of trouble for a message directed at three people. Four if you count Wil. Also, they've already communicated that to us by, you know, killing Sunni."

Her words float over me. A deep part of me resonates with the idea that the Collective, and specifically Jadore, speaks to me with their movements. First, Ethan's memories are wiped, a punishment for telling everyone about aliens and superpowers first. Now the Collective parade our parents around campus, showing off their achievements after I willfully defied Jadore in public.

Everything reeks of a conspiracy to silence me and my friends.

Well, soon the entire school will know the truth. They can't keep us silent forever.

"Are we really going to go ahead with the plan to kidnap Jadore? In front of our parents?" Jia asks. "What if they hold our parents hostage?"

Dread pools in my stomach like thick black oil. I want to vomit. I'm not ready. Yet here we are. "We have to strike. If we don't...they'll just keep finding new and better ways to torture us."

It's minus ten outside when Misty and I meet my parents and Misty's uncle in front of Rita House. We're still waiting for Jia and her family. Jia insisted we go on ahead while she fused over Paige's outfit. When Mum sees my outfit and the meager black fall coat I have to cover myself, she shakes her head. "I should have brought up your winter jacket."

"It's all right, we're only going across the road." In truth, the biting cold is no worse than my prickling anxiety about what fresh horrors tonight can bring. The longer we wait outside, despite the temperature, the less time I'm under the watchful eye of the Collective. Parents and students spill out of Rogers Hall. I'm in no hurry to squeeze inside.

Eventually Jia and her family exit the dorm. Jia links arms with Paige. She's wearing a black and white dress, fashionable and smart. Her parents are equally tasteful, with her mother wearing thick furs and her father in a long dress coat.

"Everyone looks nice, don't they," Mum says cheerfully. "And look. You can even see the stars here."

Dad strains his neck, peering up. "Look at that. You don't get this in Calgary."

"It's not often you get this clear a view," I say. "Last time was…" I glance at Misty, as I'm about to tell her about a particular summer camping trip we took to Cape Breton, when I realize the last time I had a clear view of the stars was when I was in space, caught in the clutches of a supermassive black hole.

Misty raises her eyebrows at me. "Last time I saw a view was on the mother ship. With Sunni."

Mum and Dad aren't listening to us anyway. "You look really nice. I'm sure Sunni would have said so."

She looks away, trying to hide her blush. "Thanks. Even if you're just sayin' it to be nice."

"No, I mean it." I frown. I'd been so caught up with parrying the Collective's moves against us that I'd nearly forgotten. "I have to show you something later. It's about Sunni. I don't know how but…I got the journal back."

"Sunni's journal?" Misty's eyes widen. She looks over her

shoulder at Jia. She's too far back to hear. Misty clenches her fists. "That was destroyed."

"I know. Sunni gave it to me. In a dream."

She doesn't reply right away. Misty's feelings for Sunni run deep. She has never given up hoping that somewhere, somehow, Sunni is still alive, if not corporally. "If we get through tonight, I want to see it."

My lips are already chapped. "Agreed."

The reception itself is in the cafeteria in Rogers Hall, where yesterday's assembly took place. It is, unsurprisingly, too small to accommodate every student and their visiting family. The lobby is packed, as are the stairs leading down to the space outside the cafeteria. I take Mum by the hand and lead her through the crowd, with Dad close behind. I don't want to lose them in the chaos. Especially now. The crowd is heaviest by the cafeteria doors, which are open and inviting. Delicious smells waft above the sweat of hundreds, promising hot BBQ ribs, sweet potato fries, hamburger sliders, and other hor d'orves, which no doubt will be served in the most tempting way.

As we approach the cafeteria doors, Mum says, "Your father and I are getting hungry. Honestly, I don't know how your stomach isn't trying to eat its way out of your body."

"I'm only hungry when I'm thinking about it," I mutter, and add, "What about the snacks I gave you? And didn't you say you brought some from home?"

"We ate our own hours ago. And those carrots you gave us were half stale. What is wrong with the food here? Can't you smell that? There's beef and something fried—looks like on a buffet table in there." She points into the busy cafeteria. It's dimly lit. On the side wall is a long table filled with delicious treats—probably all dosed with Gen-Grow, the drug that keeps students pliant and makes our powers stronger.

I sigh. "Mum, it's really not a good idea to get the food here. It'll make you sick."

"I see people with plates all around us and no one is rushing for the bathroom." She looks worried. "If we can't eat that, what can we eat?"

"I don't know, Mum." I've barely eaten since Jadore presented me with a mouth-watering feast designed to heighten my powers. Jia had only stale produce left from her family's last care package. We are in desperate times. "Just do your best to not eat, okay? That's how they control us, with the food."

Mum looks dubious but shakes her head. "All right. We'll make our way over there. Join us when you're done with your friends."

I nod and Dad pats me on the shoulder warmly as the two of them squeeze into the cafeteria, politely saying hello to the other parents and students mingling in the hallway and the entrance.

Misty waits with me for Lynn, Greg, and Elisha. Jia and her family have fallen far behind. By the time Jia makes it through the crowd, her parents are no longer with her. That isn't a concern: she's grinning, one hand covering the scarred side of her face, the other firmly linked with Paige's. The two of them lean in and share giggled whispers as if there aren't a thousand other bodies pushing against them.

I wave at them, and just as they're about to walk by, Paige spots us, and the two of them make their way to us.

"My parents found some other farmers, so they'll be set for a while," Jia says over the din. "Are we ready?"

Misty and I exchange glances as we have a private battle over who is going to tackle *that* one. I lose. "So, Paige. What do you think of Sparkstone?"

"Pretty nice, I guess," Paige replies. She smiles at Jia.

"I guess you don't like all the farm talk," I continue, raising my eyebrows at Jia.

Jia gets the hint and refuses to back down. "Paige is hanging out with me this evening."

"Right. So she's also going to be patrolling the party. Convincing people at the drop of a hat to leave the building when it's time?" Misty says.

"Are you part of that weird Student Watch?" Paige asks Jia.

"No. Not really." Jia quickly brushes more of her hair in front of her scarred face. "There's too many people in here, Paige. Let's take a walk around. Try and find the least busy place."

"Okay. Where's the food? Something in there smells really—"

"Nope." Jia steers her little sister away from the cafeteria. "Let's go this way."

Paige pouts as Jia navigates them towards the stairs up to the main entrance. Misty crosses her arms. "I don't blame her, but now isn't the time for...well, we have to keep our heads in the game. Whatever the Collective brought all these people here for, it's definitely not helping us."

"Yeah. It is nice to see my parents again."

Misty nods solemnly. "I wasn't sure if we would."

Then, I spot him. Ethan's hand is firmly trapped by Mira's. She's chatting enthusiastically with two elderly people across the hallway. They don't look much like Ethan or Mira, and as their relatives are supposedly delayed in airports far away, I doubt they are family. Ethan nods intermittently at his conversation partners, yet his attention drifts to me, and when our eyes meet, my feet drift towards him.

Misty grabs my arm. "Don't get distracted."

I think about pulling away, but I don't.

She senses my surrender and releases me. "He's alive. That's what's important."

The words carry a kind of insult. Sunni is not alive—yet Ethan is. "They've mutilated him."

"They've mutilated all of us," she says bluntly. "We have to survive. To make them pay."

Her words steel me. I nod. She's right. A small, selfish part of me wants to flee and sneak into his dorm, or lure him into the art studio, just to steal a few precious moments with him, but I shake my head free of it. My parents are here. I have to think of them first. Especially since they know the truth about Sparkstone.

After another five minutes of enduring the press of bodies struggling to enter the cafeteria, the three journalism students emerge from the crowd. Elisha waves, making her bracelets jangle. Her flowery, sleeveless dress nearly catches on her heel as she hurries towards us. Lynn follows in a black and white collared shirt and beige skirt, hunching her shoulders and looking uncomfortable in the crowd. Greg, frustrated by the slow pace of his friends, makes a *finally-we're-here* face at me and Misty. He wears a red bowtie with a faintly polka-dotted dress shirt and dress pants.

"Out of our way," Greg says dramatically, sneering at some students just trying to get through to the cafeteria. "This night is already a disaster. No one has an iron around here."

"I already said I was sorry for breaking yours," Elisha replies.

Greg doesn't seem to have heard her. "My pants are unpressed and therefore unready to face the alien horde."

"Don't worry, I'll protect you," Misty replies sarcastically. She does jazz hands in front of Greg's face as sparks and bits of ice dance between her fingers.

Greg smirks. "Very funny."

"It's not funny," Lynn whispers. Her nervous gaze flits over the crowded hallway. "All of our families are here. Who do you think is going to get hit the minute Misty starts throwing her powers around?"

"Hopefully Jia will do her part to get people out of here." I wish she hadn't gone off with her sister, but better to have Paige and our families away from the core of the action. I already took a big risk telling my parents the truth. Maybe that's what Jia is doing with Paige right now. My stomach is doing flip-flops. I can feel it in the air: this night has the stench of an evening that will never end. I eye the three journalism students. "Have you found anything out about what's going on tonight? What is this reception for?"

"The school is branding this as an Open House for the parents," Elisha explains. "This reception is about honouring the students who have shown the greatest promise throughout the year so far, but also highlighting the most interesting projects, as well as *supposedly* talking about the future. It doesn't look like they're selling the parents on the whole superheroes-versus-aliens story they told the student body."

"My parents didn't buy it anyway," Greg mutters.

"My dad is just hanging out by the buffet," Lynn says. "The students I talked to seemed upset their parents were here. Who wants their parents around when they're trying to train to be superheroes?"

"What about Jadore? Or the other professors?" Misty asks, folding her lacey arms.

"The rumour is Jadore's going to give a toast or a speech sometime before midnight," Elisha continues. She turns her chestnut eyes on me. "It's an opportunity we may want to take advantage of."

Misty was right earlier: we don't know when we'll have another chance. They could slaughter us all tonight. I can't let that happen. "We're doing it."

"Are you ready to do this?" Misty asks.

"I have to be," I reply. I lock my happiest thoughts in a mental vault. My teleportation power runs on hope, not fear. My footsteps feel heavy as the five of us disband to carry out our assigned tasks. Greg, Elisha, and Lynn are scouting the reception for Brigade members and security guards to come up with an accurate count. They'll relay this information to Misty and Jia so, when the time comes for the speech, they can distract or interfere with key guards to allow the maximum amount of people possible to escape. If the weather were warmer, we would have created a distraction outside. While people will want fresh air in the suffocating heat generated by nearly twelve hundred students and their families, I doubt we'll be able to convince a good number to stay outside in the below-freezing weather.

My job, leading up to the actual kidnapping, is simple. Stay near the stage. Watch for Jadore. Don't get caught or waylaid by the Brigade. Think happy thoughts so I can actually use my teleportation power.

Waving to Misty as she heads off with Greg, I join the people squeezing through the double doors into the cafeteria. The Collective has transformed the space in short order. Buffet tables line the walls, skirted handsomely in white. Blinking soft lights drape from the ceiling, failing to capture the majesty of the stars outside. Alternative rock music drones just loud enough to recognize the genre but not the band, and that annoys me, for I don't like things lingering on the tip of my tongue. I search the room for our respective families and for Ethan. It's difficult through the crowd. Every inch of the room is packed. It would take me a good fifteen minutes to make my way from the stage to the back of the room, where I believe I see Mum and Dad hovering by a tall, ornate chocolate fountain.

I manage to brace myself against the stage. White silk hugs the edge and a couple of Brigade members put the finishing touches on more backdrop drapery. A podium sits alone at centre stage. The stage is the only place that isn't occupied by students and parents. Enforcing this just behind me is a hafelglob security guard. A different one from before, but again, he gives me a friendly, knowing nod, and mouths, "Crosskey."

Now that I'm closer, I can make it out more clearly. Like the guards at the front desk of Rita House, he also has a white-stitched, cursive *a* on the collar of his black jacket. I wonder what it means. A new public signifier for the hafelglob? No, I haven't seen many others with that symbol.

I cross my arms. I'm still wearing my jacket, yet I'm paranoid about someone seeing my wristband and branding me an alien. Around me, people sip their drinks and engage in loud small talk, and as the seconds drag by, my anxiety intensifies. How am I supposed to do this? Jadore will go up on stage and I will run past the security guard, provoke her and expose her alien-ness, and teleport with her to who-knows-where. The security guard probably won't stop me. The only thing that will stop me is...me.

Everything adds weight to my fear. The crowd. The smell of the crowd. The hands of time struggle to tick in the thickness. Worst-case scenarios churn endlessly on my mental hamster wheel. They're going to gas the room. But no, why destroy the students—the assets—along with their parents? Poison, then. The punch. No one should drink it.

Yet a dozen or more parents and students have already gathered around the buffet tables lining the walls, consuming a variety of drinks, cheeses, sliders, and fruits. None of them grip their throats or writhe on the floor after swallowing. All of them laugh and enjoy each other's company.

Hostages. They're going to transport all the parents to the mother ship and demand we submit to the Collective.

Then why didn't they do that this morning, when the parents arrived?

This is the true evil of the Collective. They don't come at us with weapons or bald threats. They seed fear in all of us, and like quiet mines they wait until we misstep and trigger the real danger.

My sensitivity serves me. I begin noticing the Brigade members circling in increasing numbers. Their black jackets and red faces from wearing said jackets are a dead giveaway in the crowd. I throw my hands behind my back and accidently hit another student standing behind me. I whisper an apology as I stare at the exit. There are two Brigade members standing next to the security guards. I could slip by them and come back in when it's less crowded.

As I sweep the crowd one last time to catch a glimpse of my parents, I instead catch someone else's attention.

Shane locks eyes with me. In that brief moment, our plan to

kidnap Jadore seems to be written on my face. His pouty mouth gapes and he points. I read his lips: *Don't move.*

Nope. That bloodsucker is not getting anything from me.

I duck and slink away from the stage. I'm impossible to hide, with my hair and vibrant dress. I'd hoped to blend into a sea of formal wear, yet it seems I need a different strategy to dodge this new threat.

As I rudely creep through the crowd like a red-handed thief, Mira slips breezily into the cafeteria. The crowd almost seems to part for her. It's no surprise. She looks stunning tonight. As I'm only a few feet away, I can see her ensemble in its entirety. She holds her beige, sleeveless maxi dress in both fists as she navigates the crowd with purpose. Ethan isn't with her. Despite the heat, her hair is immaculate and her makeup is fresh. I pull at my long, frizzy locks. No matter what I do, my hair will always be a mess.

Ethan didn't mind my messy hair, I think bitterly. I stand up for a split second and Shane is still heading my way, though his gaze has drifted. I crouch and keep moving, following Mira in her wake. The Brigade members by the cafeteria entrance don't seem alerted to my presence or Shane's mission—yet.

Mira is headed for the other side of the stage. Another quick peek shows me that Ethan isn't over there. Her dress is far nicer than mine. I'm no expert on designer clothing, but it looks expensive. I sink further into despair. I can't compete with that.

Sighing, I look up—and Shane is only two feet away. He has his back to me. I quickly duck once more as he turns. Weaving and squeezing between thirty more intimate conversations, I manage to catch up with Mira. Shane is still close. I reach out and touch her arm. "Mira?"

She flinches and spins in place. Despite her initial reaction, she doesn't seem surprised to see me. "Ingrid. Something wrong?"

I shift slightly, trying to hide behind her tall form. "Hey. Just… saw you walking by. Thought I'd take the opportunity to say hello while I had the chance."

Now she looks surprised. "Oh. Hello…"

I glance beyond her. Shane is pushing towards the stage, but he's no longer looking in our direction. "Look. I haven't gotten an opportunity to…apologize. For my weirdness around Ethan when we met. I didn't know he had a girlfriend in the UK. If I'd known, obviously I wouldn't have gotten involved."

"Oh. Yeah. Don't worry about it." She gives me a shallow smile and starts to wave and turn—just as Shane whips his head towards me.

I grab Mira's arm and swivel so that once again, she blocks me from Shane's sight. "How long have you known Ethan?"

She frowns at my hand and I retract it. Shane is by stage centre. He's craning his neck among the crowd, looking for me. He finally moves away, towards the windows. I think I've evaded him. For now.

Mira glances over her shoulder where I've been staring, and then levels me with a sincere look. "I've known him a long time, Ingrid. We grew up together."

I purse my lips. That's hard to beat. I've lost Shane in the crowd now, and hopefully he's lost me, and yet now I have Mira on the hook. The stage is still empty and it's not even nine yet. I've got lots of time before Jadore's speech.

I return Mira's sincere stare. Not once have I seen her without Ethan. This is an opportunity to test her and find out what her real deal is.

"You went to school with him?" I ask.

"I was ahead of him in school, but we lived on the same street," she replies.

"And what street was that?"

"Park Drive. In Upminster. Are you familiar with London?"

I have no way to verify the information and I have a sneaking suspicion she knows it. Ethan told me over a month ago he'd forgotten minor details of his life. I should have paid more attention to those cues. "I've always wanted to go to London."

She smiles good-naturedly. "Maybe someday you will."

Another beat. She seems to be waiting for more questions.

"So you're not a student here."

"No. I have a bachelor of science. Working on my masters in biomedical engineering at Imperial College. Er, I was. Taking a bit of a break now."

"Because of Ethan's...condition?"

"Yeah. When he called me, he wasn't in his right mind. I was on the next flight. Pricey, but..." She shrugs heavily. "I had to."

Because she thinks she's his girlfriend. *He* called her? It doesn't add up.

Seeing my distress, she takes my arm. Her hands are soft and I catch a whiff of her perfume: vanilla, jasmine, and patchouli. I can practically hear the serenity of sitting at the beach, listening to the lapping waves, all in that one smell. "Look. I know you care about him. I know this must be really frustrating for you. As soon as you said you were his girlfriend, I was just as shocked and hurt as you are now. I don't want there to be hard feelings between us. I think we both want what's best for him. Yeah?"

Searching her face, I want to believe her good intentions. I want to be the bigger person and say *yes, we should both look out for Ethan.* But part of me knows that means saying *no* to a romantic relationship with him. Even with all that's happening, I don't know if I can give him up, surrender him to his old flame without some kind of fight. I don't know if I can win against the Collective. But at least I have a chance at winning against perfect Mira—as long as I don't give up hope.

Especially if Mira is an alien.

I steel my nerve. "Did the Collective put you up to this?"

All sympathy drains from her face as she releases me, as if I am a leper. "The Collective?"

"Yes. The aliens controlling the school."

"That's not...no. The aliens don't control the school. They're attacking—"

"Don't feed me Jadore's lies. I want what's best for Ethan too. But I need to know who's side you're on. Because if you're one of *them*"—I point at the hafelglob disguised as a security guard by the stage—"then we can't be friends."

Mira is physically taken aback by my words. She stammers out nonsense, clutches at the bust of her dress, and then regains her composure. "I see," she says coldly. "You're going to be like that. Never mind, Ingrid. Ethan thought you were a nice girl."

"I'm tired of being nice. I want justice."

She sneers at me and shakes her head. "All right then. You're one of *those*. Go ahead. March, demonstrate, do whatever you want. Ethan and I are leaving in a few days, so—"

My heart sinks like a stone in a black lake. "You can't. They're not going to let you go."

"Ethan isn't well. I've already talked with Professor Jadore and other members of the university board. They're going to make an exception for his condition."

"Don't you see what that really means? The only way anyone leaves here is in a body bag. Or...on a spaceship, destined for the mother ship..." My face reddens at the mention of aliens. I push past it. "If he leaves, he's going to die."

Her complexion, already pale, seems to whiten. "I would never let that happen."

"I don't know how much control either of us has over that." I swallow over the lump in my throat. "Where would you take him? Back to London?"

"If he can make the journey, yes. He needs to be somewhere familiar to him."

"And then what? Would you try and get his memories back?"

She looks confused. "Those are gone, Ingrid. Did you not listen to me, earlier? This isn't the first time this has happened. It won't be the last." She glances over her shoulder. A group of students have climbed on stage left and stand in a nervous row before the crowd. The podium is still bare. "I have to go."

"I'm going to get his memories back," I yell after her. "Whatever it is..."

She waves dismissively at me, and I am quelled by the mere action. I doubt anyone heard me or knows what I'm talking about over the thousands of other conversations happening in this crowded, smelly room, but I feel like I'm the one losing my mind. I hide my face in my hands. That isn't what I wanted.

As Mira approaches the stage, I realize she isn't the only one. Six students are gathered by stage left, chattering away excitedly. They're dressed to the nines, just like Mira. My throat tightens as Jadore appears from the crowd next to them, cane in hand. One of the students helps her onto the stage.

I quickly check my phone. We're hours away from midnight. No, it's too soon!

Maybe Jadore switched the times, because she knows we're up to something.

My paranoia kicks up more adrenaline and I squeeze my way through the crowd. Now that Jadore is on stage, more people are trying to pour into the cafeteria. If we had a fire marshal, he'd shut this event down immediately. Maybe that's all we need to do, I think bitterly as I keep a guarded hand on my purse. But who knows where the nearest fire station is out here?

Jadore stands behind the podium, adjusts the microphone, and organizes her papers. She wears an elegant, tightly fitted black dress with a deep slit up the left leg. Extremely risqué for a university professor at a professional event. Her black hair is silky and sleekly pulled back in a tight ponytail, like it was earlier, yet now the neatly trimmed ends go past her elbows.

The music fades and the lights dim even more. The din of the crowd quiets as Jadore clears her throat and speaks eloquently into the microphone. "Ladies and gentleman. Parents and students. Friends and family. As acting president and a long-standing professor of this institution, I welcome you to Sparkstone University."

There is a polite round of applause. I'm nearly to the stage.

Jadore clears her throat and shuffles her papers. "I know it's hot in here. I'll try to keep this brief." She's not even sweating. In fact, she looks comfortable. In control.

"Here at Sparkstone University, we take pride in our students." Jadore smiles warmly, and for a moment, I believe her. "You have come from all over North America—some of you, from even further—to share your excellence with us. For that, we are eternally grateful."

"Yes. Sharing," I mutter.

Rustling to my left captures my attention. Jia, breathless, catches my arm, and Misty is right on her tail.

"My parents drank the punch. There was nothing I could do," Jia whispers, nearly in tears.

"Uncle Jacob only drinks whiskey. So he's probably fine," Misty says. I stand on my tiptoes and follow her gaze to her uncle, who stands beside the buffet table across the room. His hands are free—and animated. He's whispering with another parent as Jadore continues her speech. They seem interested in each other's company and nothing else. Misty doesn't seem to mind his lack of attention, though she keeps an attentive eye on him all the same.

"Where are your parents? Are they okay?" Jia asks.

Her desperate hope fills me with dread. They promised not to snack, but they don't truly understand the danger we were in. They didn't watch helplessly as their classmates were tortured and killed. The three of us sweep the crowd until we spot them. They're right where I saw them before. The buffet table, at the back of the room. They're chatting with Wil's parents.

"Get to them. Be ready for a massive panic," I say.

Jia shakes her head. "Maybe we shouldn't do this. What if...?"

"Nope, it's happening." Misty pulls Jia into the mass of people and my anxiety intensifies. It's happening.

I glance at the door guarded by Brigade members as Jadore drones on. It's not too late. I could still run.

Keeping a watchful eye out for Shane, I make my way back to stage right.

"And for those reasons," Jadore continues, "tonight, we honour students who have shown excellence in their fields."

The six students climb onstage to a roaring applause. I wipe the sweat from my brow. Mira stands offstage, like me but on the opposite side.

"A round of applause for our honour students."

She introduces each one and presents them with a gold medal. I recognize one of the names: Emily Foller, from our tutorial group, who studies business and psychology. Normally cheery and bright, she seems unnaturally subdued this evening. Each student bows their head and receives the medal around their neck. Jadore's praise is brief but strikingly specific. They look genuinely proud to be recognized for their work. Her words ring in my ears as I listen for the best moment in jump in and ruin her evening. After they receive their medal, they walk towards Agailya. She shakes their hand gently and the student exits stage right, hopping off beside me.

With each student that whooshes by, my resolve fades. I could just *not* go on stage. We could always wait for the next assembly to prove Jadore's alien-ness.

"We have one more award, and then I'll leave you alone." The crowd murmurs a polite laugh. "Would Ethan Millar come to the stage, please?"

My throat closes and the crowd applauds, hiding my shortness of breath. One hand grips the edge of the stage as I bend over, riding out the panic attack as Ethan emerges from the crowd. Mira straightens his tie and beams at him. He gives her a little smile, flushed and somewhat surprised, and then hops up on stage. His face is flush from the heat of the room and the top button on his dress shirt is undone. His dark hair is a mess, as usual.

This can't be happening. I can't do this now.

"Ethan has shown great progress since arriving here at Sparkstone University over a year ago," Jadore begins. "His paintings have been exhibited not only in shows in Edmonton and Calgary, but have garnered interest from international buyers in London, Paris, and China. I'm not much of an art critic, but I have been informed by Ms. Agailya, who has more of a taste for this, that his art is evocative, emotional, and mature, especially given his age."

Behind Jadore, Agailya stiffens, clenching her hands together, but she doesn't interrupt the proceedings. Jadore faces him, a shiny gold medallion in hand.

As Ethan extends a hand to her to accept his accolade, a cold sweat overwhelms me and again, I can't breathe. I'm drowning in worst-case what-ifs: she's erased his mind to fill it with lies about me. The medallion is poison and if he touches it, he'll die. She's going to gas the room and we're all about to die.

If I do nothing, everyone will perish.

I leap past the hafelglob security guard, who watches me with amusement, and onto the stage. My purse jostles against my hip. My thumping is loud and unexpected: even Agailya jumps. Jadore spins around. Her large sunglasses slide down her nose, revealing her shiny, black eyes. I have trespassed on her territory. The primal look was unmistakable. One wrong move, and she'd use her ill-gotten powers against me.

"Has something happened?" Jadore asks, not taking her gaze off me.

Agailya steps forward. "Ingrid is onstage." Her tone is flat. It's a performance, though a tired one, to cover for Jadore's alien eyes.

"Ingrid Stanley," Jadore says. There's a note of surprise in her voice as she makes a half-hearted attempt to cover the microphone. "I didn't call your name. Get off."

"No." I ball my hands into fists. The time is now.

Jadore, sensing my resolve, removes her hand from the microphone. "Do you have something you'd like to say?"

"I do." I take a deep breath and one step forward as I retrieve my phone from my purse. My feet are like two concrete blocks and my coat feels stiff around my torso. Ethan narrows his gaze at me—as if trying to place my face. Being with him on stage again reminds me of the failed protest we threw, and how we played a beautiful haunting melody that summoned Campbell into our realm. Another step. I'm lighter this time.

With an accusatory pointing finger at Jadore, I say, "That woman is an alien."

CHAPTER 6

Beside her, Ethan snorts. "What?"

There's a murmur in the crowd. I don't think the back heard me. Fine. I'll have to show them.

Before Jadore can make another snide comment, I rip the sunglasses from her face, exposing her dark-orbed eyes to the entire room. This alone doesn't get the reaction I want: the room is dimly lit, and while the people at the very front of the room squint in confusion at Jadore's face, those at the back gasp in horror at my rudeness.

But I'm not done. Lifting my phone, I turn on the flashlight app and shove it in her face.

Letting out an inhuman screech, Jadore's fingers claw at her eyes as she falls to her knees. The crowd ripples as the people in front recoil in terror. I jump backward myself. For a lingering moment, beneath the brightness of my phone, Jadore's natural green skin shines through her darker, false exterior.

"There!" I shout. "Did anyone see that?"

My voice is lost to a growing chorus of confusion and outrage from everyone in the room.

"What did you do that for?" Ethan demands.

A dark dread overtakes my belly like a quickly rising tide. Ethan's misplaced concern is a million times worse than the angry crowd yelling for justice. I need to get out of here.

I quickly kneel before Jadore and grab her arm. I stare at the wooden stage and dig deep for a hopeful thought beneath the distracting shame and frustration.

Yet Ethan stoops beside her and offers her a hand. Jadore turns her head towards me, hiding her face from the crowd as she stares at me.

She's not crying at all.

She's *laughing*.

I can't find Misty or Jia or my parents or any friendly face in the crowd. All I can see are horrified glares, and my own shame reflected in them. Scrambling backward, my heel catches in my dress and I feel it tear. I have to get off this stage.

Students in the Brigade climb onto the stage and even a couple of security guards hop up lazily, though Jadore, now on her feet, waves them off. She makes a show of holding onto Ethan as he guides her back to the podium and politely returns her now bent, skewed sunglasses.

"It's all right," Jadore says dryly. "I'm all right. No harm done. Did everyone enjoy that little performance?"

Silence. Someone coughs. A few laugh awkwardly to cover up their concerns.

"My eyes aren't likely the same as yours, Ingrid," Jadore continues, now with dramatic flair. "Yet we must first accept our differences and learn from them, so we can move forward. Together."

A couple of the Brigade members behind me cheer and a

smattering of parents clap at the sentiment. Jadore rearranges some papers at the podium, readjusts her glasses, and feels for her cane. Behind me, someone sneezes.

"I apologize for this interruption. Please enjoy the rest of your evening."

That's...it?

Two students wearing Brigade jackets grab me by the arms. I jostle them away but they insist on guiding me offstage, the way I came. I stare at the floor. I feel numb. Betrayed. I shouldn't have done that. I crouch and try to retain some dignity as I hop offstage in my flowing dress, but I'm still in shock. I fumble the landing—and yet someone catches me by the arm.

"I knew I saw a wristband under your sleeve," Shane says, and jabs a long grey tube against my trapped finger. There's a pin-prick and I yelp and wrench my hand away. It's too late. A bright red dot sits on my forefinger and Shane is smiling.

He holds up the grey tube. "I should arrest you now."

Although the Brigade is still around me, I put my hands behind my back. I smoosh the blood-stained finger against my palm, hoping it clots. No one else is getting my blood today. "The wristband doesn't mean I'm an alien. You have no idea what's really going on here. Trust me. You are not on the right side of this."

He snorts. "Now I'll be able to tell what side you're on. I can't wait for the results. Don't be surprised if there's another knock on your door tomorrow morning...*alien*."

Turning away, he pockets the grey futuristic needle in his jacket. His two Brigade friends follow him.

I could take them. I could take them right to the moon.

I start to go after him when I feel a gentle hand on my shoulder.

A light touch isn't usually enough to stop me in this state, yet my body is suddenly infused with a blanketing calm. All of the fear and desperation and anger seems to subside, and the shame sets in. I can think of only one person with such a power.

"You cannot win," Agailya whispers in my ear.

I turn to face Agailya, or as she's known to the students, Ms. Grace Agailya. When I first came to Sparkstone, I thought I could trust her, even though it's pretty obvious she's an alien. But when I watched her torture and kill Tilly Newman, a girl in my tutorial who also had powers—that changed. Although she's trying to cure a plague that terrorizes her people, she's testing it on unwilling humans—including Ethan.

"But *she* is a monster," I hiss, pointing at the stage towards Jadore.

Agailya shakes her head slightly and glances back at the stage. Mira helps Jadore now—she's exaggerating a limp and fumbling with her cane as she tries to exit the stage. A crowd has gathered to assist her and offer their sympathies. I feel the crowd behind me sink away, as if they're afraid to touch me.

"No," Agailya says firmly. "You are the monster now."

The rest of the night is agony. I run out of the cafeteria, out of Rogers Hall, where I sit on the grass in the freezing air. Sure, I could go back to the dorm, but why? The fresh air, and my anxiety, keeps me highly alert. I rub my fingers over the silver wristband, trying to pry it off for the millionth time without success as I consider the consequences of teleporting back to the supermassive black hole. I decide against it. That would make time stretch even more than it already is.

Students and parents filter in and out of the building as the reception continues, though as the hours drag on, more exit than re-enter. One student, who may have had too much punch, yells, "Hey, tell us who else is an alien!" They are quickly ushered back to their dorm.

Someone's parent gathers her courage to approach and lectures me on respecting the differently abled. I endure it and nod. Because she's right. Being respectful is important. I have done a terrible wrong and I deserve every bit of shame and punishment.

I stare up at the sky and realize there is a way to relieve the pain: to admit that I am crazy.

And for one dark moment, I doubt everything.

Maybe there are no aliens and this entire time, I've dreamed up all of my adventures with my new friends. I didn't travel to the mother ship. I'm not tethered to a time-travelling guardian. I don't have superpowers. Maybe I just want to feel special and important in a new environment where I am no longer the cream of the crop—I'm just part of the regular harvest. A modicum of relief comes with this: it's easier for me to believe my mind has invented an enemy than for me to accept an arsenal of shame and disappointment.

You will perish and your name will be forgotten, Agailya had said to me once.

And yet, there's no way I've made this up. I know what I saw, what I've experienced. Sunni and Tilly and so many others are dead, and anyone could be next. Hildie, Sunni's mother, came to Sparkstone because she believed something was wrong, and she died for it. Maybe I will too, but that day won't be today.

Finally, my parents emerge from the building. They say goodnight to Wil's parents first, who shoot me a troubled stare. I stand, my legs and butt aching from my long sit.

"You must be cold!" Dad says.

"Where you out here this whole time?" Mum demands.

My parents hug me. I can tell they didn't approve of my actions, but they can equally sense that I don't want to talk about it.

"We'll see you before we leave," Mum says. "Are you sure you don't want to sleep with us tonight?"

I shake my head. All I want is to be alone. Which is impossible at Sparkstone. I wait for Misty to exit with her uncle. They're among the last to leave. They say goodnight with a breezy easiness I suddenly envy, and Misty escorts me silently back to my dorm. For once, I appreciate the silence between us. She doesn't criticize or opine. When two Brigade members start to approach us, all it takes is one icy stare from Misty and they give us a wide berth.

Jia choses to sleep with her family. I should have done the same with my parents. My brain spends the night on a hamster wheel, turning the scene over and over. I identify every moment where I could have acted differently. I imagine Brigade members coming for me in my sleep, and so at one point, I attempt to move the dresser across the room, before realizing that is perhaps going too far. That, and, Misty grumbles for me to go to sleep.

I dread the sunrise. When it comes, I hide under the blankets. I can't face anyone. My parents, most of all. I'm too afraid.

Eventually, the sounds of buses rolling up and parking on Sparkstone Boulevard rouses me completely. Students begin to spill into the quad, crying, screaming, and expressing their goodbyes to their families at top volume. My dorm neighbours exit their rooms with slamming doors, and I hear snickering and loud whispers in the hallway, accompanied by some unusual smells.

The student population has made their opinion of me clear. Rude notes, rotten vegetables (stolen from the cafeteria, I assume, because where else would these come from?), and paper bags that stink to the high heavens await me the following morning at my doorstep. I recoil at the stench. It takes me a full minute to convince my hungry stomach not to dry heave as the smell wafts into the dorm.

"Ugh," Misty says, rolling over on the floor mattress. "What *is* that?"

Agailya called *me* foolish. Well, this is just childish. "Just hooligans who feel the need to express themselves."

"Can't they express it somewhere else?" Misty presses a pillow against her face. "Close the door! It reeks!" Then, as an afterthought: "Who says *hooligans*? Are you an old woman?"

Caught under the door, half-buried beneath the filth is a stained piece of paper. Since some of the other dorms in the hallway seem to have the same announcement, I fish it out and shut the door behind me.

The paper reads:

REVIEW. Participation mandatory. Verbal and physical exams begin December 23rd.

I walk across the room and slap the announcement on the dresser. This torture will never end. Outside, I smell and hear large busses as they line up on Sparkstone Boulevard. The parents are returning home today. Supposedly.

Shaking and unwilling to face the day, I take a cold shower. I get ready for the day. I am outside my body, puppeted by some greater force who cares, because mentally I am checked out. Misty and I clean the mess outside the door before trudging downstairs and into the overcast, chilly morning.

Sorrowful students and families mill around the crowded buses. We spot Jia saying a tearful goodbye to Seymour and Noreen while Paige bawls into her hands. When Misty spots her uncle, she gives me an encouraging smile and runs towards him.

My parents are waiting for me apart from the milling crowd. Mum keeps one hand on her purse and the other on their overnight bag. They pick me out almost immediately—my hair makes it easy—and offer sympathetic smiles as I approach.

"Good morning," Mum says, with false cheer.

"I guess," I reply with equal measure.

"Aww. Did you get any sleep?"

"No."

I lean against her, and the three of us embrace. I want to stay in here forever. It is the strongest shield, especially against my own negative thoughts.

"Everyone hates me now," I mumble.

"We don't."

I pull away from them, pouting. "Yeah...but you're my parents."

"Yes!" Dad exclaims.

"You could have handled that differently," Mum says diplomatically, "yet from the way Professor Jadore treated you earlier, I can see why you'd be frustrated with this situation."

"So you believe me." My hopeful gaze darts from Mum's face

to Dad's. I need this, and they know it.

"Of course we do," Dad says. "Are you sure you don't want to come home with us?"

I do want to go home with them. There is nothing I want more in that moment. But I avert my gaze and shake my head.

Mum lowers her voice. "Honestly I'm surprised you haven't been expelled. Or suspended. Or whatever they do for punishment at fancy universities."

"They'll think of something appropriate, I'm sure." And that's what scares me. I grab my parents' hands. "Please. Promise me the second you get home, you text me. Or text me every hour, so I know you're safe."

"Every hour?" Dad looks incredulous.

"Yes. We should use a secret code, so I know it's you."

They exchange glances. I've passed into a new zone of paranoid. Even I can hear it. Fortunately, they indulge me. "What kind of code?" Mum asks hesitantly.

"Has to be something random." I glance around the quad. The day is overcast and bitterly cold. Around us, students say tearful goodbyes. Several black buses, newly painted, line up on the curbside to take parents back home. I lower my voice, in case the Collective is listening in. "*Oolong tea, freshly brewed.* Write that in the text, and I'll know it's you."

"That seems *oo long*," Dad says with a smile.

Mum rolls her eyes and nudges him. "I'll do it. Though I don't see why it's necessary. You said these aliens are blocking the cell phone radio waves, or whatever they're called."

"I just want to know you're safe. And not body snatched." I smile, trying to keep it light, but only Dad returns it. Mum looks even more concerned. "I'm definitely coming home for

Christmas." If they'll allow us to leave, that is. If the Collective is bent on keeping up appearances as a regular school, they'll have to let us go.

"Good," Mum says. "That's only a little over a month away. We can talk more then."

I hug my parents goodbye once more. Tender words leave our mouths, but my brain is miles away. All this time, we've been focussing on doing damage to the Collective, trying to get revenge on the wrongs they've committed against our bodies and minds. Yet we've been doing so on their playing field. Rats in a cage, trying to plot against our masters. We've been trying to play a game we're destined to lose.

Not anymore.

My parents board one of the black buses with dozens of other families, and I step away from the road. By Rita House, Misty and Jia stand with a few other students in our tutorial. Jia's face is puffy from her tearful goodbye, and even Misty's normally impeccable mascara is smudged.

I don't wait for a quip or sorrowful remark about the situation. The time for that has passed. I ball my hands into fists. "Misty. Jia. It's time to break out of Sparkstone."

PART TWO

The dome has cracked, but we lost three good soldiers tonight. She's closing in on us. I don't know how much longer I can keep this up. I have to believe there is something better than this place, or a version of these events where we made different, winning choices.

CHAPTER 7

I have concluded that there is nothing worse than living in a community where you believe in the truth, and the rest of your peers worship a lie.

My mother texts me, as instructed, at the top of every hour with the secret code. As far as I know, if her messages are to be believed, they made it home safely, as did other families my parents met and kept in touch with. I hear from my mother regularly after the Open House for a while, but every time I try to phone, the line is busy or I get disconnected.

Now, six weeks after the Collective ferried our parents in and out of our lives, my peers and I have settled into new routines. Regular tutorials have been suspended, as students adjust to their new roles as would-be galactic superhero saviours for a secret global entity. Just as well for us, as Sparkstone University has never been about learning. I take up running in earnest with Jia, and Misty tags along, even though it's mostly to keep an eye on the Brigade's outdoor activities.

The Brigade hosts regular rallies and gatherings in the quad and develops a devoted following for those wishing to eradicate the alien threat with their budding superpowers. About a dozen black-jacket wearing superhero-wannabes assemble in the increasingly cold weather for long periods of meditation, jogging, and LARPing. Okay, so *they* don't call it LARP, but for some reason, Shane and many other original members believe that by striking superhero poses, pretending to fly, and otherwise acting out what it would be like to have traditional, stereotypical superhero powers, they may awaken that potential in their DNA.

"I mean, that's just stupid, right?" Misty says. "They look ridiculous."

We have our own gatherings in the cold basement room in Raylene House with Greg, Lynn, and Elisha. As usual, Jia hovers near the door, my anxiety has me pacing, Greg makes wild gestures and pounds his points into the crafting table, Lynn sits perfectly still, even when she's speaking, Elisha doodles, and Misty leans against the cream-coloured walls, scuffing her boots on the floor.

"What did you do to get your powers?" Greg asks. His voice is even louder as of late. Beside him, Lynn covers her ears.

"Definitely not what they're doing," Misty remarks, folding her arms. "One of us should infiltrate them. Not me, obviously, but someone."

Since her demonstration in the quad during the vigil, it's common knowledge that Misty has particularly blast-y powers. Many Brigade members—including Shane—have approached her about joining. Although she meets each request with a threat or a sarcastic remark, they haven't gotten the message.

"I'm not spending my days leaping around in the cold!" Greg replies.

When the Brigade swallows a student into their cause, they

don't regurgitate. They eat together, sleep at the same time, and socialize only with each other. The only times we've seen a Brigade member with non-Brigade students is when they're giving a lecture about school safety, evangelizing the Brigade itself, or demanding to know if anyone has seen or heard superpowered activity among the students. It's hard to say whether anyone in the Brigade has developed powers themselves, but my best guess is no—if they had anyone powerful enough, they'd put them on a pedestal as an example, and they'd stop bothering Misty.

So the six of us keep our ears to the ground for rumours as we develop our powers in private. We've given up on starving ourselves and partaken in every meal at the cafeteria for the past two weeks. The chemical the Collective puts in the food to make it delicious also subdues the students and makes their wills pliant, yet it also is supposed to awaken or heighten our powers. That's the main reason I have surrendered to this one aspect of Sparkstone. Since I've failed to kidnap Jadore, the new plan is for me to teleport everyone out of here. Somehow. And if I'm going to achieve that, I need to be on top of my game. Misty and Jia join me in solidarity for each meal. Jia has no more food coming in from her parents, the cafes that sustained us months ago have seemingly closed up shop, and although I occasionally throw up my lunch and feel woozy, so far, the three of us have survived. Greg, Lynn, and Elisha will occasionally eat with us as well, though we try to keep our public interactions to a minimum, in case the Brigade or the Collective gets any ideas. If one cell dies, the other cell will be safe—for a little while.

Which is something I've been worrying about, ever since we got the first paper announcement about this so-called Review under my door.

Although the frequent announcements never say explicitly that the Review involves testing for superpowers, the entire school is convinced it's an official exam to determine who has the most useful power for fighting aliens. The Brigade has especially taken this to heart and in the last week alone their numbers in the quad have doubled. Jadore has shut herself in her office and participates in regular, secret meetings with select students. Those who have joined the Brigade, as far as Jia has been able to determine. We know better than to show off our powers. The strongest will be harvested by the Collective for their nefarious scientific experiments.

As rumours about the upcoming Review spread like a contagious disease, the holiday season draws nearer. There is no talk of returning home for the break, despite what I told my parents. There doesn't seem to be a break at all, which only worries us Sparks, the continued unofficial name of our little resistance. The professors, including Agailya, have been tight-lipped about leaving.

One of the only consolations of remaining at Sparkstone in its current militant state is the knowledge that Ethan, despite Mira's claim, hasn't left yet. Perhaps she had lied, or had been trapped here by the Collective's will. My theory that she is an alien working for the Collective wanes in power. If she were part of the Collective, she could probably leave on her own, right? Although Ethan has actively avoided me since I made a fool of myself, every time I see him crossing the quad, or nipping into the cafeteria, I feel relieved that he hasn't been taken from me. Not completely. That gives me hope.

I think about how I'm going to get everyone home for the holidays as Misty, Jia, and I enter the cafeteria on December twenty-first. There is nothing festive in the air. No music and certainly no generosity of spirit. If it weren't for the cold weather, you would never know it was nearly Christmas. This day is just like all the others I've experienced these past few weeks: dreary, anxiety-ridden, and increasingly unbearable.

I steel myself as the three of us line up to choose our food. At least thirty percent of the room wears Brigade jackets. They've been upgraded: around each left arm is a coloured band. Most are blinding red. I see a splattering of yellows. I manage to find Shane. His is silver, with a blue stripe in the centre.

He notices me staring and cracks a rude smile. Since the family visit, he's leered at me from afar and I've caught him pointing me out to his jacketed peers. The Brigade never posted the results of the blood tests, and while I'm continuously glad they haven't accused me of being an alien despite my wristband, I can't help but feel they're waiting for the right moment to drop that bomb.

Someday, I'll craft the perfect revenge on Shane. But first, soup and cheesecake.

As we walk the crowded rows with our lunches, I feel my fellow students staring and whispering. I keep my eyes on my soup to avoid engaging with anyone. My attack on Jadore has not been forgotten. Shame and social exile seem to be my primary punishment. Ahead of me, Misty gives as good as she gets. Rumours fly about her powers. No one wants to cross her and be burnt to a crisp or frozen in an ice block. Her demonstration at our candlelight vigil made it clear that she's not to be trifled with. She glances back and me and flashes a sly grin. She's enjoying this way too much.

Jia, on the other hand, looks paler than usual. She trails behind me, her hair falling in her face and into her food. Her nervous gaze rests on the back of my shoes. Paige hasn't texted in the last two days and neither have her parents.

Misty finds a table near the back of the room and waves us over. Three students are enjoying their lunch there until they see me heading towards them. They exchange a knowing look and without saying another word, they take their trays to a neighbouring table.

Jia watches them go as she settles into a warm seat. "Couldn't you have found somewhere else?" she asks Misty.

Misty shrugs. "Place is crowded. It's their problem if they don't want to be part of our cause." I sit down next to her, across from Jia.

My face reddens. "Technically it is our problem. It's my fault that we have so much bad PR and no one wants to be seen with us. Have you heard anything from Greg, or Lynn? Elisha?"

I've been keeping an eye on the three of them since they started eating regularly at the cafeteria. Elisha has reported feeling sick most days, though her creativity has gone through the roof. At our last meeting, she had a rush of ideas and crafted ten business plans. Greg seems more high-strung than usual, though that could just be his personality mixing with the stress of the situation. Lynn seems to have retreated into herself, and whenever we have a meeting, she's always late. Apparently, she prefers to be outside—even though it's been nearly zero degrees every day. Whether any of this is precursor behaviour to superpower development, I can't say.

Jia shakes her head. "I'll head down there after lunch. I want to know if they've heard anything new about the Review."

Misty shrugs again. "People think we're crazy for accusing

Jadore of being an alien. But what can they do to us, really? Bad mouth us to death? Put on jackets and join a stupid club? The Collective isn't going to kill us—yet. Especially not now that you've made a mockery of yourself. That would just look suspicious. Besides, the three of us are more powerful than any of them." She waves her finger around the cafeteria. "Even if eating this stuff dopes us up...we are still stronger than them."

I don't comment. I don't feel strong. I haven't been able to successfully teleport for weeks now. Given my state of mind, it's been hard to feel hopeful. Each day that passes is another that I have been unsuccessful at evacuating the school.

"For now," Jia says. "Enough people join the Brigade—enough people with powers that pose a real threat—then we have a problem."

Kimberly sees us from across the cafeteria, waves, and brings her tray towards us.

I slurp up the delicious soup and bite into the freshly baked roll that accompanies the meal. The food smells more delicious than usual, despite me knowing what's in it. I've never tasted anything more heavenly, and I'm pretty sure I had the same lunch yesterday. "It only took one meal for me to have enough strength to teleport to a black hole in the centre of the galaxy. We need to come up with a strategy to get everyone out of here as quickly as possible without...setting off any nukes or bombs, so to speak."

Kimberly places her tray next to Jia and plops down. "Bombs?" She lowers her voice. "Are we blowing up the school?"

"No," I reply, just as Misty says, "We could..." and Jia adds, "Once everyone is out."

"Man. Dark," Kimberly says, shaking her head. She has

occasionally joined us in our Spark meetings. She is Ethan's closest friend, or was before Mira showed up. With Mira monopolizing Ethan's time now, she's latched on to us. "I'm just trying to finish my papers. And a painting. I started a painting. Like I have anything else to show for this Review? I know, everyone is saying it's a chance to show off your superpowers to Jadore. Literally everyone on my floor has been striking Harry Potter poses, screaming, and running up and down the halls, expecting magic to shoot out their eyes. Even the non-Brigade people, though they wouldn't admit it to the Brigade." She grins at Misty. "I guess people just want to be like the famous Misty Carter and blast stuff."

Misty smirks. "And? Any success?"

"I heard a rumour that Emily Foller started a fire with her mind. She also likes to put thirty bajillion candles in the bathroom while taking a shower. Wasn't she in your tutorial? The Brigade has definitely been to her room more than once in the last couple of days, so maybe they've got her now."

Jia looks grim. "We'll add her to our list of people to watch out for."

"I also heard that Karsten Berg can change his skin colour. See?" She points to a pale-skinned young man with patchy blue spots.

I squint. "Kinda looks like paint."

Kimberly shrugs. "It's not the only thing I've seen or heard that's weird, but it's hard to say if any of it is true. Shape-changing, people turning into ooze, enhanced math ability, telekinesis. I think that French student, Felix Debois, can recite 68,000 digits of pi."

"I suppose not every superhuman power is...useful, in the context of war."

"Ms. Agailya was speaking to some students in the quad the other day. I think she's still running a tutorial even though they've been suspended. Apparently she said that no matter what abilities you develop, they're all special, and even if you can think or run or compose music just a little bit faster than before, that they'll find a way to put you to good use in the fight against the alien invasion." She glances between the three of us. "What do you think about that?"

Misty's sees through Kimberly's ranting in a way that I don't. "Let me guess. You've developed a useless power."

"Actually," she says. "I haven't developed anything. And if you're to be believed, eating in the cafeteria intensifies my powers or mutates my body or makes me weak-willed. Well, I haven't experienced any of that. I think I've gained twenty pounds though. That's about it."

"Maybe you're a late bloomer," Misty suggests. "And of course we're *to be believed*."

"Sure. Fine. I'm just suggesting that maybe the aliens overestimated how many of us actually have superpowers. Or as you put it. *Useful* powers."

Kimberly returns to her regular chatty self and I consider her words as my paranoid gaze scans the cafeteria. The Collective is smart, but it's also been sloppy. Sunni's mother ventured from Texas to here because she didn't believe the fake correspondence the Collective had been throwing at her. Jadore obsesses over Campbell and has hesitated on critical occasions when she's held my fate in her hands. It took a risk to bring all of the parents here—and for what? It did a second round of blood collection—why?

My attention snaps back to reality as I spot Ethan enter

the cafeteria. It's like every fibre in my body lights up at his presence. He scouts the cafeteria line and heads instead for the fruit basket on a side table near the entrance. His clothes are wrinkled and ratty. He runs a hand through his hair, chooses a banana, and he heads for the exit. I haven't spoken to him since I assaulted Jadore—and every time I've even come close, Mira or a nearby Brigade member has swooped in to run interference. He probably thinks I'm looney. I don't blame him.

"He's been holed up in his art studio for the past three days," Kimberly says, noting my interest. "Mira won't stop hounding him. She keeps coming to me, asking me what to do. I keep telling her, I don't know, aren't *you* his girlfriend? Former girlfriend." She adds the last part for my benefit, and then twists her lips awkwardly. "Sorry. I don't know what you consider yourself to him now. Is it still a relationship if only one party remembers it happening?"

"It was real. It still is real to me," I reply quietly. "But I can't force something that may not be there anymore."

Kimberly smiles. "He fell for you once. Who's to say it wouldn't happen again?" She looks to Misty and Jia for support. "Wouldn't that be romantic?"

Jia mutters a polite yes, while Misty levels Kimberly with a dead-eyed stare. "I think we have more important stuff to work out."

"Sorry. Yeah. Misty's right." I can't sit here anymore. "I'm taking a walk to make sure I keep this food down. Meet you in my room in half an hour or so?"

"That enough time to snoop around?" Misty asks Jia.

Jia nods as she picks at her salad.

"Snooping! Aww, can I come?" Kimberly asks. "Maybe *I* can turn invisible!"

"No," Misty says as Jia says, "You never know," as I pick up my tray and leave the table.

❋❋❋

I grip my stomach. I feel queasy, but not enough to barf up my lunch. The sky is bright and clear, though it's nearly freezing. I walk briskly along the path towards the Lewis Arts Building. Not many students are out, and those who are move off the path to give me space. Even the Brigade members, who have taken to patrolling outside every building on campus, keep a close eye on me. As if the Collective's cameras aren't enough.

It's true that I need the walk to keep the food down. For the past few days, however, I couldn't stomach the thought of Ethan believing I'm a tinfoil hat conspiracy theorist, trying to stir up trouble. Especially since he might leave at any moment. I mean, I am trying to stir up trouble. I'd just prefer to do it with him by my side—or at least with his support.

I pull open the door to the art building. My palm buzzes as the technology within identifies me, yet it doesn't deny me access. No one minds the front desk in the lobby. I'm struck by the mural spanning the entirety of the wall to my right. I admired it on my previous visit. Earth, from space. I have seen the real deal from the mother ship, and the artist has managed to capture our beautiful planet's likeness. Whoever painted it deserves a real medal. Just not by a fake university. By a real institution with real merit.

I take the elevator behind the desk up to the third floor. There's a camera in the elevator. Its red eye greets yet another camera at the end of the hallway when the elevator doors slide open. I step off and listen. I don't hear a soul.

Have people become so obsessed with trying to manifest their powers that they have abandoned art entirely?

The second door on the right is ajar. I knock gently and the door squeaks open. I push through. Ethan isn't here—no one is. Since the door's unlocked, I assume he hasn't gone far.

This is a shared space, yet I see Ethan's handiwork everywhere I turn. Canvases large and small lean against the walls. Most are unfinished, at least to my eye: there's a theme of hurriedly painted blues, dotted with black. Ethan's style is more refined. I remember him enjoying painting women in fantastical settings. Yet the entire studio is filled with these abstract paintings, all of them false starts. Some look like they've been thrown across the room in a rage. On the sole easel is a large, blank canvas.

A pile of crumped up sketches lay abandoned at the foot of the easel. I retrieve one at random: it's a bunch of charcoal scribbles around roughly drawn circles. I discard it and pick up another. Similar, but in this one, there's one circle with multiple rings. I blink and drop it as it makes me dizzy.

Footsteps in the hallway light up my senses. Brown shoes. Stalky weighted, surely footed. A friendly whistle of a half-familiar tune. It's Ethan, and I don't know how I know, yet it's what my superhuman senses tell me, and I have no reason to doubt them.

"You shouldn't be eating that. Did you eat that sandwich I gave you this morning?"

Ethan—and Mira.

If she finds me in here, snooping around Ethan's paintings...

A dozen unfinished canvases lean against the wall behind me. I scramble to tunnel through them as the door opens.

"I'm fine with my fruit," Ethan replies. He sounds exhausted.

I'm laying on my stomach, arms splayed out in front of me. I press myself against the wall and roll over onto my side. I can see them through a gap between two large canvases. Mira looks sharp and cozy in her white shirt, worn jeans, high-heeled boots, and a floor-length multi-coloured knit cardigan tied together at the bust with a single string. Her hair is tied up in a messy bun. Next to her, Ethan's unkempt sweat pants, baggy shirt, and bed hair makes him look five years older at least. He throws a banana peel in a trash can by the door.

She closes the door after them. Ethan beelines for his easel and heaves a frustrated sigh. "Where was that sketch...?"

"What are you trying to paint?" Mira asks.

Ethan mutters an unintelligible reply.

"Hmm?" she says, inching closer. I tense. She's facing my group of canvases.

He kneels and rummages through the crumpled sketches. "Just...something I've got in my head." He picks up one, turns it this way and that, and throws it over his shoulder. "No, no. That won't do."

Mira sighs. "You're tired. Let's go for a walk. You should get fresh air."

He ignores her and disappears from my view. A moment later, he returns with an already wet paintbrush dripping with blue paint. He begins boldly stroking the blank canvas.

"Do you want me to mix you some colours? Create a palette for you?"

Ethan shakes his head.

"You're running out of paint. I'm going to—"

Ethan's paintbrush clatters to the floor, splattering blue on the old wood. The crease between his eyebrows deepens as he whirls on her. "You're always telling me what I should be doing. Fresh air. Food. Sleep. Well, I think I know what's best for me. Right now, all I want to do is finish this painting."

"Painting is all you've been doing for days," Mira replies patiently. "Haven't you painted enough of these already? I don't want to see you waste away in here."

"Maybe I want to waste away," Ethan mutters. He stoops to pick up the wet brush and faces his unfinished masterpiece again.

"I'm not going to let you. You're just tired. Eat something, take a walk with me, and you'll feel better. Then you can finish your paintings."

Ethan shoots her a look of disgust. "I was just out for a walk. You're always hovering around. Don't you have anything better to do? Why are you even here? Go home. Finish your masters. Unless I'm a more interesting project for you?"

Mira, taken aback, purses her lips. Ethan starts painting again as she watches, formulating her next words carefully. "I'm sorry. This is just the way it has to be now."

I bite down on my hand.

Ethan, equally surprised, glances over at her. "What do you mean?"

"You don't remember. But you did something before you came here to Sparkstone. Something so terrible that your brain is blocking it out. That's why you don't remember me, or your family...and you have trouble keeping new memories."

"What did I do?" He holds the paintbrush pointed at her like a weapon.

I can barely contain myself. Ethan told me, over two months

ago now, that he suspected he'd done something terrible back in London, only he cannot remember what, and that it may explain his spotty memories.

Mira backs away. She's nearly in tears now. "If I tell you…it'll send you into a spiral. Whenever you remember, that's what happens. The pain of it is so great that it physically eats away at you. Your mind is protecting you from this trauma, yet it's not healthy to remain in this cycle of remembering and forgetting and remembering again. Please. I…I'm willing to live through it again with you, but I can't let you wither away in bed. Let me help you, ease you into your burden, in a safe way."

"You're mad. Mad! I'm leaving." He shoves the still-wet paintbrush behind his ear and heads for the door.

"Ethan." Her tone takes on a more authoritative, sultry edge. It halts him in his tracks, like magic. "I've talked it over with Professor Jadore and Ms. Agailya. It's taken me some time, because of everything that's going on. All the politics and the games the administration plays. They wouldn't let me leave once I arrived on campus. But it's settled, finally. In a few days, we'll both be on a plane back to London."

Ethan looks as surprised as I was when Mira first told me this, six weeks ago. "I don't care if it's the holidays or if this is some kind of ploy to distract me. I'm not going anywhere. I have work to do."

"You can do it back in London. Where you belong. Isn't that what you remember most?"

"I…" He presses his palms against his temples. "I don't know. I remember London. I remember being there with you. All of our dates, our…time together…yet I *feel*…empty." He gestures to his messy, abstract paintings. "These don't feel empty to me. This scene here, that's real."

"*This* is real." Mira takes Ethan's hands and shakes them. "Why can't you let me take care of you?"

Ethan trembles. His knees buckle. My hands hurt from biting down on them. She cups his face tenderly and strokes his hair.

"Remember when I used to sing to you?" she asks softly. She hums the first few bars of a song so beautifully I feel it in my gut. I don't recognize the tune, yet it's haunting and a swirling deep blue. My eyes well as Mira's hum becomes a full-bodied song on her lips.

Ethan begins to hyperventilate. He drops her hands violently and throws off her attempt to calm him by covering his ears. "Leave me be!"

He exits the studio in a furious rage, slamming the door behind him.

"Ethan. Ethan!" Mira opens the door and screams after him. Frustrated, she stomps around the studio and knocks over the easel. The wet canvas tumbles to the floor and the easel crashes on top of it. She covers her face with her hands, squats, cries, and paces the room.

"What am I going to...?" she mutters breathlessly, shaking her head, and then runs out of the room.

I lay on the floor, shallowly breathing, until the echoing sound of her light footfalls have faded and whirring of the elevator has stopped. I shouldn't have come. My mind flits to an even worse scenario that could have come to pass: Ethan discovering me here among his canvases, eavesdropping on his personal life and still-fresh wounds.

Did Agailya choose Ethan for her sick experiment because of this trauma Mira is keeping from him? Has he always been this way? Or do his still-dormant superpowers cause this trauma, which attracted the attention of the Collective?

What if he remembers me—but in doing so, remembers this trauma, and it kills him?

I wait another five minutes and then climb out of my hiding spot. Wil and Misty had periodically warned me not to get involved with Ethan. Something is off about his brain, Wil had said. Maybe they're right. He brushes off Mira, whose intentions seem to be good. What if I'm destined to become her, doting on him, turning him into a project?

I have enough projects on my plate. As I walk past his half-painted memories, I decide that I can't be one of them. I have to let him go.

CHAPTER 8

By the time I'm back at my dorm, all I want is some peace.

So of course, I open the door and I enter a screaming match between Misty, Jia—and Wil.

"You're not letting me finish!" Wil says.

"Would you two just cool it? And you, you shouldn't even be yelling, you want the Brigade and Jadore to march up here and find you?"

"Obviously I don't want that. But *he* would know, wouldn't he?"

I slam the door shut, cutting through the argument. "What is going on here?"

The three of them stare at me in shock. Well, Misty and Jia look surprised. Wil probably knew I was coming. He smiles a little. He appears relaxed, so unlike his usual uptight self. His cargo pants are wrinkled and dirty and the white t-shirt is full of stains. Only his leather jacket looks new, which makes me even more suspicious. None of us have money for clothes and Sparkstone isn't exactly a shopping destination.

"Whatever it is you're arguing about," I say, rubbing my temples. "Can you—?"

"I know that Wil erased my mind," Jia says through gritted teeth.

Oh. Oh no. My face says it all, because she continues: "You knew what he did"—she points at Wil—"and you didn't tell me?"

My stomach sinks. "I'm sorry Jia. I didn't know...how to tell you. Or if you'd believe me. Or if it was my place."

Jia's lips tremble as she stares at the floor. Her hands waiver in and out of sight. She shifts her weight, like a dancer about to take flight, and says, "I thought we were friends."

"We are. Nothing would—"

But she doesn't wait for another explanation. Jia disappears into her invisible world. I feel a rush as she hurries by me, and I wave my arms to stop her, but I'm too slow. The door slams behind me, seemingly of its own accord.

Misty levels a death stare at Wil. "Great. Thanks. How are we supposed to find her now? You realize that if she's caught by—"

"She'll be fine," Wil says confidently.

"Is that so?" Misty continues, circling him. "Can you see the future now too?"

"I'm not here to argue with you. I just stopped to talk to Jia. To...apologize. And you've turned it into this big thing."

"It is a big thing. You erased her mind. Repeatedly!"

"What was I supposed to do?" Wil demands. "I couldn't get rid of her crush on me. It was so buried in her mind, it was part of her identity. You don't know how much it was tormenting her. I could feel my rejection of her *inside* her mind. It was like I would walk into a room and just my presence was a rejection to her. And *I* didn't want to feel that anymore. The first time, I was scared, but then she kept working up the resolve to tell me how she felt, and I had to keep erasing it, hoping that next time, it would work..."

"Are you even listening to yourself?" I ask.

Seemingly remembering I'm there, Wil sighs and shakes his head. "Yeah. I am. Look, this happened a long time ago now—"

Misty raises her eyebrows. "It was like, a month ago, Wil."

"Okay. I...should have known better. I'm sorry. I really, really am. I did a lot of stupid things in the past. To you, Jia, Kimberly. Others. I'm just trying to make up for them now. Okay?" He glances at me, seeking forgiveness and understanding.

What Wil did to Jia—what he did to me—is a reminder of how close we are to using our powers out of fear and desperation, instead of to help our fellow students get out of this hell. I want to believe his apology. I want to believe he's changed and offer him the forgiveness he craves. But he hasn't been gone that long—and that's really the crux of it. He left us and manipulated us for his own selfish reasons when we really needed him.

Maybe if he were truly sorry, he would have stayed.

"Where have you been?" I demand.

"Around," Wil replies vaguely.

"We are in the middle of a crisis. Even more so than usual. Why didn't you answer when your parents tried to call you?"

He frowns. "How did you know they tried to call?"

"Because I was standing in front of them." Blank stare. "The Collective brought them here, to Sparkstone, Wil. They brought all of our loved ones here. Why, we don't know."

"They...brought our parents here?"

"How could you not notice?" Misty asks, slumping down on the bed. "The place was packed."

The realization creeps up on me as Wil struggles to come up

with an adequate answer. "You didn't know because you weren't even on campus. You've discovered a way out."

Wil hesitates. "Yes. I have."

"Good," I reply. "Tell us about it. We need to start evacuating. Immediately."

He nods briskly and slides past me to open the door. "I will. But first I should settle things with Jia. Or at least see if she'll be willing to talk to me, or if she needs her space. I've abused your trust. Her trust. I know you all need time to forgive me. I promise after I'm done here, I'll return and we can talk about defeating the Collective, once and for all." He swiftly exits.

Defeat the Collective once and for all? Misty and I share a look—I don't have to be a mind reader to know we're thinking the same thing. "Uh...didn't that sound just vague enough to placate us?"

The two of us rush the door and burst into the hallway. It's empty. Because of course it is.

"Wil!" I shout.

Misty mutters some choice words under her breath and pounds the door jamb. "Should have known better than to let him leave."

"Maybe Jia took him into her invisible world," I say, with more hope than I feel.

"Yeah. Right. No way would she want to be alone with him now." Misty returns to the room. "I'm done with relying on him. We were just coming back from Raylene House when he found us and then followed us back here. We can smooth things over with Jia when she comes back, if she'll hear us."

I follow Misty back in my dorm and shut the door. "Did you have any luck with Greg and Elisha and Lynn?"

Misty looks grim. "Yeah. Maybe. Lynn wasn't there but Elisha was already drawing up battle plans. Greg was his usual self. Elisha had to take out her earplugs just to talk to me and Jia. Does that count? Apparently Lynn slept outside last night and the Brigade had to escort her back in and when asked, she said it felt better out there. Do you know how cold it was? Below freezing."

"That's pretty weird."

Misty surveys our messy dorm. "If they actually have superpowers, I don't want them sleeping in here with us. Crowded enough as it is."

Sending one of us to guard them this evening isn't such a terrible idea. In the past, the Collective has taken students at night, and the next morning all that remains is a pristine, cleaned-out dorm room. That's one of the reasons Misty, Jia, and I have been sharing a room. Although I seem to have some protections with my mysterious connection to Campbell, the time-travelling, interdimensional alien, the same is not true for Misty and Jia. I've tried and failed multiple times to figure out why I am tethered to him—and what exactly he wants with me. It's especially hard since he's been unusually quiet these past several weeks.

"They also confirmed what Kimberly said. Emily Foller, Felix Debois, Karsten Berg, and even Laura Laska—remember her? We pinned that awful protest we did on the cafeteria on her. They have powers, and they've joined the Brigade. Elisha was able to confirm four more people, already in the Brigade, who have developed powers. What they are, we don't know. And...I hate to tell you this, but Shane is one of them."

This is very bad. It's one thing for a bunch of students in jackets to run around pretending to be superheroes. It's another when those same people believe they have the authority to boss us around and can carry out the enemy's work. With Wil gone, there's only three of us, and maybe only two if we can't get Jia back. More than ever, I feel like the world is on my shoulders, that it is my personal responsibility to save the entire school from itself.

"You haven't teleported in weeks," Misty says flatly, reading my reaction. "And look, I don't want to nag on you. What happened with Jadore, it sucks. It's messin' with your head and I can understand that. But you can't let them win." She folds her arms. "Is that a good enough pep talk to get the wheels running?"

I smile a little. "We can find out."

"Pick somewhere on campus. I will park myself there until you show up."

More than anything, I just want to teleport home. "Are you sure? I was gone for like, three days once."

Misty retrieves Sunni's journal from the bed carefully, as if it's a priceless artefact. For the past couple of weeks, reading and deciphering it has been her personal project. She's been tight-lipped about the contents and I don't want to pry until she has found something useful—if anything. "I have this to finish. Anyone who gets in my way will regret it."

"Okay. I'll teleport to the music room." It's indoors, and if it's anything like the art studio, there won't be many takers. I start the stopwatch app on my phone for good measure and take a deep breath. "I guess I'm ready."

She smiles thinly. "Don't get sucked up into any black holes."

"Thanks for putting that in my head before I disappear."

Her smile becomes more genuine. "You're welcome."

I hold out my hand and she gives it a brief shake. That alone makes me lighter. Misty and I have come a long way, from bickering and petty fights and misunderstanding, to this, now. I close my eyes and I think about the strength of our bond as I feel myself getting lighter, and the room becomes far less substantial and fixed in space.

I conjure every detail of the music room and think of my kiss with Ethan there. He snuck out, and despite the watchful eye of the Collective, I defied the rules and followed him to the quaint music studio to play the piano. He is so talented. Was so talented.

I promised myself I wouldn't think about him. Yet his lost potential, and the thought of him retrieving it someday, pain-free, fills me with a euphoric hope. Then I can tell him about my powers, not in the middle of a life-or-death situation, but on my own terms. We could be happy, someday, if we can both make it through this.

I'm no longer in my dorm room. I'm drifting...

Where is the door? Not that one. Don't get caught. Don't look them in the eye. Now—

I slam against a hard, cold wall. I take inventory. I'm alive. I'm awake. The air is warm and musty, but in a familiar way. My feet ache, as if I've been running on concrete in my heeled boots all day. Although my brain feels like mush, I force my eyes open. The music room.

And then it comes rushing back. I wanted to teleport here. I was in my dorm with Misty and I said I wanted to practice and so I chose this location.

Fortunately, the music studio—really just one room of three in a trailer mounted on a foundation—is deserted. The instruments haven't been touched in a while. Keyboards line the back wall and guitars hang like decorations, never to be played. Daylight streams in from the window at the front. I peek through. It's still sunny out and the quad is packed with students. Brigade students—I lose count after twenty—adopt fighting poses and squinch up their faces and splay their fingers, as if expecting lightning to spring forth. Others jog in unified lines across the quad. I wonder how many of them are harbouring secret superpowers.

Remembering my phone, my stomach does flip-flops as I retrieve it from my pocket. My phone clock says only two minutes have passed. The date is still the same. That's got to be my best record yet. I bring up the stopwatch app—and I nearly drop my phone.

The timer has been running for eight hours, twenty minutes, and five seconds.

I hit stop. A wave of exhaustion hits me then as I stare at the digital numbers. I wrack my brain. What have I been doing for eight hours? I brace myself on the sill. The last thing I remember is leaving Misty's room. Then, a blurry daze. A dark hallway. A sense of dread. Someone was chasing me. There was nowhere to hide...

The door opens and I spin around, startled. It's Wil. He smiles in greeting. He's changed his jacket. It's brown and filthy. "There you are. Banana. Cameras have been fixed. No feed in here, obviously."

I stare at him, mouth agape. "Did you just call me *banana*?"

He hesitates. It takes a lot to rattle Wil, and I've just made him nervous.

"Did you talk to Jia?" I ask. "Where is she? What if she doesn't come back from her invisible world? How are we supposed to find her? You didn't try to mess with her head again, did you?"

"Jia." He shuts the door. "I see."

"I don't see her." I look around. "Do you?"

He nods curtly, but not in the affirmative. Just an acknowledgement that he heard me. "Right." And then he opens the door again.

"No, no, no." I quickly slap a hand on the door jamb. "You're not leaving until you tell me about this magical way out of Sparkstone. I'm assuming it's magical, because you're acting really weird, and I'm not going to let you lock me in a tight space again while you try to play hero."

Wil's expression reveals nothing. He isn't rude or impatient or angry. There's something about his behaviour that's off-putting. He simply nods at me like a stranger on the street as he gently moves me aside and heads for the door.

"Hey! You can't ignore me!" Nothing.

The music studio is one of three in the trailer. Outside this room is a small entryway with the door leading outside. There's a faint beep as the front door opens—it's Misty. She's taken aback by Wil, and then by me.

"Excuse me," Wil says, as he passes in front of Misty, and exits the trailer.

"Did you find Jia?" she asks.

I try one more time. "Don't leave, Wil. We need you."

He falters at the entrance. "That's why I'm going."

Misty tries to stop him, but Wil shakes her off as he lands on the grass and continues around the building, completely ignoring her question.

She mutters a choice word about him under her breath. "What was he doing in here?"

"He said he fixed the cameras." My brain is sluggish. I hope that means the Collective can't see us right now.

"We should go after him and tie him up before he does more damage," Misty says. "So? This is a success, right? You're here. You didn't lose three days."

"Yeah." I try to feel happy about it, despite the elapsed body time. "I haven't tried teleporting with another person. That's the real test."

"You can try it out with me."

I nod. My eyes feel heavy. "Maybe later."

"Take a nap before dinner?" Misty suggests.

"We need to start getting people out of here ASAP," I say in the middle of a yawn. "Tonight. Before the Collective can make any other moves."

"We should move Greg first," Misty says. "With his loud mouth and good connections, he'll turn some heads on the outside. And he's annoying, so really this is a win for everybody. How many people do you think you can handle?"

It's tough to say. "I should start with one." I hesitate. "You're sure you don't want to be the first one to get out?"

She considers it sincerely as we head for the exit. "My place is here. I meant what I said before. I'm going to kill Jadore. I can't do that from the outside."

Part of me feels relieved. Without Misty, I'd feel far more alone here. "Let's see how Greg feels about an extracurricular trip."

❋❋❋

Although I'm eager to get moving, my body isn't. When Misty and I return to my dorm, I slump on the bed and when I lift my head, it's nearly five hours later and I'm feeling more refreshed.

We agree via text to meet Greg in the lobby of Raylene House at three in the morning. He'll let us in and we'll find a storage closet, where I can attempt to teleport with him to a place of his choosing. I'm trying not to think of everything that can go wrong. I have to keep my spirits up if I'm going to pull this off. I eat a hearty supper, even though I'm not that hungry. I endure the whispers and the stares, knowing that one day soon, I'm going to be the one saving their lives.

At eleven p.m., when Misty and I are curled up in bed—Misty with Sunni's journal and its secrets, and me with my thoughts— the door opens and closes seemingly on its own. I side-eye Misty, but neither of us say a word as the floor mattress *thumps*, the blankets float into the air, and cover a Jia-shaped person. Her breathing slows into a steady sleep. At least she came here, and didn't try to sleep alone. That is *something*.

I drift in and out of restless slumber myself. At two-thirty a.m., my phone alarm blares. Even though I'm expecting it, I sit up with a start and shut it off. Misty leaps out of bed as well and flips on the nightside lamp. She's fully dressed and ready to go. "Let's go. Jia?"

Jia rolls over, away from us.

"I know you're mad at us. But this is super important. We're meeting Greg and I'm going to attempt to teleport him out of here. We can't do this without you."

"You can keep secrets from me so you can do this without me," she mumbles sleepily.

Misty and I exchange exasperated looks. "How many times do we have to apologize before you'll forgive us? Be mad at Wil instead."

She curls up into a ball and pulls the blanket over her head.

I sigh. "Maybe we can do this without you. But I don't want to. We're a team. I'm sorry I didn't tell you about Wil."

"It's not your fault that he messed with your mind," Misty adds. "Blame him. Get revenge later. Just like we will." She heads for the door. "You can stay here in your bed if you want. But we're going to save someone's life. I know you're good at that. You can come if you want. Up to you."

"You don't have to guilt me into it," Jia mutters, and throws off the blankets. She too is fully dressed.

"I didn't mean to sound—"

Jia flickers out of existence once again, and the bathroom door slams shut.

"I'm sorry, Jia!" I say, hoping to add some sugar to Misty's salty attempt to convince Jia to help us. No reply from the other side.

Misty raises her eyebrows in surrender and I sigh. I know we all need time to forgive and heal, yet time is not on our side right now. If I can't successfully teleport Greg outside of Sparkstone before the Collective solidifies their hold on us...we're all doomed.

Fifteen minutes later, the three of us are firmly entrenched in Jia's invisible world and quietly making our way downstairs. Awkward, given that the three of us must remain in contact with each other to remain invisible. The invisible world is blurrier than the visible, and each step takes more effort, as if gravity is also different here. Sound is dampened, as if we are underwater, and the comforting heaviness of the air settles on my shoulders. Jia navigates with ease. She's done this many times. In fact, she seems far more at home here than in the visible world.

Jadore let slip during our battle with the Hunger that most cameras on campus have infrared capability now. If Wil were here, he'd just disable them. Instead, Misty and I can only make careful use of our wristbands to temporarily interfere with the camera's audio signal.

The front desk is manned by a hafelglob, who only casually glances at the door as we carefully open and shut it and head into the cold December night.

I tap a button on my wristband. There are cameras outside too. "For the record," I say, "I don't know if 'getting revenge' on Wil is the best attitude to take."

Misty narrows her gaze. "He did the unthinkable to Jia."

"I know." Something about the way Wil acted keeps bothering me. In my dorm, he had been apologetic. Troubled. Yet in the music studio, he had been robotic and dismissive. "Jia, what do you think we should do about Wil—if he ever comes back?"

"I just want this to be over," she says. Her voice sounds small and faraway.

"Do you want me to teleport you out of here, instead of Greg?" Truthfully I feel Jia's powers are more useful here at Sparkstone. We can protect and move people around relatively easily. Even if the Collective has infrared cameras, they can't necessarily tell who is sneaking around without sending a person to check it out. However, if Jia wants out, I can't blame her. If I were her, I'd want to escape.

"No," she replies finally, with sound resoluteness. "To protect my family, I'll stay."

Raylene House is not far. Every careful step I take in this blindingly freezing night is one step closer to victory. Yet our attention is diverted by movement and voices near the music trailer up ahead. I count ten Brigade members, recognisable with their glow-in-the-dark jacket armbands, and three other hulking figures that, from their gait, seem to be hafelglob in disguise. Their flashlights and phones sweep the grass and the foundation of the building, as if they're searching for something.

"What are they doing?" Now I'm really concerned. We were just there, before supper. Did they know I teleported? What if they were looking for me? Didn't they see me in the cafeteria, and in my dorm room? What if they knew we were snooping around outside?

"Let's not find out. Can we go around?" Misty whispers to Jia.

She nods. Just because we're invisible doesn't mean we're soundless. Best to err on the side of caution.

"Greg's wondering where we are," Misty whispers, holding her phone gingerly.

"He's early. Can he come outside and meet us?" I ask.

Misty thumbs a reply and a few minutes later, says, "'There are two Brigade students standing by the door. Can't leave. Waiting in my room.'"

"Can we sneak past them?" I ask, mostly to Jia.

She huffs a sigh, which I take as an affirmative.

Misty's typing a one-handed reply when her hand slips. We swear at the same time as the phone drops out of the invisible world and onto the very visible grass. The three of us halt our slow parade while Misty quickly retrieves the phone.

Excited cries echo from around the music trailer several feet away. We break into a run, holding onto Jia with dear life. I glance over my shoulder and realize that all of the Brigade's flashlights are pointed in our direction.

"Go, go, go," I hiss.

A distorted voice blares from a megaphone. "Stop! Troublemakers!"

"How can they see us?" Misty whispers.

"Just go!" Jia shouts.

The lights grow brighter behind us as the Brigade closes in. More shouting, including Shane's voice: "They're heading that way! I think there are three of them!"

They shouldn't be able to see us. Jia's power renders us invisible to the naked eye, and we should have been far enough away not to attract them with our whispering. They're closing in fast. I wrack my brain. I need complete stillness to teleport, so that's out.

"Wait! The wristbands!" I hiss.

The other neat trick the wristbands can do: create a full-body environment suit that hugs every curve. Not the most flattering of outfits, but it can hide our identities. It worked the first time, when we confronted Jadore on the mother ship. Unfortunately, she managed to find out who we were anyway.

"We are armed and we will shoot!" comes the distorted, projected voice once more.

Jia skids to a stop and we are forced to oblige the quick change in pace.

"What are you doing?" Misty whispers. "I don't want to be *shot*."

"Neither do I," Jia says, and she turns in place to face the onslaught. We turn with her, and their flashlights narrow in on us. It's hard to see their faces in the intense, blinding lights. None of them run by—they really do know where we are. We shield our faces.

They slow to a stop before us, lights trained on our location.

There's some murmuring and someone steps out in front of the gathered mob. He takes off a pair of goggles and shines his light below his chin and grins. It's Shane. And he really wants us to know that.

"Come out, come out wherever you are..." Shane says wickedly. "Oh wait. We *do* know where you are."

"Oh, there's no point in this," Misty says, and lets go of Jia.

"No wait!" Jia says, but it's too late, because Misty is visible.

Shane's grins insufferably. "Hello, Misty Carter. Care to explain your late-night stroll?"

"Maybe I should put on a uniformed jacket and ask you to explain all of your movements. I'd find them equally fascinating," Misty retorts.

Heaving a sigh, I also let go of Jia.

"Figured as much," he says, as soon as he sees my face.

The space between Misty and I is person-sized until Jia, huffing a sigh, voluntarily steps out of her invisible world.

Shane unhooks a radio from his belt and begins sauntering away from us as he mutters a report. Three other Brigade students draw towards us, holding up long black rods along with their flashlights.

"You want to fight me?" Misty challenges them. A flame erupts in her palm.

Surprised, the three Brigade members recoil.

"That's what I thought," she says. "Talk to me when you've fought real aliens."

But they aren't to be intimidated. The three Brigade students exchange glances and their black batons cackle with electricity. So the Collective has *really* armed their Student Watch.

"It's all right," I say, holding up my non-powered palms,

giving Misty a look. "We're just going to take a step back. You stay where you are, we'll stay right here. Okay?"

I reach for Misty's hand and quizzically, she puts out her fire and takes my hand as together, we take one giant step back from the Brigade. They don't power down their batons.

I lean towards my two friends and say under my breath, "I think I can teleport us out of here."

"If we just turn invisible, we can escape without these bozos noticing," Misty hisses.

Jia looks annoyed as she points to Shane's head. A pair of infrared goggles sit in the midst of his curly hair. In fact, all of them are equipped with an identical pair. Seems like Jadore warned them about us and took no chances.

"The cameras have infrared tech too," I say. I take Misty and Jia by the underarm. My supper was large, but my feet are still barking from my earlier unremembered adventure and my brain feels like it's been awake for days.

"You can do it," Misty says.

Shane spins around again to face us. He's still speaking into his radio. "Roger that. Over and out." He gestures to his team. "Yep, bring 'em in."

I hear them first, but I don't react in time. Two Brigade members grab me by the arms. A third—Shane—tugs hard on my hair and something sharp sticks into my neck. The world spins. Misty and Jia face similar struggles. Jia manages to elude her attackers and begins to run—but is stunned by a baton. Down she goes.

My stomach is queasy. My head spins. I hit the grass hard and reach for the night sky as darkness claims me.

CHAPTER 9

I fall face first into my bed, yet it's not mine—it's Sunni's. I leap up, terrified I've disturbed the sheets, and she's sitting in an armchair, legs crossed, hands neatly steepled. She's been expecting me, because she's always expecting me, and I can never say the same.

"You haven't opened the door," she says to me, because that is what she wants.

I scramble to sit up, but my feet are caught in the sheets. "I don't have time for dreams. Misty and Jia are in danger. The Brigade—"

"You think your problems are more important?" Sunni replies. She grips the armchair in one choppy, sudden movement. "Your time is running out."

"I'm doing all I can!" I can't seem to untangle myself from her sheets. They snake of their own will around my legs.

"You have done *nothing*," she says. She's standing on top of the chair now.

It's true. What have I done since come to Sparkstone? Toy with Jadore, call her names, engage in pointless conversations with an all-powerful alien, begin and end a romance, and alienate my friends. She's right, and now, the Collective will win, because I have done nothing.

I stop struggling, which only frustrates Sunni more as her sheets pull me into the black hole forming in her mattress, and I'm tumbling again.

Sunni's voice echoes all around me in purple soundwaves. "This is what I have done. This is the beginning of the end."

A blinding explosion rocks the darkness and sends me flying. I'm in a warzone. The open sky over the quad is filled with large spaceships. They spit shuttles from their underbellies, filled with soldiers ready to conquer Earth. A half-destroyed dome surrounds the entire campus.

I try to stand, but another explosion knocks my balance, and dust and bits fill the air. My ears ring. The spaceships are bombing entire buildings—buildings they built to house us, mold us to their wills. I spin in circles trying to find a friendly face and I see only dark uniforms, fishmen, and collaborating humans equipped with ray guns.

Outside the library is massive metal ring. A localized fog surrounds it and at its centre, an electric blue rippling power undulates. The portal is guarded by armed fishmen, either guarding or waiting their turn to step through.

"Sunni?" I scream. My voice is lost and another explosion knocks me out of the scene and into a hard-backed waiting room chair.

Before me, a hazy doctor's office. Agailya injects a clear liquid from a syringe into Ethan's arm. He winces and then his expression becomes blank. When Agailya removes the needle, Ethan stands robotically and marches out of sight, until his form becomes mist.

I chase it, and then I'm swimming in a lake. It's familiar—I've swam here before, on family vacations to Nova Scotia. Around me, slick-skinned humanoids with gills and scales break the surface and make horrible screeching sounds at a hovering spaceship bearing the Collective insignia. They raise spears. I cover my ears, but in doing so, I'm pulled under. It's all right, because somehow, I can breathe.

Sunni floats beside me. We are gently descending deeper into the depths. I am not afraid. Bubbles appear as we breathe underwater.

Our feet touch the ocean floor, and yet it's just regular earth now. The water is now air and we're back in the Sparkstone war zone. The explosions have stopped, the spaceships are moving away towards more urban centres, and the night is crawling with foot soldiers.

They're all coming at me—including Ethan. He's in a Brigade uniform. He has a silver and blue armband. He's leading the charge against me. I don't move, because I feel I deserve his wrath. I was a terrible person in front of him, and I cannot forgive myself—

An unseen hand takes mine and drags me through the quad. A mess of blonde hair fills my vision. Sunni. I pick up the pace as we run hand-in-hand. The story floods me then, as it does in dreams: this is the end. We are the last of the hunted. The rest of the students have joined the Collective, as soldiers or as labourers in their devious cause to take over the universe. All universes.

Together we reach the front gate. It's closed. We head for the toll booth door, as that's the only other way through. But we're trapped by a mob of Brigade students. Some wield futuristic alien guns. Others wield fire with their bare hands, their eyes flaming with the desire to kill. The rest hold alien spears with sharp ends that cackle with electricity.

"We're trapped," Sunni quivers. She reaches for my face. "I'm sorry, my love."

Ethan appears at the forefront of the Brigade, armed with a two-pronged spear. With one swift motion, he stabs me in the chest.

And yet, it's not really me. Suddenly I'm no longer holding Sunni's hand, nor am I trapped by the Brigade. I am standing off to the side of the scene, once more an observer and not the observed.

"Misty?" It's Sunni who speaks, but it's not my Sunni. My Sunni watches the scene beside me as Other Sunni kneels before Dead Misty.

The Brigade surrounds her, and Other Sunni screams.

"Is this the future?" I demand.

"It is the present," she replies emphatically. "Please. Open the door. NOW."

I sit up, gulping stale air greedily through my mouth. My body tenses. I'm not in my dorm room.

Fluorescent lights buzz and one flickers overhead. My back is killing me. Grit digs into my palms and I smell the unclean floors of my tutorial room. Chairs line the wall before me—all empty. Outside, it's black. I feel my jeans for my phone.

"We confiscated your possessions hours ago."

The deep, chilling voice frightens me. I gasp and scoot backwards. Jadore sits cross-legged on a chair behind me, her manicured hands resting perfectly on her knee. Her white suit jacket and matching skirt have been recently pressed and her lipstick is a deep purple. Different sunglasses sit upon her nose—they're still large, to protect her alien eyes, yet they curve up like cat's eyes in the corners. Stylish. Her cane rests against the wall beside her.

I try to recall the last thing I remember: Shane knocked us out. Sleep weighs me down yet I slowly climb to my feet. "Where are Misty and Jia?"

Jadore smiles and doesn't reply.

"You seem to have recovered from your wounds, from when we fought you and the Hunger," I continue, wiping my hands on my front. "From what I remember, Misty really did a number on you."

Again, Jadore says nothing.

"All right. Keep pretending. For the cameras, I assume." I glance at the ceiling. I don't see any obvious recording devices, but I always assume they're there. "But if you don't tell me where my friends are, I can assure you, there will be consequences."

I'm all guff, and she probably knows it. She heaves a satisfied sigh, and only then does she rise to her feet. She reaches for her cane—unsteadily, I notice; she nearly misses it—and makes her way to the door. Feeling for the entrance, she knocks three times, and steps back.

The door promptly opens, and the Brigade piles in, single-file. Seven chairs line the wall, and seven jacketed students, all of yellow rank or higher, march in. Shane leads them. He looks overly pleased with himself. His hair has been slicked back since

I last saw him—who knows how long ago that was—and his beard is freshly trimmed. Behind him, I recognize a couple of others, including Emily Foller—her eyes are now a crisp orange—and Felix Debois, as twitchy as ever. They all take their seats, except Shane, who stands with his hands behind his back.

"We are present, Mistress-Commander," Shane says.

I make a face at Jadore. "Mistress-Commander?" The hafelglob—or at least Ohz—calls Jadore *mistress*, but she's given herself a military rank now?

"Show some respect, alien," Shane sneers. He unholsters a long black rod and holds it up menacingly.

Jadore cocks an ear. "Violence will not be necessary. You will cooperate, won't you, Ingrid?"

We both know that I won't, whatever I'm here for. I start thinking about places I can safely teleport to, and hopeful thoughts I can call upon in a pinch.

"What have you done with my friends?" I ask Jadore again.

"Your fellow traitors have been detained separately," Shane replies instead.

"I wasn't talking to you," I say.

"You're a filthy spy and an alien infiltrator. You will address me." Shane advances slowly. I notice the top of his baton glows blue-hot.

"You should address her with that weapon," I tell Shane, gesturing to Jadore. "She's the alien who has been murdering students."

Jadore raises a carefully crafted eyebrow in the Brigade's direction. They smirk in return.

"Is there something funny about murder?" I remark.

Shane is about to deliver a retort when Jadore lifts a hand.

"Ingrid is right. A serious accusation, murder. Not only am I an alien in disguise, but I'm a murderess too. The list keeps getting longer and longer, it seems. I should return the favour. Shane, what is it you told me about Ingrid's wrist?"

Jadore knows perfectly well what's on my wrist. Shane lowers his baton; he's more than happy to show off his authority, with or without violence. "She's got one of those alien restraints on there."

"Interesting," Jadore says. "Those are very hard to come by. Hard to remove too. Only our alien servants wear them, to control and restrict their movements."

I roll my eyes. "Do you call the hafelglob *servants* to their face, or only behind their backs?"

She sneers, and then smiles, because she's not done. She's enjoying this exchange far too much. "Your friends are undergoing their Review. And we are still verifying their humanity." She says the last part to Shane, to please him. "Hopefully we can put that matter to rest soon. In the mean time, a practical test is required."

"Is that why I'm here?" I ask. "This is my Review?"

"Mistress Commander, permission to interrogate the alien. This trial is...pointless," Shane says.

Jadore slams her cane into the tile floor. I hear the tile crack. The seven Brigade students gasp and recoil in their chairs. Even Shane looks disturbed.

"It is not pointless. Ingrid is powered—even though her humanity is in question. Yes, Ingrid, this is your Review. Though first, some housekeeping. Shane found you and Misty Carter and Jia Fields sneaking around the music trailer last night."

Last night. I bite my tongue. It's still dark out. Have I been unconscious for twenty-four hours? No wonder my body aches.

I hate to think what they've been doing to me this whole time.

"We all know what you've done with William McBride," Jadore continues, nodding towards the Brigade knowingly.

"Okay," I reply with uncertainty. Best not to feed that fire.

"If you tell us where you've hidden his body, we will be lenient. After all, our witnesses say it was an accident."

I'm in such shock, I can't answer. Campbell had said that Wil would die. Yet I'd seen him less than twelve hours ago. Er, longer than that, I suppose. I keep my mouth shut. The more I say, the more I incriminate myself, and the weaker I seem to make our cause. I stare straight ahead, counting the dragging seconds until this whole ordeal is over, though my hands are shaking. I clasp them in front of me.

I have to think of something hopeful, quick.

"Nothing?" Jadore asks. She looks up at the fluorescent lights. "Perhaps your friend Jia knows more. I should have someone ask her."

"I don't know what you're talking about," I say, unable to stop myself.

"Clearly," she says icily. "You were seen with him. Arguing. Murdering a fellow student is a crime on this planet."

"Yes, it is," I reply, just as coolly.

Jadore is undeterred. "Tell me where you put him, and I can make the Review easier on you."

"I prefer to be evaluated on my own merits, thanks."

She lets out a long sigh and gestures her cane at the Brigade. "When we're through here, tell the students I will give bonus points on their Review and extended curfew privileges for the person who comes forward with information about the whereabouts of William McBride's remains. He was spotted behind the music trailer—ensure the area is dug up again."

"Yes, Mistress-Commander," the seven of them say in unison. Shane speaks the loudest.

Wil left the music trailer and walked around back—and then what? I should have followed him. I could have stopped him. If Jadore is to be believed, Wil is dead, and if they find his body, they will use it for their nefarious, scientific purposes. He was acting so strangely—did he know he was going to die at that moment, and deliberately took action to ensure his body wouldn't be found?

"Now," Jadore says. "We can begin."

She places a hand on the wall and follows it to the door, where she knocks three times briskly. She steps back as two Brigade members bring in a familiar hafelglob in human form. It's Ohz. He looks like hell. His right eye is blackened and bruised. His nose is disturbingly crooked and recently dried, brown ooze trails from his nostrils. Although this is not his true form, I feel sorry for him, as he truly seems to be in a great deal of pain.

When he sees me standing there, however, he goes berserk.

"How...?" He struggles against the Brigade members as his wild gaze darts between me and Jadore. "Did you...?"

"That's enough," Jadore says, annoyed. "You are not permitted to speak in my presence. Understood?"

"Yes, Mistress," Ohz replies, and one of the Brigade students escorting him jabs him in the side with a baton. It sparks and shocks Ohz. He yelps. The air fills with the smell of hot garbage. The baton has burned a hole through his clothes, right to his flesh, leaving a blackened, circular wound.

Jadore returns her attention to me. "I've been led to believe you are quite skilled by now. At teleportation, that is." She says this for the benefit of the Brigade.

Again, I say nothing.

"Your test is this. There's a flag in a windowless, locked room in Rita House. Do you know the place?"

I do. It's on the top floor and students can book it out for private meditation, prayer, or yoga. I give her a curt nod.

"Travel there and bring back the flag. You'll bring along Mr. Ohz for...supervision."

Ohz doesn't look pleased with this assignment. He wrings his greasy hands as if I am the gross one. His eye is swelling shut and his terrified gaze is locked on me. I don't want to meet the person that did that to him.

"Give me your wrist," Jadore says.

No way. When I resist, Shane grabs my arm and holds it out. Jadore reaches into her suit pocket, and now I'm frightened. Instead of a weapon, she pulls a cheap looking digital watch. Confused, I settle somewhat.

Jadore quickly feels for a bare spot and straps on the watch. Shane presses a button on the side and thick red numbers appear: 15:00. 14:59. 14:58...

"Shane," Jadore orders. "Give me a moment alone with the alien traitor."

As the other six Brigade students rise to their feet, Shane hesitates. "Are you sure, Mistress-Commander?"

Her lips curl into a smile. "I'm blind, not helpless."

"Uh, yes, of course, Mistress-Commander. Troop!"

All members of the Brigade march single-file out the door, and promptly shut it behind them.

Jadore lets out a breath, waits a beat, and then grabs my arm.

Before I can resist, she taps a sequence on the small buttons on my wristband—the sequence that disables the camera audio.

"If you're not back in fifteen minutes, I'll start cutting off fingers," she hisses in my face. She grins. Her teeth are tiny, pointy spikes. "Guess who I'll start with?"

I try and fail to let my worry show. I steel myself. She's just made a fatal mistake, showing me she's acting for the cameras now. She told me during our last extended, truthful interaction that she's trying to undermine the Council in charge of the Collective. Perhaps her failure with the Hunger means she's just as much a subject in this experiment as the students. "Tell me what planet you're from. Maybe I'll pay that a visit."

She laughs. "You wouldn't last ten seconds in my swamp. The air would rot your lungs."

"They hated you that much, they forced you to leave?"

"I was *lifted*," Jadore hisses. She jabs my sternum with a sharp fingernail. "Remember your betters, now, and run along. The clock is already ticking."

Reluctantly, I take Ohz by the arm, who endures the exchange with trepidation. He tenses under my grasp. I don't like this either, but I'd rather test my teleportation abilities with him than one of my friends. I take a long look at Jadore, trying to think of something witty, but coming up with nothing. I close my eyes and breathe deeply, thinking of my parents and how happy I'll be when I'm reunited with them as I carry us out of reality.

Focus. Remember.

My head feels heavy, as if I've been rudely awakened from a deep, satisfying sleep. I'm in motion. Moving down a tile-floored hallway. Every few paces, there are doors on my left and right. My hands graze them absently. It seems the most natural thing to do. Red door with a squiggle. Tap! Blue door with a line. Tap! They are all cold to the touch. That means I'm not welcome inside, not today at least.

I have a vague memory that I am with someone. "Ohz?"

He can't have gone far. A whooshing sound underscores my footsteps, like the sound of an air conditioning unit or far-off traffic. Every so often, the floor rumbles, and I think I hear people talking from behind one door or another, but when I crane my head to listen, the sound dissipates. The hallway is lit just enough that I can see the way, although I can't tell where the light is coming from, as the ceiling is a dark, still cloud, ready to unleash rain.

At the end of the hallway is yet another, adjoining hallway. To my left, doors. To my right, even more doors. Squinting down both paths, I see the hallway forks again and again at random intervals.

I'm in a maze. A never-ending labyrinth of doors. And I have no clue which one is mine.

"Crosskey!"

I swivel and gasp. It's Ohz. Or, I'm pretty sure it's him. I haven't seen him many times in his true form. A beige, fleshy mass of rounded tentacles writhes from a fleshy blob about half my height. Besides the tentacles, the most terrifying part of the hafelglob is the mouth, which takes up most of its body. Three sets of small, sharp teeth spiral into the creature, and as his mouth opens to inhale a raspy breath, droplets of salvia pool on the floor beneath him. How he digests is beyond me, and not something I care to think about.

"Does Crosskey know the way?" he asks, in a gurgling voice.

I turn back to the fork. "Left."

I don't feel confident about the choice—yet it isn't the wrong choice. I can't say how I know that for sure. This place is familiar to me. I have walked it many times now. The more steps I take, the more I remember panicking on my very first arrival. I ran and screamed and no one helped me. I banged on so many doors that the walls began to shake and I'd slumped on the floor and cried for hours before finding the right one. Other times, I didn't think about it, I just trusted my instincts.

And then, my last visit returns to me. The drudgery of the trek had exhausted me. I knew what I was looking for but every turn I took was wrong. Something was hunting me, and I had to double back three times before finally reaching that glowing, red door...

Right. A glowing door. I shake my head and smile. Of course it's a glowing door, it's a glowing door every time. Why was I so worried?

"It's going to be all right," I say over my shoulder to Ohz.

"Ohz does not doubt Crosskey," he replies. "Only she can lead us to victory, yes."

His strange faith only serves to bolden my step. At the next juncture, I take a right, and then a quick left, then straight ahead. Ohz keeps up heartily. The sounds of his slurping, slithering body behind me are at first unnerving, but one gets used to the unusual.

It is impossible to keep track of time here. The stopwatch on my arm is stuck mid-count between 13:24 and 13:23. I'm tired, but I'm not more tired than when I started walking. My belly aches for a hearty meal, yet I could have used one when I was in the tutorial room. No wonder I was exhausted upon returning from my last trip. Time is at a stand-still and so is my body, yet when I return to the real world, it all catches up with me.

The more I walk, the warmer I feel, and I also take that as a good sign. Although the corridors feel infinite, every door is unique. Each door has a colour, a symbol, and a unique handle. Some have windows, and some don't. A few have peep holes. I attempt to look through one, though I see only darkness. A strip of light shines through the bottom of some, and I have an urge to knock to see who is home.

I'm passing down a long stretch of hallway. To my right, a row of three doors are unusually identical, except for their symbols. The first has five stars, the second six, and the third, eight.

"Well that's weird," I say, to no one in particular.

Ohz gurgles behind me, neither agreeing or disagreeing.

I'm about to continue on when goosebumps ripple across my skin. I have the feeling I'm being watched.

"Getting close?" Ohz asks. His gurgling is also on edge. Can he feel it too?

Now I remember why I was worried—why I would return to the regular world with a start, as if waking up from a bad dream.

Because this maze has Minotaurs.

I put a finger to my lips, hoping he understands the gesture, and I turn left down a short hallway and then turn the corner again. I flatten against the wall. Beside me, Ohz copies the gesture, though for him, it's more literal. His tentacles suction quietly against the wall and his body decompresses. The tips of two of his tentacles twitch uncontrollably. I frown at him.

"Sorry," he gurgles, in the lowest volume he can muster. "Can sense...them."

I chance a peek around the corner. At first, I see no one, but something more primal is warning me that danger is afoot. Then, two beings in grey robes, walking side by side, pass in a parallel hallway. They are eerily silent, yet they gesture and nod at each other as they walk. I don't get a good look of their faces, yet their hands are tiny and grey like their robes, which appear a size too large. They don't appear hostile, yet I remain still. After all, I'm not supposed to be here. I get the feeling they can sense me if I get too close—or in their way.

I flatten against the wall once more and wait a few minutes. Once Ohz's tentacles stop twitching, I figure it's safe. I check, and they seem to have gone.

Yet something has changed.

I creep out of our hiding spot and jog down the hallway to the adjoining corridor. Before, there had been three nearly identical blue doors with differing stars. Now, the blue door with six stars that I had touched earlier—it's gone. A blank wall has replaced it seamlessly, as if the six-star blue door had never existed.

"Should keep moving," Ohz mutters.

"Yeah." I stare at where the door was, that blank space, and I press a hand against the wall. Immediately, I recoil and yelp, and a resounding sense of dread fills me.

"Crosskey?" Ohz asks, slithering towards me.

"S'okay," I say, attempting to keep my distance from him. My hand turns a bright red. A millisecond longer, the burn would have been far worse. I blow on it, and gesture for Ohz to keep up. I shouldn't have touched that. I made a noise, and they'll hear.

I let my base instincts take over. Ohz seems equally on edge now, and despite his mass, keeps on my tail. "They know we are here," he says, at one point, some time later.

"What are they?" I ask.

He has no answer for me. Perhaps he cannot communicate it.

I start to slow down, even though my animal instincts tell me to run faster, away from the lurking predator. I'm close to my door.

Wiping my brow of sweat, I turn left once more—and it's there. A red door, with the picture of a white flag. There's a four-digit number in thick red lettering beneath it: 13:2, with the fourth number being a hybrid between four and three. It matches my stopwatch perfectly. The entire door glows a soft light blue.

"This is it." I hold out my good hand to Ohz. He places a long tentacle on my palm.

I turn the round handle. A blinding white-hot light and a terrible screeching sound meets me.

To my left—movement. A grey-robed, horrible-faced monster appears, hand outstretched. He's nearly caught me!

I step through the door, pulling Ohz along, but he's heavy and the creature is upon us and—

THURMP.

I'm a feather, descending gracefully back into my body. I'm standing, not laying down, which is disorienting at first. I reach out—my left hand hurts terribly; what happened?—and touch a wall.

I open my eyes and see white. White walls, white floor, white door. It's a small room, smaller than the tutorial classroom I just came from. Was that where I was? My memories of my trip from there to here are fleeting, yet fragments remain. A blue door with stars. Endless hallways. A friendly presence. Being chased.

I had someone with me—Ohz.

He's not here.

But the flag is. The white fabric is mounted on a pole as long as my arm, and attached to a base that stands upright on the floor. I pick it up with my good hand. It's light.

To my left is the door. I try the knob and endure the pain in my burned hand. Locked. I pound on it. "Hello! Someone's in here!"

Nothing. Big surprise. I check the ceiling. No obvious cameras in sight. There's a fixture above me—perhaps there's a camera in there. The Collective wouldn't do an experiment like this without monitoring the results. I wave. Best to give them a show. I am cooperating, after all.

I blow out air. What happened to Ohz? My first time teleporting another person, and I couldn't even get that right. How am I supposed to evacuate an entire school when I can't even take one person from one place to another?

I pound on the door some more. Maybe he ended up somewhere else. "Ohz? Hello! Anyone?"

I nearly check my phone, but then, remembering it was confiscated, I look at the digital watch. Nine minutes left. I have no idea what time it is here. I hope it's not hours later, or days. I wonder how much body-time has passed. At least I've managed to remember more of my missing time, and I've arrived in the right place. I'm just contemplating my return trip when the door unlocks, and in bursts Ohz, out of breath.

"There you are!" Phew. I don't know if it's part of the test for me to return Ohz as well as the flag, or if he's just my chaperone, but I'm relieved he's in one piece, and in human form. Not only that, his face appears to have mended. His blackened, bruised eye has disappeared and his nose is no longer crooked. No traces of that oozing brown substance in his nostrils. His clothing looks clean as well—no burn marks from where the Brigade had tortured him into silence. "I guess you ended up outside. That's never happened before, but I've never done this before with another person, so I guess..." I'm rambling. "Your eye looks better."

Ohz is confused. "Eye?"

"Yeah. Can you regenerate your appearance?"

"Um...Crosskey is not making sense. Listen. You have allies with me, and many others. You may have noticed. Crosskey is not to be afraid of us. We want to help."

"Okay...how?" I don't remember him being this talkative when we were in the strange hallway with the stranger aliens. Why bring this up now, in front of the cameras. "Ohz, maybe we should just cool it with—"

He steamrolls over me. "Listen carefully to Ohz now. The portal is complete. It is beneath the library. Mistress will put Crosskey on the amplifier and fry her to channel her power and open the portal. Crosskey will be harvested."

My stomach turns. We destroyed the Hunger, which was not only a literal cloud that extracted information from prisoners, but a power source for Jadore's portal. She wants to use the portal to infiltrate other universes to dxpand the Collective's influence. Or...her influence, at least. That would explain the increased activity around the library, why it has been off-limits for weeks now. We were there, what, two months ago? Rows and rows of old books and haunting green lighting had disturbed my dreams for many a night.

But I can't be strong enough to power a portal, even with an amplifier, whatever that might be. She must also realize that if she puts me in danger, Campbell will materialize. Unless that's also part of her plan.

It's then I also notice the white *a*, stitched into his jacket collar. Just like the other hafelglob guards in Rita House, and the one by the stage during the Open House reception. "What does this symbol mean?"

He seems relieved and pleased that I've finally asked him about it. "Allies. To Crosskey."

"You can tell me more about this when we're safer," I say slowly, glancing up at the ceiling, searching for hidden cameras. This isn't the time or place for Ohz to be professing his allegiance to me. Time is ticking. "We should—"

"No place is safe, Crosskey," he says bitterly. "It is glorious and awful. Other planets have not been this...exhausting. Not since wristbands are remotely controlled. Crosskey is lucky hers is modified. Otherwise...she would be fried meat by now."

Yes, we are lucky to be wearing these stupid wristbands that can't come off, I think bitterly. Lucky that Wil modified them for us. Now he's missing, possibly dead, and mostly unwilling to help us further. Realizing I have an opportunity, I fiddle with the buttons to block the audio signal of any hidden cameras.

"Tell me the truth, then, Ohz. When will Jadore harvest me?" I demand.

"When Crosskey proves herself. Then she will be placed on the amplifier, and Mistress will hook her up to the controls and send energy to her brain, and—"

"Ohz. What do you mean, when I...prove myself? Do you mean after you and I teleport back to Jadore?"

He stares at me blankly. "Crosskey has an appointment with the Mistress, now?"

"Yeah." I lift up the flag and wave it around. "This is what I'm here for. Did the trip make you feel sick? The first time I teleported, I threw up. You get used to it."

Lumbering, limping footsteps approach in the hallway. Ohz speaks more quickly now. "Never mind this now. Ohz has said his piece. Must hide now. And not to worry. Ohz hid body for Crosskey. Ohz never betray Crosskey. Mistress will be furious. Ohz never betrays Mistress...until today."

"What body?" I demand.

"Mind-Friend body," he replies, confused.

I grab Ohz's arm. "Wil's body? Ohz, did you kill him?"

He looks worried. "I only—"

A garbling voice in the hallway calls to us. "Ohz? Mistress and funny humans want to see you. It's very urgent."

"Busy! Tell her Ohz will go later!"

"It's very important!" A security guard in human form appears at the door. When he sees me, he falters. Like Ohz, he wears the white ally symbol on his jacket collar. "Oh. Crosskey?"

"Hello," I say politely.

"Ohz. Mistress wants you in tutorial room two-one-six. Asked to hand you over to funny humans for show." He sneers. "As if they can—"

Just then, two Brigade students enter the room, carrying batons. They beeline for Ohz. He looks genuinely afraid. "Get away. Ohz is busy on business!"

"C'mon, alien," one of them says.

"No!"

He backs against a wall as the two of them close in. He fumbles with his wristband; he isn't fast enough. Single-mindedly, the two Brigade students activate their batons. One gets him in the side. The other strikes him in the face repeatedly. Ohz crumbles to the floor but lifts his head to me.

His eye is severely bruised. His nose bleeds a thick, brown oozing substance and slants brutally to one side. It looks just as fresh as it was when the Brigade brought him down to the tutorial room...

A creeping chill overtakes me then as I too slide down the wall, taking in the scene as if I am outside of my body.

The Brigade students take no notice of me; they're too preoccupied with lifting Ohz, who has submitted to them, and carrying him out of the room.

My heart pounds I grip the wall with my burned hand. I can no longer feel it, for this shock is far greater. But...how can this be?

Am I...in the past?

I stare up at the cameras. Are they getting this?

If that is the Ohz that I teleport with—where is the real Ohz?

If I return to Jadore without him...will I fail the test?

The flag is slippery in my hand as I think of happier times, and blink out of the room.

CHAPTER 10

I wobble on my feet, like a newborn waking from a deep sleep. Every time I teleport, it's like arriving in the middle of a dream. Something you'd think I'd be used to by now. My brain fills me in: I'm in the tutorial room again. I'm exhausted. My feet feel like they've been walking for hours. The stopwatch is going again: 4:21. 4:20. 4:19…

"You've returned," Jadore says, with a hint of a surprise in her voice.

I hold up the white flag. "Here."

Jadore stands in front of the well-used whiteboard and adjusts her sunglasses. She gives the flag a mere glance. "Where is Mr. Ohz?"

The hafelglob in disguise isn't in the room. Besides Jadore, there are only the seven Brigade members, including Shane, plus the two that brutally attacked and escorted Ohz here, to the tutorial room. I look upon them in a new light, terrified. Frantically I start to pace, hands on my head, trying to process the horror that I can barely remember.

The infinite hallway. Gurgling noises. My name, called

repeatedly. Dark robes. Screaming. The vacuum of space. Something slimy around my arm...

Shoving my jacket sleeve up, I see a dark red bruise, similar to the light burn on my hand. It's wide and long, tentacle shaped, complete with suction marks.

"I was just...speaking with him..." My throat feels cold.

I left him, and not just once, but twice. Once, in the hallway of doors. And again, in the past.

I didn't just teleport. I travelled through time.

Shane, fascinated, grabs my bruised arm and holds it up to his eye-level. I wince and he takes no notice. "Gross." He unbuckles the stopwatch and ensures it is no longer running. "Mistress-Commander, the alien servant didn't return. Her arm is bruised."

"Yes, thank you," Jadore says quickly. From inside her jacket suit pocket, she pulls out a familiar tome. It's Campbell's treatise. The one she took from my room.

"Hey. That's my—"

Shane bars my advance with his baton and shoots me a devilish look. He's daring me to take another step.

Jadore peruses the tome, taking her sweet time flipping through the fragile pages. Some of the Brigade members exchange confused glances. Good. Let the doubt fester in their minds. I wait for one of them to speak out, but they don't. They're too afraid.

"*Reading* anything interesting in there?" I ask. The last time she dared show that book in my presence, she was trying to force me to summon Campbell, so he could translate it. Perhaps she's been able to muddle through on her own, which is worse.

After a minute of complete silence, she lowers the tome. "Yes, as a matter of fact." She shakes her head and flips the page. "You know, I can interpret certain shapes and symbols. Which this particular treatise is full of."

"Extremely rude," Shane says to me, shaking his head with disgust.

So is stealing, I want to say. "You don't need me to call anyone to translate that for you, do you?"

The fact that I haven't heard from Campbell in a long time, and that Jadore is seemingly uninterested in finding him, settles uneasily within me. I feel like I would know if something happened to him. And yet, Jadore stands there, smug as can be as she flips through his treatise.

Speculation will get me nowhere. Campbell told me that several months from now I'll still be alive, and I'm to wait for him at the portal. Whatever has happened, will happen, he said, so like it or not, I will survive this dreadful interaction.

"Your plan won't succeed," I continue, trying to rile her. "Ohz told me about your power supply problem. However you plan to use me, it won't work."

Jadore releases a slow, low hiss that she turns into a frustrated sigh. "As I said, Ingrid. I will manage. With or without your cooperation."

The barely veiled threat is clear. "I did what you asked of me. Assure me that my friends are safe."

Jadore raises an eyebrow. "I made no such deal with you." She snaps the treatise shut. "You performed this task, but it was done poorly. If I were to grade you, you have barely passed. We will review the footage. Seeing that you failed to bring back your companion, I'd say your iteration of power is too unstable. However...that can be corrected in time for the launch of phase four."

My mind spins. Will they notice that I arrived in the past, before they asked me to complete this task? Is there a flag up there, right now?

How can she say I did poorly when I literally *just* time travelled?

What if Jadore discovers I can time travel?

What if she forces me to travel to the past...and do something terrible?

I am beginning to understand Wil's decision to leave.

"Shane," she continues. "Walk with me. I have a new plan. Have your people escort her back to her room."

"Mistress-Commander?" Shane asks. Jadore nods for him to speak. "Forgive me, but with teleportation powers as strong as hers...even if they are unstable, as you say...wouldn't it be prudent to keep her sedated? What's preventing her from traipsing off to her fellow traitors and planning an attack?"

Jadore's dark lips twist into a sly smile as she heads for the door. "She has nowhere to go. And even if she does...if she cares at all about her friends, she won't dare leave."

I open my mouth to protest this—when her words suddenly hit me. If I manage to leave Sparkstone, no one on the outside will believe my story. And if I leave at all, she'll hurt my friends.

And if I do nothing, she will use my powers for her own gain, and everyone will die.

❁◉❁

The Brigade escorts me back to Rita House and up to my dorm room. I am met by several students who glare at me, because I am a pariah, doomed to be forever guarded and alone. They return my phone, though it's already dead, and probably suped up with spyware. Felix Debois shoves me inside my room, and slams the door. I plug in my phone and then try the door, but it's locked. I pound on it.

"Locked doors are meaningless!" I shout.

I'm blowing smoke. They know they have power over me.

My anxiety has me pacing frantically, and I begin tidying the room, because using the energy productively helps me think clearly. If I teleport, they'll hurt my friends. Maybe even my parents.

I run to my reflection in the bathroom mirror. I'm alone, and muttering to myself doesn't make me feel equipped to handle the situation. Can I concentrate on Wil, and see if he hears my thoughts? No, apparently Wil is dead. Would Jadore lie about that? No, she would have said he was locked up with Misty and Jia. She is searching for his remains—wherever they may be.

Can I contact Campbell? The tether between us lingers. Before, I summoned him by singing or playing the piano—activities he enjoys—or he appeared when I was in trouble. Well, I'm in real trouble now. I close my eyes and sing a slow ballad, gripping the cold sink to steady my nerve.

I open my eyes. Still alone. Damn it. I am paralyzed once more by inaction, trapped by my fear of what if and what now.

They're going to win, a small voice inside me says.

"I can't let that happen," I reply to no one. "I can't."

There is another option: teleport away from here, despite Jadore's threat to kill my friends.

But where? A police station or news outlet that would believe my story? My parents? I desperately want to go home, more than anywhere, but other than personal comfort, my parents can't provide the kind of help me and my friends need right now. What if, by the time I make it back, everyone is already dead? I'm not powerful enough to control *when* I return.

Jadore is right. I have nowhere to go, and no one powerful enough to help me.

I am on my own.

I run my burned hand under water. It doesn't hurt as much as it did before. The tentacle burn on the same arm looks worse. I dab it with a soaked facecloth, and then I decide to take a cold shower.

After changing into a fresh t-shirt and pair of jeans, I put my boots and coat back on and settle down next to the door. I have to be ready, you see. The Brigade could return at any moment. Jadore could barge in carrying my friends' heads. Ethan might finally remember me, and whisk me away to the music trailer again...

I doze, my mind racing with these possibilities, but I'm startled awake that evening as the door beside me clicks open. I scramble backwards—but it's not the Brigade, or Jadore, or even Ethan. It's Misty and Jia, and only Misty and Jia.

The door shuts and locks again, and I barely notice.

"You're back. You're not dead." Tears flow down my face.

Their faces are pale and the bags under their eyes say it all. They don't want to talk to me. I back against the wall as Misty collapses in bed and Jia crawls to the floor mattress like a parched woman to water. They're still wearing the same clothes we snuck out in, though theirs are far more wrinkled. I see no visible cuts or bruises, but that doesn't mean they haven't endured torture. As soon as their heads hit the soft pillows, they're snoring.

Whatever tests they were subjected to—or whatever

torture—I fear the worst. I sit against the wall all night, imagining it, until I tire myself out. When I come to, stiff and sore, it's still dark, though the alarm clock on the nightside table says it's nearly seven. They're both in bed, but Misty is staring at me, bleary eyed.

"Are you okay?" she asks.

The words are a jolt to my stomach. I'm wildly awake now. "Are you?"

"Yeah." Her voice is croaky.

I crawl over to the bed and lay down next to her. She rolls over to face me.

"You look awful," she says.

"I feel...awful." I try to come up with a better descriptor, but can't. "Tell me what happened?"

"Ugh. They took us to a classroom with no windows and just left us there. For a day? I guess that's how long it's been. They tried to rough us up. They got a few good shots in." She lifts her shirt and shows me some reddened, circular baton wounds. "The Brigade got the worst of it."

"I'm glad you survived."

"Me too. Jia was invisible almost the entire time."

The two of us listen for her snores.

"Is she still mad?" I ask.

"Yeah. I guess. Tried to talk to her...but she was just...out of it. They also sedated us. Didn't knock us out, just kept us mellow and quiet. Mostly me. They know I would have blasted my way out of there otherwise."

I frown. "So you didn't have a Review."

Misty shakes her head. "You?"

"Yeah." I fill her in: my teleportation adventure, Ohz's demise, the time travel, and even my dream with Sunni. "It sounds so stupid...and unlike her...but it sounds like Dream-Sunni wants me to cooperate with Jadore."

"No." Misty shakes her head. "It's a trick. Or, not a real prophetic dream."

I don't know how to explain the difference to Misty. It was a special dream. And every strange thing Dream Sunni has shown me has come to pass in one manner or another, even if the results were less fantastical. "She keeps telling me to open the door. I thought I already did that. I let Campbell into this world. I accepted her journal. How many doors can there be?"

"She's trapped in the spirit realm. She wants you to open the door to the afterlife. Or...to here."

"If that's the case, I wish she'd just tell me how to do that. Teleportation is my thing, not reaching into purgatory. You didn't find anything in the book, right?"

"A lot of it is in code. It's hard to translate. There are entries in here about the Collective invasion—but it describes attacks that have never happened. If I'm reading this right, she talks about a... wall? A dome? She tried to sabotage it. I don't think it went well." She looks frustrated. "Unless these are dreams she was having. I just don't know if it's the *same* book as the one she had before."

The book I pulled from the dream is more worn. "Could I have pulled it out of the past? Just as it was destroyed?"

"I don't know. Did you?"

There is one other possibility. "What if this isn't our Sunni's book? What if this is Sunni...from another universe?"

Misty frowns. "C'mon. Be serious."

"I am being serious. Campbell's treatise talks about the multiverse. Jadore is building a portal to connect to another universes. She told me herself. What if my dreams haven't been from Dead Sunni. What if they're from *another* Sunni?"

I know it's a stretch—and yet, it's not. Somehow, Sunni was able to give me an object through a dream. A marriage of both our powers. I imagine if either of us are able to cross that divide, we could have already. Maybe it's only a matter of time before my powers are strong enough to bring something larger and more sentient than a book.

She holds my stare in disbelief. "I just can't believe that there would be another Sunni. Another Collective, carrying out the exact same invasion. It doesn't seem right," Misty says slowly. "Maybe I'm reading this wrong. I'll try cracking this code again or die trying."

"Don't say that."

Misty sighs. "I'm not going to let them kill us, Ingrid. Stop bein' dramatic."

"I'm not being dramatic. I was really worried that they'd done something terrible." I roll onto my back and bite my lip. "But they won't, if I don't teleport out of here. Jadore said I'm not strong enough to use for her nefarious project, so she's let me live, for now. That will buy us enough time to come up with a new plan."

She sits up in bed and grabs me roughly by the arm. "You need to teleport us out of here. Right now!"

"Misty. Who knows who they'll kill if they realize—"

"The Collective is going to kill all of us. You are letting your fear and your superpowered ego get in the way of saving those who actually still fighting this thing."

"I couldn't even bring Ohz from Point A to Point B. I won't sacrifice your life to save us!" I retort, wrenching away my arm.

"That isn't your choice to make!"

"I didn't save you before so you could die now."

Misty is taken aback. "Excuse me? You can't even hear yourself, can you? You don't get to decide my fate. It doesn't rest with you, or anyone, even if you think we're all alive because of you." She slides out of bed, hands on her forehead. She's trying to keep cool, and she's struggling. "Do nothin' if you want. But you could literally end a planet-scale invasion by goin' out there and seekin' help. The cost? Sacrificing a couple of people in the thick of it. Potentially me. Potentially Jia. You have to be okay with the idea that we're not all going to make it through."

I sit up on my elbows and avert my gaze. "Wil is dead. That's who the Brigade was looking for by the music trailer. They can't find his body, but they've seen it at some point. So we've already lost him. I just don't want to lose you too."

She stares at me for a long moment. "I've already decided how I want to die, Ingrid. Hands blazin', sending Jadore back to her maker. Make your peace, and when I come out of this bathroom, let's just say, I hope you're gone."

As she shuts the bathroom door, I pull the covers around my legs. I can't abandon my friends. There has to be some other way to foil Jadore's plan from within the school that doesn't put my friends in jeopardy. Surely not everyone has joined with the Brigade yet. I lean over the side, peeking down at Jia. She's on her stomach. The blankets have long been abandoned on the floor.

"Jia. Are you awake?"

Her breathing doesn't change. When I don't get a response, I slump back on the bed.

Maybe Misty's right. I should just go—and let them deal with the consequences. It just seems so heartless to leave them here at our darkest hour, with only the two of them to protect each other.

The Collective is going to win, the doubt within me says again.

Footfalls in the hallway alarm me, though it's the pounding on the door that rattles my bones. "Wake up." It's Shane.

Misty throws open the bathroom door. Neither of us move. She holds up her hands, still wet from the sink. One freezes and bits of ice swirl around her palm. "Get ready," she whispers.

Just as she's about to take a step towards the door, outside, there's fumbling with the lock. Misty and I exchange terrorized looks. "Does someone else have a key...?"

I shake my head as the door unlocks and swings open. Shane steps boldly inside. He quickly takes inventory of the room: Misty at the door to the bathroom, one hand on the jamb; me, sitting up in the bed in shock, and Jia, murmuring in her sleep.

He gestures to three other Brigade members, including Felix, in the hallway. "Make it thorough."

They march with purpose into the room. Jia sits up, confused, as the Brigade turns the room upside down. They open drawers and spill all my clothes onto the floor. One heads for the bathroom and runs the sink, checks the toilet tank, turns on the shower, and looks under the mat. The third feels up every crevice and cranny, as if searching for illicit goods. It's an inspection, and neither Misty, Jia, nor me make a move to stop them—because the three of us are the most dangerous weapons in the room.

"What is this all about?" Misty demands.

"Don't speak to me," Shane retorts.

Immediately, Misty's hand erupts into flame and she holds up her fist. "Don't you speak to—"

Before Misty can splay her powers about the room, Felix jabs

Misty in the side with a blue-hot baton. Misty growls at him in French and falls to her knees. He has some choice words for her too in his native tongue, though it only infuriates her more. Her hand smokes out as she steadies herself on the floor. The scent of it attacks my nose.

I whirl on Shane and I grab the nearest blunt object—my hairbrush—and I'm about to take a swing when Felix hovers the baton over Misty once more.

"Cooperate," Shane says in a low, warning tone.

The brush shakes in my hand. If I leave, they die. If I resist, they get hurt. Slowly, I lower the brush.

"Stay here with them. They can get their breakfast when we're through," Shane instructs his troop. They nod and salute, and then he gestures to the door with his baton. "Let's go."

I glance back at Misty. She's still on her hands and knees on the floor, glowering at me.

In my heart of hearts, I know she's right. Yet I can't. I just can't.

I submit to Shane and follow him into the hallway. He shuts my dorm room and nods to two Brigade students guarding it. One of them is Emily Foller. She greets me with cheer, as if we're not living in the same dystopian nightmare.

I don't know what to say. I turn and Shane follows me closely down the hallway, down the stairs, past the hafelglob at the security desk. There's just one, and he trains his eyes on me as I pass. Our gaze meets. I note the white symbol on his collar. An ally.

Does he know about Ohz? How can I tell him?

As if he can sense my thoughts, he nods slightly, but he makes a fist and shakes it, as if to say, *Don't give up.*

Shane doesn't even give the hafelglob a second glance.

Outside, I pull my fall coat around me. Shane looks comfortable; his Brigade jacket must be fiercely lined, though his ears are beginning to look rosy. I suppose his facial hair provides him some measure of warmth. He gestures for me to follow him across the road.

"Where are you taking me?" I demand.

To my surprise, he replies. "To the cafeteria. Breakfast. Mistress-Commander has ordered you a special diet to refine your abilities."

"And you are you my personal chaperone?" I ask dryly.

"Yes, from now on," Shane replies. "And if you try anything on me—"

"You don't have to make threats." I pull my jacket tighter around my middle. It's below zero and daylight has just broken. That's when I remember. "It's Christmas Eve."

Shane raises an eyebrow. "I suppose."

"You don't care?"

"I don't celebrate." He frowns. "Why does an alien care about Christmas?"

Yes, what a mystery. I told my parents I'd be home for Christmas. They must be worried sick about me. The Collective has probably been blocking my calls—maybe they've been sending fake messages to them. My parents would know a real message from a fake one, with the code we established. I have to get back to them.

You wouldn't risk the lives of your friends just to see your parents, that little voice within says nastily. *Just give in now and save yourself some time.*

When I don't reply immediately, he does a double take. I've

piqued his interest. He pauses on the road. "So. What planet are you from?"

I try to think of the funniest or grossest science fiction planet and then decide that such a reference would be beyond him. "You wouldn't be able to pronounce it."

"Ah. You think I'm too primitive."

"You said it. Not me."

"You know," he says, lowering his voice and hiding his mouth with his hand, "perhaps you and I could come to a certain... understanding. Let's just say that the Mistress-Commander is incredibly generous to those loyal, select few. You pass me a few freebies: small bits of information about your real mission... and I could make this whole captive supervision thing far more pleasant."

"More pleasant than this?" I gesture to a Brigade troop marching by, doing a rude call and response about killing aliens with superpowers. They march to the end of the road and turn, heading back towards the town of Sparkstone. "I wonder what Jadore would say about her most loyal soldier trying to strike a deal with an alien."

"Maybe she'd reward me for my genius."

I see another armed Brigade troop coming towards us, from behind Rogers Hall. This mass of uniformed Brigade members is different. They're with an even larger group of non-uniformed students. They carry identical suitcases, as if they're all taking an overnight trip. Some of the regular students look afraid and others look excited, but most importantly, they are being escorted somewhere, in broad daylight. Kimberly is among them in a dark winter jacket with a lined fur hood. Her gaze darts about the crowd, searching for companionship. She tries to strike up a conversation with a student next to her, but gets the brush-off.

I watch them go. "Where are those students going?"

"That's on a need-to-know basis."

"That's me, I need to know." I start off in their direction, but Shane hooks me by the arm and spins me against his chest. He sticks the baton in my stomach.

"One wrong move," he says, "and I'll turn this on to its max setting."

"Do that, and Jadore will murder you for killing her most valuable resource."

He scoffs. "You're nothing."

"No? Well this nothing can teleport you into space." I close my eyes and remove all tells from my face.

I hear the buzz of the baton as he charges it up. "You have five seconds to stop."

"It only takes me two." I take a deep breath and imagine floating above Earth, near the mother ship. That's a nice view to die to. The image itself is so hopeful. The mural in the art studio had captured it perfectly. I call it to mind—

He throws me to the ground just as the end of the baton erupts in a blue-hot electric light. He's breathing heavily. "I felt that. Don't do it again. Now get up."

"Come with me if you want. I have nothing to hide," I say. "But don't touch me again."

He doesn't stop me this time as I hurry after the students, though he does follow. Kimberly is on the outer edge of the mass, and when she spots me approaching, she waves vivaciously.

She's not the only one who sees me. One of the Brigade guards, with a yellow stripe on her jacket, raises her baton. "This is Student Watch business. Keep your distance."

Shane is on my tail and he waves her down. "She's my charge."

She nods and falls back into formation. Shane walks about a foot away from me, not far enough away to have a private conversation, and close enough to grab me if I start causing trouble.

"I'm so glad you're not dead. I didn't know what happened to you," Kimberly says. "Where are Misty and Jia? Did you find out what happened to Wil? Why is that Shane guy following you now?"

I roll my eyes. He keeps his gaze on the horizon. He's totally listening in.

"I did my Review with Jadore. My powers are strong. But now I get to have a personalized guard with me wherever I go. Because I'm dangerous, I guess. Misty and Jia are...fine. Tell me what's happening here."

"They're moving us all to MacLeod Hall," she says in a loud stage whisper. "I didn't even know they had dorms in there. I don't think they do. I think they converted some of the classrooms. Did you see the Review scores? I didn't see your name on the sheet they posted. I saw your friend Greg's name, though. He got like eighty-five percent! I didn't do so well."

With Shane nipping at my heels, it's best I stay away from the other half of our resistance. If he scored high, perhaps it means he has manifested powers. I feel sick in my stomach. "Is that why they're moving you? Because of your low score?"

"That's the talk, as far as we can figure out." She gestures to the group. "They tested me for everything. Psychic ability, shapeshifting, fire-starting... Did you ever see that movie, *Firestarter*? With young Drew Barrymore?"

"I take it you can't start fires with your mind?"

"Nope. That would be cool. And scary." She sighs. "But I don't seem to have any of those powers. So they gave me this new meal plan and an exercise regimen and of course more tests. Me, and all these other people. This arrangement apparently sucks though, because I don't get my own room anymore."

I do a quick count of the crowd. There are about thirty students. "No one here has superpowers?"

"Not that we know of. I mean...they told us we're supposed to. That's why we were selected to be here, at this university. Now they're telling us we *probably* have superpowers, it's just going to take more work to get them out of us."

I shudder as my imagination runs wild with dark possibilities. I also realize that Ethan isn't in this group. As far as we know, he hasn't shown any powered ability, unless losing all your memories is a superpower. Perhaps he is protected as a subject in Agailya's experiment. "Kimberly...I'm sorry. They shouldn't be doing this to you."

"I guess. We all want to have superpowers, though. We can't really complain. They're treating us really well."

"Sure."

Kimberly gives me a sceptical look. "I know what you're thinking. Not in a psychic way, of course. But you're an easy read, even as a cold read. Yeah. We're suckers for going along with this. Is this super weird? I guess? I just want to make a difference. Fight the good fight. Be useful. Like you and Misty and Jia and...Wil."

I slide my arm through hers. "Why be useful when you can just be Kimberly? You're fine as you are."

She smiles. "Thanks. But wouldn't it be cooler if I was Super Kimberly?"

I purse my lips. She always manages to see the good in everyone and in every situation. "The moment you feel uncomfortable, or you see something wrong—you get out of there. Okay? Come and find me or Misty or—"

"Or Wil?" she asks, hopefully. "Ingrid, Shannon Belair, who lives across from Jia's room, heard from her other friends that Wil...someone saw his body behind the music trailer, but then the Brigade searched it, and no one can find him. What happened? Is he...really dead?"

"That's what they say," I reply slowly.

"Yes, but is it true?"

Shane drifts closer to me. He's desperate to know as well.

"I don't know," I answer. "He was acting really weird the last time I saw him. And if he were here now, I don't think he would be happy about this...strategic roundup."

Kimberly isn't often quiet. She leans in close to my shoulder. "Did he do something bad?"

"Yes," I reply. "Did he tell you anything?"

"He did come to see me, before he left, over a month ago." An embarrassed smile blooms on her face. "He said he was going far away and he was going to make up for his mistakes. And he..." She trails off, casting a suspicious glance at Shane. "I know he's not perfect. But I forgive him. Not because he asked me to, or because he was desperate for it. He just seemed...ready. To be forgiven. If he really is dead now...at least we were able to give each other that." She blew out a sigh. "Really eloquent, Kimberly. Do you know what I mean?"

"I think I might." Though I also can't put a finger on *what* made him different. From her behaviour, Kimberly knows more than she's willing to say in front of Shane, though I don't press her for it. Her time with Wil is hers alone. "I'll get to the bottom of this. I promise. Just...don't get too excited about this superpowers stuff. You can still help by just being you. And by staying alive. Okay?"

She nods though her enthusiasm has been tempered. "Do you think his parents know?"

I squeeze her arm and think about my parents. They know the truth, even if they may not believe it. If I die here, they may never know what really happened here. Any reply of mine would be a sob, so I say nothing.

Kimberly glances at Shane again and pulls gently away from me. "You should go. Don't worry about me, okay?"

I step back. "You know I will."

Waving me off, her eyes are full of doubt. I remain in place on the road as the Brigade escorts thirty non-powered students toward MacLeod Hall.

I grip my stomach. I haven't eaten in days, but I feel like throwing up.

"I gave you your time. Now c'mon," Shane mutters.

If I go now, Shane will detain Kimberly and question her about Wil. She's already being scrutinized for not having powers. The Collective may kill her outright if she's of no use. Have I just damned her with our conversation?

Have I damned all of my friends?

"Go on," Shane says. He has his baton out again.

Despite his threat, I amble along the road once more as I remove my phone from my jacket. It's about half-charged since last night. Outside Rogers Hall, I can smell breakfast. Sausages. Eggs. Bacon. My stomach rumbles.

I could enter and eat my prescribed meal. Operate under a

routine and submit to the Collective's tests as the noose tightens around my friends' necks. Lay down beneath the cameras, receive more warnings from Sunni, get up, allow them to exploit my weakness, over and over again.

Until one day, I wake up in a war zone of my own creation, because I did nothing to stop the evil in the gallows.

Quietly, I set my phone to airplane mode and begin the timer app.

"What are you doing?" Shane demands, peering over my shoulder.

I slide the phone back in my pocket. "Checking the time."

He eyes me suspiciously and then grabs me by the arm. The doors to Rogers Hall are several feet away. "Go in."

I wrench myself away. "I said before, don't touch me."

"And I said, *get in*." The baton cackles as he swings it at me. I nimbly dart away.

"No thanks." With my newfound resolve, I think about home, and give into my deepest desire. Just as Shane advances on me again, I exhale and drift out of his reach.

The train station isn't home—but it's close.

The platform of Anderson Station is nearly deserted. It's night now and a train is just pulling away. I pull out my phone to check the time and the stopwatch app, but it's dead. I don't have a charger, identification, or money—just my now-useless dorm key. A cold wind whips through the rafters of the covered platform and some roosting birds flutter their wings.

Despite the late hour, there are a few cars in the parking lot.

I hurry down the stairs and cross the tracks to step onto the icy pavement. I stick my hands under my armpits as I search for clues about the time and date. The large electronic sign flashes between "MERRY CHRISTMAS" and "-13 C." It must be late Christmas Eve.

Behind me, a woman steps off the platform and digs her keys from her purse. I stop her. "Hey. Sorry. Do you know what time it is? My phone's dead." I smile awkwardly and try to seem non-threatening.

Startled but happy to oblige a fellow young woman, she takes out her phone. "It's eleven-thirty."

"Only a couple more hours until Christmas morning," I say with false cheer.

She raises her eyebrows, but continues to oblige me. "Yep." She pauses, equally aware we are alone at the station. "You said your phone is dead. Do you need me to call someone for you? The next train isn't coming for a half hour."

"Oh…no. I'm okay. Really. I live nearby." Now my smile is genuine. It really is still Christmas Eve. And now, a stranger is offering me help. The magic of the season, my personal good fortune, or perhaps because I am special and chosen—it's all finally working in my favour.

After thanking the woman once more, I run across the parking lot and then into the adjoining public park. The air is crisp and clear. It's nippy but I'm running now, elated. At this pace, it will take me fifteen, maybe twenty minutes to reach home. I laugh into the dark night, startling someone on the other side of the park walking their dog. I'm nearly home.

As my footfalls pound the path leading into my community, my mind races as reality settles in. Yes, it's still the same day, but

I left this morning—and now it's late evening. Anything could have happened today at Sparkstone, and I have no way to check in with my friends. They could be dead.

This sobering thought is replaced with a stark, distant memory of Campbell, who gave me a hint about my friends' fates. He said Jia would be consumed not by loss, but by the replacement of something dear. Misty's power would grow by leaps and bounds, but in the ashes of her destruction, she would rise again. Wil's fate has already come to pass: he is dead. Ethan, dear sweet Ethan, seemed to have no discernable fate. Perhaps that's because of his memory loss.

Yet Misty's power hasn't grown stronger recently, as far as I've been able to tell. And Jia is certainly in mourning—Wil's mental trespass, and her battle with Jadore, leading to Jia's disfigurement—these are all major losses for her. I don't think anything of hers has been replaced.

If these things have not yet come to pass—then maybe they too will be alive by April, when I'm supposed to meet Campbell at the portal.

Unless they have come to pass today, while I'm away.

I pick up the pace as I exit the park and cross the four-lane highway to enter my home community. If I can return without the Collective knowing I'm gone, just a few minutes after I've left, I could start removing students one or two at a time. Shane and the Brigade would never have to know. It's not ideal, but it's better than nothing. I think I can do that. Perhaps I can return all of the students to their homes before the Collective even realizes what I've done.

Then...then we can get real help. From the government or the military or both. Prove that the Collective is the real threat to humanity and drive them from our galaxy once and for all.

Ethan will be safe. My friends will be free to explore their powers on their own terms.

And me...I'll be a hero.

Jadore was wrong. I do have somewhere to go and people *will* listen to me.

My nose is plugged by the time I reach our street. My heart pounds in my ears but I'm not out of breath. I'm laughing again and silently thanking Jia for her patience with me, because without it, I would not have been able to run this far, for this long, to reach my street. The road is empty and the houses are done up with Christmas lights, most of them tasteful. Only a few cars are parked on the streets this time of night. I quickly cross the street to enter my cul-de-sac. Nerves swell up in me then. Four long months—that's how long it's been. The last time I went for a walk here, I remember being so nervous about going away to university and leaving everyone I knew for a random town that had forced me to accept it. It seems so long ago. How little I knew.

I tread carefully as I approach my house. Relief fills me. The lights are on upstairs and in the living room. On Christmas Eve, we'd attend a community church service or have dinner with the neighbours. After, we'd stay up until close to midnight, watching *It's a Wonderful Life* or *White Christmas*. By now, if they're following tradition without me, they'd be in the living room in front of the TV right now, sipping mulled wine and eating copious amounts of popcorn mixed with red and green M&Ms.

My stomach rumbles and I lumber forward, propelled by my base instincts. I take the porch steps two at a time. The yellow porch light activates at my presence. I turn the screen door handle, then the knob to the front door. It's not locked and that in itself fills me with panic. Anyone off the street could walk in! Dad refuses to lock it until he goes to bed.

The door opens easily into the entrance hallway. Before me, the stairs. To my left, a sitting room. To my right, a hall table with a framed picture of the three of us and a pile of bills. Down the hallway is the kitchen and the TV room. I stand on the welcome mat and take a deep breath. Every home has a distinct colour palette within its smell, and I take in mine. It's a fresh, warm smell, brought in by the custom wood in the entrance hall table and the custom dining table off the kitchen. The flavours of the season weave in there too: the full-bodied wine and the spicy brown cinnamon. Although the popcorn was made over an hour ago, it lingers, and I'm salivating for it.

I don't take off my shoes. I drift down the light wood floors of the hallway, to the TV room, where I hear Jimmy Stewart's rich drone. I know the part instantly. It's the bank run scene, where the Building and Loan is packed to the brim with townsfolk, eager to cash out their shares because they're scared. But their money isn't there, it's in Joe's house. We can't let Potter take over this town, and that drives me forward too, even though I know how it all ends.

I'm home. I did it. I'm free. It's like I've never left.

George Bailey's speech at the bank run is cut short. "Hello?" my mother calls out.

The *clunk* of a plastic bowl on a hard surface follows the sounds of two people standing up in a hurry and rushing into the hallway. First Mum, wearing a blue flower-patterned blouse and sparkling earrings. She's still dressed up from her night out.

Dad is wearing a plain red sweater, probably the closest thing he owns to a Christmas sweater.

At first, they say nothing. They stare at me, equally confused. I realize, I'm a mess. Hair askew. Shirt, dirty. I smell like someone who has been wandering around outside. That's not like me at all. I've literally walked in off the street, unannounced, on Christmas, from an expensive university where I told them there's no escaping from.

"Hi....Hey," I say. "I...didn't have time to shower before. I'm just..." My throat tightens. "I wanted to come home."

Her jaw closes at that. Mum and Dad exchange glances. "Home?"

My grin widens. "Yeah."

But they don't share my enthusiasm. "Are you sure...you're in the right house?" Mum asks. I can tell she's being diplomatic. It's the tone she takes when she's feeling threatened or about to go on the defensive.

"Yeah...?" The stairs are to my left. I touch them to ensure they are real. This doesn't feel like a dream. I don't see Sunni. I blink a few times for good measure. Nope. Still real life.

Mum's eyes narrow. "Do you need to use our phone? We still have a landline," she offers, pointing to the phone sitting in its dock on the kitchen counter.

A cold dread creeps up from within. Goosebumps ripple down my arms. I swallow over the lump in my throat. "This isn't some kind of bad Christmas prank, right?"

"You think we're pranking *you*?" Dad asks. One hand finds his hip as he leans into the door frame that separated the hallway from the TV room and kitchen. His tone is not friendly. It's concern.

"Okay," I say. I have to assume the worst. I take a deep breath. "Prove to me you are Craig and Margaret Stanley. Right now. Tell me something only they would know."

"Excuse me?" Mum says.

"You might be a hafelglob in disguise." As soon as I say it, I hear myself, how silly I sound. "Remember, I told you, at Sparkstone about them? Of course I will prove that I'm really me. When I was five years old, we were camping in Baddeck, it was August or something. We decided to go for ice cream. There were so many different flavours at the shop and I wasn't used to making that kind of decision, but the woman serving us was so nice she let me try like twenty different samples, but by then I was so full that when I actually picked one, I ate one bite and then threw up? Remember?"

"How...how do you know that?" Mum demands.

"Maybe we can take you to the nearest police station," my dad suggests. "Or shelter? Do churches have places for people in need? It's Christmas, I'm sure there's something open, maybe downtown..."

I can't believe what I'm hearing. "What? Hello? It's me."

Blank looks from both of them. "It's...you," Dad says, unconvinced.

Do I really have to tell them who I am? "Yeah. Me. Ingrid. Your daughter."

Now they're really concerned. "You're not Ingrid," Mum says flatly.

"What do you mean? Yes I am." It's so ridiculous to say, I'm smiling again, though inside I'm dying. "How do you not know me? I mean, yeah, I look awful. But see?" I rush down the hall and pick up the framed photo, and walk it back to her, frame pressed against my cheek, pointing to myself inside the glass. I can't believe I'm doing this to my own mother. "See?"

Her gaze darts between the two and she shakes her head, recoiling. "I'm sorry."

My arm is heavy. The framed photo clatters to the wood floor. "Mum?"

She grips the door frame, still shaking her head. "I don't know who you are. But you are *not* my daughter."

CHAPTER 11

"What...? Yes I am." My voice is quiet with shock. My own mother believes I'm not hers.

Mum reaches for Dad's arm. Her eyes widen with sympathy. "I'm sorry, you...must have wandered into the wrong house. We have a daughter, yes, but—"

"Margaret," Dad says shortly. It's a warning. "We're sorry. Is there somewhere we can take you? Someone you can call?"

My mouth is dry. The first two people I can call are standing right in front of me and they don't even know who I am.

The Collective did something to their minds. They brought in all the parents to Sparkstone—at great expense and risk—and they must have done something to them, because they were fine when they left, they even texted me the safe word...

I open my mouth to explain this, and the words fail me.

"I'll go start the car," Dad says.

Mum gives him an alarmed look and my gut sinks. She doesn't want to be alone with me. She thinks I'm a crazy stranger. On one hand, I can't blame them. Dad points a thumb to the kitchen and the two exchange silent gestures, which ends in Mum giving me a frustrated look as Dad disappears into the TV room. The garage door within opens and closes, and like that, he's gone.

I think fast. "I'm sorry. I guess...I...shouldn't have come here."

Mum looks noticeably relieved. She nods nervously, glancing at the door. One hand hovers over her dress pants. There's a right pocket with the outline of a cell phone. "Are you going to be all right?"

The question is polite but restrained. She wants to help, but she doesn't know if I'm a burden. I did just come into her house and spout a lot of nonsense about aliens. And a lot of personal information about the two of them, not to mention me. I wipe my eyes and nod.

Keeping a close eye on me, she wanders into the kitchen, to the counter where her black leather purse lives eternally. She quickly finds her wallet and pulls out a green bill. "I don't know what kind of trouble you're in, or how you came to know all those things about my family. Maybe you're a friend of Ingrid's. Maybe you hacked into our accounts and somehow acquired our personal information." She stiffens at the thought. "It's Christmas, though. And regardless of what you believe about that, it's a night where we reach out to each other in the darkness for comfort. I can't give you what you are looking for here. But we can take you somewhere that can provide for you."

She holds out the twenty-dollar bill. It's crisp and new.

"Go on," she says. "It's all right. It's a gift."

I take it carefully from her and hold it gingerly. "Thank you."

She smiles thinly. "You just wait here and my husband will get the car ready. He'll take you wherever you'd like to go. The train station, the police station, a woman's shelter, perhaps." She gives me the once over, for the twentieth time. "Would you like a glass of water?"

All I can do is nod. My whole body is numb.

She disappears into the kitchen and I stand there, watching her. She side-eyes me as she opens the fridge. Her movements are slow, deliberate. I turn away and saunter towards the front door. It's still open. I hear my father's muffled voice in the garage. He's probably on his cell, talking to someone who can "help" me.

"Oh, I should probably get you some gloves as well. Just stay right there..." Mum sets a full glass of water on the kitchen counter and disappears deeper into the TV room, out of sight, and I hear the garage door open and shut again.

I pick up the photograph of Mum, Dad, and me and saunter back to the front door. I'm right *there*, standing between the two of them in front of the tree in our front yard. We're all smiling. Happy.

How could they have forgotten me?

As I return the photo to its place, I accidently knock the bills to the floor. Swearing, I scramble to pick them up before Mum returns from the garage. Why they don't just opt for electronic bills, I'll never know. I arrange the papers neatly next to the photo, and then mess them up a little.

One letter in particular has fallen out of its envelope. The cardstock is heavy and creamier than the rest. This isn't a bill. Its matching envelope doesn't have a return address—it doesn't even have my parents' address on it. Only their names.

Glancing towards the kitchen to ensure I'm still alone, I unfold the heavy letter.

Dear parent/guardian of Sparkstone Student,

Thank you for your recent visit to Sparkstone University campus. We hope you found the experience illuminating and informative.

In accordance with foreign occupancy policy 3, subsection 401, we are writing to inform you that you and your student have been subjected to extra-planetary substances that may cause changes to your neurobiology.

By the time you read this letter, our micro-fibre technology will have activated markers consumed during your visit. Intimate knowledge of your child/charge, their physical features, and their stay at Sparkstone will be disconnected from your neural network. We have correlated these markers with samples obtained from your child at some point during their stay with us. According to our extensive research, we feel this is the cleanest and most humane approach for all parties as they contribute to our exhaustive pursuit of all knowledge in this universe, and the next.

Rest assured that your contribution to the Collective has not gone unnoted. When the Collective has assumed control of Earth, you may apply for bereaved status and receive adequate compensation.

Thank you for your cooperation.

And then I'm walking out the front door, down the porch steps, and into the cul-de-sac. The twenty-dollar bill flaps aggressively in the winter wind. It's snowing softly now. The flakes settle on my eyelashes and my nose and my hair, and I keep walking until I've cleared the cul-de-sac and I'm on the adjoining street. Houses stretch in either direction. The train is a twenty-minute walk away. I might freeze before I get there, as I have only my fall jacket and no gloves and no friends and no family to help me.

My tears freeze on my cheeks. I wipe them away. No, I have one ally. Just one.

"Campbell?" I whisper. I wet my lips. They are already chapped. "Campbell?"

I scream his name into the cold night and hear it echo through the neighbourhood. I swirl instinctively around, remembering my parents and their offer of help. Will they come out after me?

I wait. I feel no familiar tugs on the cord that binds me and the mysterious time-travelling alien. I hear nothing from my cul-de-sac. My parents aren't coming for me. No one is.

So that's it then. They've won.

How easy it would be, on one of the longest nights of the year, to disappear into the darkness. My parents are safe now. They don't know me. Sparkstone University is far to the north. They might as well be in a different country. The Collective is fast, but I am faster. I can go anywhere I want. I am free of all of it. The responsibility of the fight is no longer mine.

I hold up the twenty. I can barely feel my fingers so I pinch the bill with my fingernails to ensure it doesn't blow away. People have started new lives with less money. If I pretend not to care, if I shut out all of the people in need at Sparkstone, assuming they're still alive—I have a real shot at a second chance.

"I can do it," I tell the twenty-dollar bill.

Yet the sentence was empty, like my belly.

My parents don't know who I am.

They think I'm some kind of homeless stranger with a dangerous delusion.

And yet, they still gave me twenty dollars. They gave me a chance to leave peacefully.

Who would I be if I just left Misty and Jia and Ethan and

Kimberly to fend for themselves against an alien threat?

Unworthy of my parents is who.

There are over a thousand students at Sparkstone University. Some hafelglob are sympathetic to our cause. Perhaps some professors like Agailya could be counted as partial allies, given the right motivation. It will take me way too long and arouse too much suspicion to teleport everyone individually, and I don't know if I'm powerful enough to transport over a thousand people at once. I crumple up the twenty, stuff it into my jean pocket. I have one more card to play. It's a big one, but it could save everyone. If the price of my friends' freedom is mine, so be it. I think of their faces as I prepare to return to Sparkstone.

To save my friends, I must surrender to the Collective.

I arrive inside the Sparkstone University Library. No one has been here for some time. I saunter the room as my eyes adjust to the dim light of the rising sun. Chairs are stacked on round tables. Computers chug along in sleep mode. I smell the familiar mustiness of books, even though there's a depressing scarcity on the wooden shelves lining the wall.

I'm filled with a resolute calm as I make my way to the door leading to the underground library. It's locked. There's a paper sign: closed for repairs. If Wil were here, he'd be able to open it. Or Misty—she'd probably blast the lock. Jia would keep us safe while we did our sneaking.

I could find Misty or Jia and ask for their help. But to what end? They'd try to talk me out of going to Jadore. They'd tell me to just teleport people out of Sparkstone one or two or three at a time—but what's the point of saving a smattering of students when I can save them all in one bold move? Where would they go, when their parents don't know them? They'd want to come back here and fight. We'd be back where we started. No, this way is best. For everyone.

I turn around and walk across the library to the entrance. There is one person I can say goodbye to before I turn my life over to the Collective. If he's still here at all, and not back in London with his *girlfriend*. Ethan doesn't know who I am, and he probably still hates me and thinks I'm a terrible person after what I've done. If he could only see that I'm not a terrible person and witness the responsibility I'm carrying on behalf of the world...

"No, no," I hiss to myself. "I won't do that to myself. Just focus."

Once more, I turn on my heels and head for the locked door. I think I have one more in me, although I keep imagining myself teleporting into a stack of tall bookcases.

Suddenly, the door before me clicks. Do I extra superpowers? No—it opens and Mira emerges. Cautiously at first, and when she sees me, she freezes.

We lock eyes. Neither of us can think of an explanation for our presence fast enough.

"Hello," I say slowly.

"Hi, Ingrid," she replies with equal care. She lets the door close behind her and it clicks again, yet she makes no move to leave. She wears a long Bohemian skirt today, something I would have in my wardrobe, and a long-sleeved white peasant blouse. Around her torso, a brown purse sits heavily at her hip.

"Are you...looking for something?" I ask. "Or part of the repair crew downstairs?"

"It's dark down there," she says vaguely. She clasps her hands in front of her. "I just came back up to find a torch."

"You don't have a flashlight app on your phone?"

She smiles sweetly. "I'm not much of a phone person. I'd better go."

I block her path. "Maybe if you take me down there, I can use my flashlight app. We could help each other." My phone is dead, but she doesn't know that.

Mira's eyebrows knit together. "I don't think that's a good idea."

"Why not?"

"It's a big place down there. Too easy to get lost if you don't know where you're going."

"Say I do know where I'm going, what then?"

She takes a few thoughtful steps towards me. "You really don't want to know what's down there."

"I already know," I say, blowing out a sigh. "What I want to know is why *you* know."

"I could ask the same of you."

"Do you really want to continue going in circles like this, or do you want to tell me the truth about who you are and why you're here?"

"You've always suspected something sinister about me," Mira says, pacing around me casually. She protects her bag with one hand. "You never believed that I could possibly be Ethan's girlfriend, here from London to take care of him. Here to take him back home, when he's ready to leave. Tell me, is it because you don't think I'm worthy of Ethan?"

"I think the whole story is too convenient."

"And losing all memory of you and his life here isn't?"

This is pointless. A distraction from my true mission. If I start thinking about Ethan again, I'm going to lose my resolve. "Tell Jadore that I'm not here to make trouble. She can stop carrying out whatever terrible torture she's got planned for my friends. I came here because I know there's a portal in the secret underground library. I want to negotiate the terms of my surrender. And only my surrender."

Mira's face pales. "What?"

"Stop pretending you don't know what I'm talking about. You're obviously an alien, working with the Collective, here to keep me away from Ethan so I don't mess with Agailya's experiment. Look, I don't want Ethan to be hurt. I don't want anyone to be hurt. I know what the Collective did to the parents. If I agree to help Jadore with her plan, she has to restore our parents' memories and set everyone here free. Those are my terms."

For a long moment, Mira says nothing. She glances at the underground library door, and then to the front entrance. It's almost entirely day now. The early sunlight touches us both, yet now I notice how pale and luminescent her skin is. Her body language shifts as she evaluates me. She stands up straighter. The bag no longer weighs her down. Her feet scooch closer together. Tilting her head, she seems to be contemplating whether to leave me here alone, or if I am to be trusted at all.

"First of all, it isn't Agailya's experiment anymore," she says finally. "It's Jadore's. She took over after you destroyed the Hunger."

My jaw nearly falls open. "You *are* an alien."

"I'm not human, that's right," she replies sourly. She bristles at the term.

"I knew it!" I jump in victory. I don't even care that it makes me look childish. I'm grinning. "Let me guess. You're like Agailya."

"Yes." Mira doesn't look as thrilled as I am. "We are ahmei. The Many In Water, roughly, in the English tongue." Her face brightens as she speaks about her heritage, and she hesitates, as if remembering whom she's speaking to. "Listen when I say that you do not want to go down to the portal. It's crawling with hafelglob loyal to Jadore, and many other species you can only dream of. Saying the place is unpleasant is putting it mildly."

"Then why were you down there?" My mind explodes with worst-case scenarios. "Where is Ethan? What did you do with him?"

"He's sleeping safely in his dorm room. He was up all night painting again." Genuine concern grips her. "If he continues on this path..."

"So you spy on Ethan's behaviour and report it to Jadore for the vitaphage experiment. That's why you're here."

"Spy is a strong word, especially since I'm a scientist," she says bitterly.

"So you really aren't his girlfriend?"

"No," she admits quietly. "Implanted memories. To ensure he would accept me and allow me to monitor his movements and behaviour as much as possible. It still proved difficult, as you saw, when you were spying on us in the art studio."

Of course she knew I was there. Agailya has always struck me as empathic at the very least. "All that stuff you said about trauma and leaving in a couple of days...?"

"All true," Mira said with an even-keel levelness that catches me off guard. "His particular genetic makeup makes him an ideal candidate for the experiment. The trauma is very real and his frequent memory loss is part of that. We are going to study this in-depth on the mother ship to see how this may be impacting some of the results we're seeing in the trial. That is...if Jadore will still let us. She is prone to changing her mind. He is responding to the injections as projected, far better than other subjects. His outlook is...promising."

Her words deeply trouble me. She's going to take him away. Perform more experiments on him. If Ethan doesn't have Mira to care for him, that means he has no one on this side of the world. If the trial goes terribly, he may die alone too, just like Tilly did in that sterile glass chamber on the mother ship.

He won't die alone if you surrender, I tell myself. If I can convince Jadore and the Collective to let him and everyone else go in exchange for me and my allegiance, then we have a chance.

"Just take me to Jadore," I say quietly. "I'm ready."

"No."

"Why not? Never mind. You don't have to take me. I can take myself there."

Mira scoffs and looks disgusted. "What a waste."

"What do you mean? I'm here. This is my best play to save Ethan and my friends and the entire school." I glance at the door and shake my head. "Finish your sick experiment and leave Ethan be, alive, because you're about to return to your home planet."

"You aren't the centre of the universe!"

Her words take me aback. "I didn't say—"

"No, you didn't have to. You say it with your selfish actions, every day I have been here. You went up on that stage to 'save' Ethan and everyone in that room, because you believed *you* could take on Jadore single-handedly. You could have escaped Sparkstone at any point with your ability—and you have—and yet you returned. Why? Because you believe only you can save everyone. You are not at the centre of this web. It will not unravel because of you and your actions. Surrendering yourself here and now will not fix the invasion, because Jadore and the Collective would never honour any terms like the ones you laid out for me. When they want something, they do not wait for consent. They only exploit opportunities."

Sweat beads on my forehead. My very soul feels attacked and my world, small. "I can negotiate. I can make sure—"

"You can't. None of us can." She lets out a long breath. "You mean well. But one supposedly selfless act here will not make a difference. Making a bargain with an enemy with less to lose than you do...it's...pointless. The Collective doesn't have the same moral code you do. So you can't expect them to adhere to yours."

Campbell said I was chosen. Sunni had told me that the Collective was expecting me, that she was waiting for my arrival, because it heralded a turning point in their private war. It took me a while to believe her, but I quickly embraced this life, because what young woman didn't want to be the centre of a great fight for her freedom?

"I know you have no reason to believe me," Mira continues. "But I thought as you did, for a while. Why would I join Agailya's Collective research team to find a cure for the vitaphage? Why would I join an organization that created the plague we have fought for generations? Did you know that they originally developed the vitaphage to control the ahmei people? Just to shorten our lifespans, reduce our population, so they could access our mineral and vitamin-rich oceans?"

Pale-faced and mouth-dry, I shake my head. "Why did you join them, then?"

"I thought that if I gave the Collective my allegiance, I would turn the tide in our eternal quest to save our people. Instead, they bury me in bureaucratic nonsense and restrict our resources, so that even when we believe we are winning, we are just another cog serving their interests. So some of us, like me, join the Collective to learn, and to pass on what we have learned, in the hope that someday, someone will prolong our misery and restore the lifespan of our ancestors. Because a miserable life, no matter how long, is better than the vast nothingness that awaits us all in death.

"Oh, we do little things to undermine the Collective as a whole. Yet it's inevitable that they will have dominion over the galaxy. And all galaxies, everywhere. And there is nothing you alone can do about it, especially if you cooperate with them."

I drift without knowing I'm walking, and I lean against a computer table. "So it's hopeless. No matter what I do, they will win."

"Only if you walk through that door now believing that sheer willpower is enough. On your own, you are DNA and circumstance."

That's what Agailya said to me before, but about Campbell, not Jadore. Inside, I know I am more than that, though her words ring true. This entire time, I have believed that my friends and I are stronger together. Yet I have consistently acted without them, withheld information, and put my faith in a tethered alien that put me on a pedestal. I came here to offer Jadore my precious powers on a silver platter...without even saying goodbye.

"I will leave you be," Mira says gently. "I will check on Ethan and try to keep him alive."

She starts to leave, but I launch myself from the table. "Wait."

Mira hesitates silently, raising her eyebrows.

"You don't have to continue helping the Collective," I say. "You can join me and my friends."

Mira smiles sadly, as if she has been offered this opportunity before. "I cannot openly oppose Jadore. The situation is too fragile. I am loyal to Agailya. She has risked much, just giving me this form and surface privileges. But I can give you this." She reaches into her bag and retrieves a flat plastic key. "This will open that door. It wouldn't be prudent for you to teleport in there without knowing what you're getting into. I suggest this evening, when there are fewer members of Jadore's staff down there." She gestures to the underground library door. "In return for me giving you this, you must promise me two things."

"Okay," I say hesitantly.

"First, you must promise you will not cooperate with the Collective. They are on the verge of expansion with the completion of this portal, and it is only a matter of time before they strap you to it and force you to do their bidding."

Numbly, I nod. Ohz told me that much. "And the second thing?"

"Whatever plan you concoct to destroy the Collective, you must leave Ethan and Agailya's experiment alone." Her grip on the key tightens. "If you destroy the data we have collected, you are dooming my race to extinction, and Ethan's suffering will be for nothing, and to the ahmei, there is no greater crime than preventing or cutting short the suffering of another."

I grit my teeth. I have already sworn to myself I would leave

Ethan be, but knowing what I do now, how can I? How can I leave Ethan in the care of aliens, in his fragile state?

Wil told me once that I can't save everyone. This whole time, I've been trying to do just that. Must Ethan die so that everyone else can live? It hurts too much to consider. At the same time, I can't let Ethan's life be for nothing.

"I agree to your terms," I say, meeting her gaze earnestly.

She considers me for a moment, and then seemingly convinced of my sincerity, she hands over the key card.

"How do you know I won't go back on my promise?" I ask.

"I suppose I don't," she replies. "But I still have hope."

I nod and pocket the key. "Thanks...Mira."

"I am Gayarnu," she says.

That name, I know. As the alien leaves the library, I remain, stunned. Gayarnu was the name of Agailya's assistant. The one who helped Agailya torture Tilly.

I just made a deal with a torturer and promised away the life of the man I love.

What kind of person am I?

After five minutes, I too exit the library via the front entrance. My feet carry me into the quad. It's freezing, but sunny. Goosebumps ripple down my arms and legs and my fingers feel the bite of Mother Nature. It's a snowless, joyless Christmas Day. I see people in dark jackets at the other end of the quad, but they're too far away to notice me. Who knows what the Brigade has done to my friends since I left—who knows what they'll do to me when they realize I've returned. Yet, I don't feel like going back to my dorm just yet. What am I going to tell Jia and Misty? *Your family doesn't remember you. I nearly surrendered to the Collective. I made a deal with Tilly's murderer.*

I close my eyes and a strong breeze over comes me. I brace myself against it, sticking my hands in my armpits for warmth. My first tendency has been to keep hard information from them, because I don't want to see them hurt. And where has that gotten us? Here, on the brink of a dystopian nightmare.

I need a plan—a real plan—that stops Jadore, her portal, and the Collective once and for all.

As I walk down Sparkstone Boulevard, I notice a figure in a dark jacket running toward me at top speed. I hesitate on the road. Adrenaline courses through me. I haven't slept in who knows how long. I'm not going to be bullied by Shane and his Brigade, not today. I pick up speed and run at them.

It's not the Brigade. As the person comes close enough for me to recognize, I skid to a stop. "Wil?"

The person before me looks like Wil. Same height, same bone structure, same bald head, same glasses. Yet something about him, once again, is...off. His clothes are filthy. Baggier. He's lost weight. One of his lenses is cracked. He looks like he's been roughing it somewhere. Strapped around his chest is a giant backpack—the kind hikers or campers would use to transport survival gear.

He seems equally hesitant about me. "Ingrid. Ingrid." He says my name with increasing surety, and then grins. There's genuine relief in it. "I'm back."

"I see that," I say. Yet if this is Wil, whose body did the Collective glimpse and then lose behind the music trailer?

What if this *isn't* Wil?

"How did you get here? Or leave? Did you even leave?" I demand.

"Uh. Yeah." He laughs. "Yeah, I left." He glances around the quad, breathing in the crisp, wintery air, as if anticipating an attack. I don't know if I've ever seen him this giddy. "Catch me up on what's happening."

I cross my arms. "You first."

"It's chaos out there," he replies unhelpfully.

This is too suspicious. "Prove to me right now you're not an alien."

He looks surprised. "Right. Sorry. I'm just trying to get my bearings. It's been...interesting." Like it's no big deal, he pulls out a giant machete from an opening at the top of his backpack.

"Whoa. Whoa." I leap backward. "Where did you get that?"

"Long story." He holds out a palm. "Sorry, my knife is at the bottom of my bag. So I'll just..." Carefully, he runs an inch of his palm across the blade. A thin red line beads from his skin. He holds it up as the blood drips from his palm onto the grass. "Satisfied?"

"Yeah," I say distantly. I can't take my eyes off the weapon. "So, do you need me to do that too, or...?"

"No, no," he says with a chuckle. "Still a mind-reader over here. Well. That's a simplified explanation, but you know what I mean."

"Right." Now I'm nervous about being in the open with Wil and his new sword. "Wil?"

He picks up on my anxiety and carefully guides the blade through the opening at the top of his backpack. The blood on his left hand soaks into the backpack strap.

"I know. You're still mad at me."

"Why are you here?" I ask finally. "You could have stayed away. Been free of the Collective."

"If only that were true," he replies. "I came back because I'm ready to help. And, maybe I'm wrong, but so are you. I guess I've been pretty vague and cagey lately. But I've been all around this campus, and if you can believe me, beyond it. I've got a lot of intelligence that will useful for destroying the portal Jadore has locked up in the library."

"You know about that?"

"Ohhh yeah. And more. We need to gather whatever allies you have to attack Jadore and put an end to this invasion. I know it'll be hard to believe, but...I'm different now. I've been through a lot. And I'm not the same person I was when you last saw me. No more mind tricks. Just truth."

I want to believe him. Everything about him looks and feels different. If I bring him back to the dorm, Misty and Jia are going to flip.

He shrugs. "Up to you."

I take a deep breath. I can't police Misty and Jia's reactions and hide Wil from them. Sooner or later, we have to confront our issues and do what is best for the mission. "Let's go back to my room. We can bandage that hand for you and I'll fill you in. Then you can tell us what you were up to. Deal?"

Wil nods. "Deal."

❈◈❈

The hafelglob working the security desk in Rita House nods at me with respect as I enter with Wil and we bound up the stairs. I note the security cameras as we climb to the third floor and let ourselves into the main hallway.

"They can't see us," Wil informs me.

"You blocked them?"

"Temporarily. I won't let them see or hear us as long as we're together here."

"Isn't that like leaving a trail of breadcrumbs to our location?"

"I wouldn't be here with you if it hadn't worked in the past."

I chew on that as we approach my dorm. Surely he must know what I'm thinking, though he doesn't let on. From within the room, I hear two female voices. Misty and Jia are in there. I let out a sigh of relief. They're not dead. Not yet, anyway. Wil looks resigned, but determined. I take the dorm key from my jacket pocket and unlock the door.

Inside, Jia is towelling off her hair. Misty is putting on dark lipstick with a compact mirror, sitting cross-legged on the bed. No one guards them; they seem perfectly well. The room is a complete mess: clothes, blankets, and toiletries all over the floor. As soon as I enter the room with Wil, they stop what they're doing.

"Wil," Jia says. Surprised, she throws the towel on the floor and backs against the wall, pale-faced and uncertain. "But we thought you...?"

Misty isn't as sympathetic. "Get out!" she shouts at Wil. "Ingrid. Where have you been? We thought you were dead."

"Both of us are very alive," Wil says chipperly. I side-eye him and he gets the hint. Now is not the time for a sunny disposition. He maintains a respectful distance. "I'm just here to help. For real this time. No more deception, or mind-controlling. Those days are done. I promise."

"Right," Misty sneers. "You don't honestly believe he's changed, do you Ingrid?"

I'm torn. There is something fundamentally different about Wil that I can't put my finger on. "I don't condone his actions.

But Wil says he has important intelligence about the Collective that he's gathered during his time away."

"How do we know it's not fake?" Jia asks. "Or that this isn't a trap? How are we supposed to trust our own minds?"

Misty stares daggers at Wil. "How do we know he's not a dangerous, shapeshifting alien?"

Wil holds up his bleeding hand. In the bathroom, I wad up some toilet paper and pass it to him apologetically. "We aren't really equipped for this."

"It's all right," he says. Deftly, he sets down his pack and wraps the toilet paper around his hand. "It'll do for now."

Misty and Jia both look apprehensive about this turn of events. I can't imagine what they've been through over the last day; how much worse things have gotten. "I teleported out of here when Shane took me to breakfast." As quickly as I can, I recount my teleportation to Calgary and the fallout with my parents, Mira's confession and her hands-off offer of help, and Ohz's observations on the portal itself.

Jia turns away. I knew she would take the news about our parents harshly, but I promised I'd only tell her the truth from now on. Even Wil seems disturbed by the turn of events.

After I'm finished, Misty takes a deep breath. "The Brigade turned this room upside down three times yesterday. They patrolled the entire campus. They interrogated hafelglob janitors, random students. It was the kind of thing you can't easily hide, but everyone was so afraid, they did nothing to resist or stop it. Shane kept us here in this room, had our meals delivered, and we're pretty sure he only just left his post outside the door a few hours ago to get some sleep."

"We didn't see any Brigade outside, or hafelglob, other than the one at the desk downstairs," I say slowly. "Could they have realized I'm back, and they're planning some kind of attack?"

Wil looks grim. "I think I can answer that. In ten minutes"—he checks an analog watch on his left wrist—"oh, shoot. Later than I thought. Five minutes. In five minutes, Jadore will launch phase four of the Collective's plan. A lockdown. We have a very narrow window to strike. Jadore is about to carry out an official test of the portal. Everything we've faced so far is a picnic compared to what will come through, if she succeeds."

"What is she bringing through?" Misty asks.

"How is she going to power it?" I ask. "We destroyed the Hunger. I'm not there to power it."

"Actually, Ingrid...that is her plan. The lack of security is not an accident. They're about to deploy for the lockdown, and they were even considering sending a strike team to Edmonton and Calgary to search for you. By now, she'll know you're back. Now, in a few hours, she will attempt to capture you and force you to use the portal. If she's successful—or if you succumb—an army greater than any we've seen will slither through and the invasion begins for everyone. For real."

Now I'm the one doubting Wil. "How do you know this?"

"I've been sneaking around her office and the mother ship," he replies. "I've picked up a lot of intelligence, and believe me, I would have come earlier to warn you. It hasn't been easy getting around undetected. And it's not like you can hide from her now. You did appear in the library, where there certainly are cameras."

Then Jadore would have seen me talking to Mira. I mean, Gayarnu. Will they get in trouble for giving me a key card to the underground library?

"How have you been getting around?" Jia asks in a hoarse whisper.

"I had a shuttle. It crashed. Like I said. It hasn't been easy getting around undetected. And no, I can't get another one. It was hell trying to steal one before."

"We can't fit a thousand people on a shuttle anyway," I mutter. My mind races as I try to stack our priorities. Get everyone to safety. Destroy the portal to prevent the Collective's final invasion plans. Defeat Jadore. Destroy the Collective itself—except for Agailya's research. Retrieve Ethan's memories somehow, without killing him. I take a deep breath.

Misty slaps her fists together as they light up with fire and ice respectively. "So Ingrid teleports into the library, we bust some butts, we destroy the portal, and we kill Jadore. What's wrong with that?"

Jia nods. "Easier said than done, but that seems like the right plan."

Wil leans against the wall, folding his arms, seemingly deep in thought. He's staring at me again, strangely, as if in doubt. He doesn't offer an opinion.

"If we do that, just the four of us, it'll be a repeat of the last time we went down into the library," I say. "We got overwhelmed by Jadore's forces. We need more help. We need...our own army."

"You've met my fists, right?" Misty holds up her hands. One flames brightly and the other emits small, sharp ice shards that start to melt as soon as they hit the floor.

There's a knock on the door as a slip of paper slides through the thin space at the bottom. We wait until the footsteps are further down the hallway before retrieving the message.

Dangerous shapeshifting aliens have escaped quarantine. Effective immediately. All dorms are now on lockdown. Do not go outside. Trust no one.

Simultaneously, Misty and Jia take out their phones as they light up with an identical message.

"Sometimes I wonder if the real invasion is on our forestry, with all the paper memos they send," Wil mutters.

Outside, there's a commotion of outrage and synced heavy footfalls. I hurry to the window and Misty and Jia are close behind. Twenty—no, thirty Brigade members march in rows of two down Sparkstone Boulevard. The higher ranks carry large ray guns. The lower ranks carry long, two-prong spears. Just like in my dreams. Every few rows, there are fishmen, squishing along, also armed with guns and spears. Normally they serve Jadore and guard the mother ship. They're also in specially fitted Brigade jackets, but stitched in the back are the words "FRIENDLY."

He glances out the window and nods, taking the Brigade in stride. "So this is it. The beginning of the end."

This is what I have done, Sunni said in my dream. *This is the beginning of the end.*

Suddenly, it clicks. I rummage through the room and find Sunni's journal tucked under the bed. The binding is so worn, it nearly falls apart in my hands.

Misty sees where I'm going immediately. "No way. Is that even...?"

"Before we completely destroy the Collective's plan for expansion," I reply, "I think we need to call in an expert."

Wil is intrigued. "I feel like you have a plan. Do you?"

A few weeks ago, I would have been afraid to answer, or I would have offered a reckless, stupid plan. As I stare down at the last of the Brigade marching up and down Sparkstone Boulevard, I glance at Wil, Jia, and Misty in turn. They are powerful. And so am I. But the four of us ourselves can't defeat the Collective alone.

It's dangerous. It may not work. But together, it just might be possible.

It's time to open the door.

PART THREE

He is a collaborator. A traitor to us all.

And to think I...

[PASSAGE REDACTED]

If I leave before I get the chance, I will still avenge my love's death, in the next life.

-an excerpt from Sunni's Journal, Verse 4212.

CHAPTER 12

Shane opens Jadore's office door and a grin slides across his massive face. "Well. Look who's come slithering back. See? I told you the Mistress-Commander was right. Bring her in."

The disguised hafelglob from the front desk of Rita House grips my arm and pushes me into the cramped office. It's been a while since I've been in there. If anything, this is Shane's domain now. The desk remains the same, yet the chair behind it is far plusher. Two Brigade students stand on either side of the desk and I recognize them: Emily Foller, with her bright orangey-red eyes and pleasant face, now seem all the more devilish as she greets me with a fang-toothed grin. I notice the faint ripples of scales on her forehead, and how her hairline has receded to reveal the beginnings of small horns.

On the other side of the desk is a face I haven't seen in some time. It's Laura Laska—the girl we pinned our failed protest on, who Wil manipulated with his mind. She looks furious. Her frizzy, shoulder-length brown hair is a wild mane around her face, and her many freckles seem darker somehow, more like spots. She takes me in briefly and then stares at the wall, as if my image offends her. She tilts her head, as if listening to a far-off sound.

Shane makes his way around Emily and takes a seat in the plush chair, steepling his fingers and leaning back as if his work here is done. "You did good work," he says, to the hafelglob security guard. "We watched you, on the cams." He gestures to Jadore's closet, where a massive tower of computer screens perched on a tiny desk show a highlight of feeds from locations around campus. One of them is the main lobby of Rita House. Shane chuckles. "The way you aliens run—hilarious. But when he realized it really was you, and he climbed those stairs two at a time? And you chased her..." He shakes his head and his belly rumbles with laughter. He looks to Emily to see if she shares his sense of humour, and she reciprocates with a big, toothy grin. "Anyway. I need to get a copy of that. I'll make sure Mistress-Commander knows about your heroics. Maybe you'll get something special for your loyalty. What's your name?"

Beside me, the hafelglob in disguise tenses. "Hojshz," he mumbles.

Shane stands, though he looks a little intimidated by the sound of the name. "You can leave her with us, Mister...er... Mister *Hos-jew-shh-zee*?"

"Hojshz," the hafelglob says again, unimpressed and unhelpful.

"I'll just call you Mr. Hose," Shane says awkwardly, and tries to cover with a polite smile. "Back to your post. I'll send some people to check on the other traitors. Who knows what plan they're enacting while we're in here, trading laughs."

"Understood," Hojshz says. Obediently, he shuffles out of the cramped office and shuts the door behind him.

"The Mistress-Commander is going to reward me," Shane says, more to himself than the three of us in the room. "See what they gave Emily? Don't her augmentations look great?"

I appraise Emily's new inhuman look. Combined with her supposed pyro powers, the modifications are apt. "These didn't develop naturally?"

"They're all in the DNA, is what they tell me!" Emily says. She can barely contain her excitement. "They just gave it a little nudge."

I stare at the ground, thinking of Kimberly, and how badly she wanted superpowers. What terrible experiments are they doing to her and the others who didn't initially show powers?

Shane opens a desk door and rummages around. "Now I just have to find that sedative. I'm not taking any chances with you, not this time."

I steel my nerve. "Shane, if I didn't teleport away with that hafelglob, I'm not teleporting now. I'm officially offering my surrender. To you, to Jadore. No more games."

He looks up at me, with a mixture of suspicion and confusion. "Oh no. You think for a second I would believe you? Emily!"

She steps forward and her eyeballs turn completely red. My skin crawls. It's as if someone has turned the thermostat up to sun-level degrees, and only for me. I scratch at my arms, my torso, and my legs, and remove my jacket quickly, throwing it on the floor. My bare arms are the colour of a tomato. The burn on my hand and Ohz's tentacle imprint are barely noticeable. I can smell my hair burning. I feel like the acid in my stomach is boiling. Shane laughs again, deep and hearty, and Laura's lips twitch in amusement.

"Stop!" I yell. My eyes are watering. I grab Emily by the shoulders for support, yet her clothes feel like hot magma. I collapse to the floor. The smell of the floor burning at my touch overwhelms my senses, and now my synesthesia is a kaleidoscope of reds, oranges, and browns. My fingernails curl at my thin shirt. No help is coming. I am on my own.

"I hear...boiling," Laura says distantly.

"Okay," Shane says. "Enough. Cool it."

I don't feel the relief immediately. I lay there on the floor, staring up at Emily, who looks pleased with her work, and Laura, who looks almost vindicated, and the dim ceiling light. Maybe that's why she joined the Brigade—she must know what Wil forced her to do. Sweat pools on my forehead. My arms are still beet red as I reach for my jacket and attempt to salvage my dignity.

"Try anything, and you'll see that's only a taste of one of the Brigade's powers. We have many in our arsenal that I'm dying to test out. Including mine." He grins. I don't know what his power is, but obviously it wasn't enough to stop me the first time when I teleported away.

My tongue is heavy. I'm desperate for water. There's a water bottle on the desk, taunting me. I can't show my weakness now. "Tell Jadore," I rasp, "I have information."

"I bet you do," Shane says.

"Maybe," I continue, my voice a little stronger now, "I'll take you up on your deal."

He cocks his head and leans forward on the desk. "That was a limited time offer. Now expired. Because you used me and left me. Why do you think Emily got the enhancements, and I got nothing?"

"You'll get them soon," Emily says, genuinely enthused.

Grumbling under his breath, he shoots her a jealous look, and then says, "What kind of information? Tell me now before you pass out from dehydration."

Shane has got me pegged. I grip the desk to steady myself. My brain feels scrambled. Think. Remember. My friends' lives depend on me. "Tell her—Campbell spoke to me. I have information about the multiverse. Which one is ripe for harvest. I can...tune her portal to it. Imagine. Transporting an army, not just from planet to planet, but from universe to universe."

Laura doesn't meet Shane's inquisitive gaze as he turns to her, seemingly to verify this information. Instead, she nods. I notice the glazed look in her eyes, as if she has extreme cataracts. "Hard to tell. Could be the heat. But no extreme change."

I realize she must be listening to my heartbeat—to see if I'm lying. I focus on my conversations with Campbell, and the lessons he imparted. Everything that will happen, has already happened. I wipe the dripping sweat from my brow as I hang my jacket over my arms. Like Agailya says: I will endure.

Shane considers me for a moment, heaves a sigh, and fishes a radio from his belt. He goes to the window and leans against the wall. It takes every ounce of strength for me to stay conscious. Shane punches some buttons and then says, "This is Lieutenant Shane Richmond. Requesting to speak with the Mistress-Commander. Urgent. Code black."

It only takes a few seconds; I hear Jadore's sultry, deep voice come through the scratchy radio. "Speak."

"The alien traitor, Ingrid Stanley? Says she has information on Campbell. And multiverses. Our truth-teller says she's legit. You said to call that in if—"

Jadore cuts him off. "I'll be right there."

"Oh. Sure. Just...in the office. Over and out." He tosses the radio on the desk and blows out a sigh. "You've got her attention," he mutters to me. "But if this is a trick, or a trap, Emily here is extremely excited to try out her abilities again."

"I don't intend to give her that chance," I reply respectfully.

"No change," Laura adds.

"We'll see." Shane sits resolutely in his chair.

Each moment is excruciatingly long as we wait for Jadore. My mouth is parched, and when I can barely stand, Emily finally offers me a sip from the water bottle. I drink greedily, embarrassed at my desperation. This only amuses Shane more. He picks up a weight laying beneath the desk and starts doing reps. It looks extremely heavy, yet he lifts it with ease. Laura, like a statue, remains in place, and Emily tries and fails to engage Shane and I in conversation, as if she didn't just torture me.

I've started to feel a little more normal when Laura perks up. "I hear her."

Shane nearly drops the heavy weight as he struggles to sit upright in his chair. Laura straightens her posture and keeps her gaze downcast. Emily stands with her hands behind her back with a pleasant smile. Jadore's heeled footsteps and the sound of her cane echo in the hallway as we silently await her arrival.

I grip the desk and recoil as the door opens. Jadore twists her lips as she catches her breath, her human nostrils flaring. Her head systematically moves from left to right, quickly taking in those present in the room. She stops at me. Down the hall, I take note of two armed Brigade students. They are probably just for show, as Jadore's lightning powers are more than capable of neutralizing any threat.

Shane stands. "Mistress-Commander. I'm here with my two most trusted people, Emily Foller and Laura Laska. And right before you is the traitor. Traitor, if you—"

"Shut up," Jadore says. Her black pencil skirt has been recently ironed, but her sleeveless white blouse looks wrinkled. She came here in a hurry. "Ingrid. Are you wasting my time?"

"No," I reply.

Jadore cocks her head. "Truth?"

"Yes, Mistress-Commander," Laura says softly.

Holding out a fist, Jadore slams the door shut, frightening Laura and Shane. I clench my teeth. I can't show my fear—even if she can smell it. "Tell me everything."

"I have terms. You have to—"

She squeezes her fist tighter. "Tell me. Now."

"I know you want to hook me to your amplifier and bring in your armies to begin the next phase of the invasion. I know there are parts of the treatise you can't read. I can translate them. Reveal the best multiverses, ready for you to visit with your portal. Which I am prepared to power, if we can come to appropriate terms."

"Terms," Jadore mutters. But I have intrigued her. She lowers her fist. "You weren't ready when I tested you. You could barely bring back a hafelglob."

"You clearly didn't look at your recordings that closely," I say. "Maybe you should check the timestamp of when I arrived in the flag room and compare it to when I'm in the tutorial classroom. And then you'll see that the Ohz I'm speaking to there isn't the same Ohz I left with."

She hesitates and then points at Shane. "Verify that."

"Yes, Mistress-Commander," he replies, uncertain. He grabs his radio and awkwardly leaves the room, shooting me a jealous look. "What are you saying?"

"I don't have exact time metrics, but it's my guess that I arrived five minutes in the past, retrieved the flag, and returned to our present in a reasonable time frame."

Jadore sets her lips in a firm line. It's hard to tell for sure, but I've intrigued her enough that she hasn't killed me. "What does this have to do with Campbell?" She flicks some hidden button on her cane, and a blade flicks out the end. It's dripping with poison. Laura makes a soft gasp behind me. "And why would you turn yourself in now, if you really have this power?"

"I don't want my friends to suffer," I reply. "I think we can reach an equitable agreement. One that doesn't involve you killing everyone I love, and one that doesn't involve me time travelling back to your...what did you call it...your *uplifting*?"

Her knuckles turn white as she tightens her grip on her cane-spear. I have her now. "The treatise makes no mention of this ability in you."

"I think the name Crosskey can be interpreted far more broadly. It's just the next stage of my power. Crossing physical space. Crossing time. Crossing the multiverse. Especially since I know exactly which universe to target, and how, thanks to Campbell."

Shane returns to the room. "Tech department confirms it. The timestamp is seven minutes earlier than the one where she left."

Jadore slams her cane into the floor. "Why did no one...?" She releases a low hiss. "Never mind. They cannot keep me out for long." She points the bladed end of the cane at me. "Is that all you want? A guarantee of safety for your friends and family?"

"More than a guarantee. I want you to remove every student here on campus. Especially the ones who haven't developed superpowers. My friend Kimberly, for instance."

Shane pales. "Please, Mistress-Commander. You can't really…"

Jadore holds up a hand. "Continue, Ingrid."

"You don't need them, Jadore," I say. I'm feeling more confident by the moment. "What are you going to do with a bunch of teenagers and college students who could kill your troops? Sure. You can harvest them and distribute that DNA to your worthy subjects"—I gesture to Emily—"or you could just have me. Willingly cooperating with you, as you venture onto new worlds, new universes, with far more exotic creatures for you to exert your influence over."

"That is quite a pitch," Jadore says. "It sounds very…practiced."

I inhale slowly. The less said, the better. "I'm tired of running, Jadore. I just want this to end."

Jadore nods slowly. "Truth?"

Behind me, I hear Laura's boots scuff the floor. "Truth."

Letting out another low, slow hiss, Jadore retracts the blade in her cane. "You surrender to me. To *me*, you understand? You will activate the portal, and do my bidding with it. In return, you have my word that your friends and family will be safe. *From me.* I cannot speak for the Council as a whole, as I do not rule it."

"I understand."

"That isn't all," Jadore says. "As a token of your surrender, you will also give me Wil. Dead or alive. Whatever he is now."

My knees buckle. It's unacceptable. "No. Never. I don't know if he's—"

"She's lying," Laura cuts in. Shane grins.

"We have no deal," Jadore says curtly. "Our cameras picked up you and Wil, back from the dead it seems, having a very animated discussion in the quad. Take her to Conrod Building.

Prepare her for transport. We will harvest you now."

"Wait." I close my eyes. I dig deep inside myself. *I'm sorry, Wil. I tried. I really did.* I glance at Laura. "I don't know whose body you saw before, but you're right. He's alive. He's done... awful things. To Jia and Kimberly, and you Laura, I don't know if you remember. You are asking me to betray him..."

"He's too dangerous to be left alive. Didn't I hear one of you say that?" Jadore asks.

It hurts—because it's the truth. "Yes..."

"It's only a matter of time before he's hunting you. Turn him over to us, and we will extract his intellect. Most of the Collective's harvests don't go to warfare. We have many humanitarian efforts." She smiles.

"I didn't know that," I say evenly.

"Of course you didn't. You are naïve."

I ignore the insult and focus on Wil. He can probably hear my thoughts, right now, if he isn't too far away. "I can't just...give him up without him knowing immediately I've betrayed him."

"Tell me," Jadore says slowly, "did he send you here?"

My stomach turns. "No..."

Shane gestures to Emily. "Perhaps you need a second round of persuasion?"

Emily advances on me again. Jadore makes no move to stop this hideous plan.

I hold out my hands in surrender. If I'm blasted again, I'll die. "All right, all right. He's made some kind of plan. To attack the portal, in the library. They're going to enter the underground and try to sabotage if not destroy it."

Time seems to stretch. Eventually, Laura says, "It's true."

"And you're here as a distraction," Jadore surmises. "Yet they didn't surmise you had an interest in surrendering—to soothe your noble spirit."

I avert my gaze to the floor and say nothing.

"Very well. I take your silence as compliance. Here is the new plan. You will come with me to the portal. We will do a… test, you can call it, of your ability. When your friends come to sabotage the portal, you will help me and not them. I will take Wil. Your other friends are free to leave. As long as they survive the inevitable skirmish." Jadore's smile widens as I consider her offer with earnest. "Do we have a deal?"

My heart is pounding. This is really happening. "We do."

Laura comes up from behind and grabs me by the arm. "Truth—though she's terrified." Then, lower in my ear, "I *do* remember his little suggestions, and no one believed me until I joined the Brigade. If Wil isn't dead, he will be by the end of today."

I purse my lips. There is no turning back now.

"I had this amplifier built especially for you," Jadore mutters, as she tightens the chains around my wrist. "The Hunger would have surrounded the portal itself. It wouldn't have needed amplification."

I vaguely remember a cloud surrounding a portal in Sunni's dream. It's not the future, she'd said, it was her present. "Do you really have to chain me up here now?"

I stand on a raised dais, facing the massive portal: an elongated horseshoe, more than twenty feet tall. It is steel-coloured, though it is probably made of stronger stuff. It's inactive right now, and on the other side I see Shane, Emily, and Laura, having a whispery, animated discussion marred by the echoey nature of the warehouse. The portal itself is surrounded by consoles, also arranged in a horseshoe pattern. More black consoles have been set up to my left, likely to monitor the amplifier, where I've been conveniently chained. Shaped exactly like the portal, but turned on its head, the amplifier is far smaller. Jadore has chained my arms to each end of the horseshoe shape.

The low, green light fills the warehouse. Just a few short months ago, I was here with my friends, searching for Campbell's treatise. The place had been filled with endless rows of old books and book shelves. Now, it's empty, save for the portal, the consoles, and this amplifier.

Soon, it will be crawling with Jadore's army, fresh from who-knows-where, ready to take over Earth.

A slight smile touches Jadore's lips. "I am going to run a test. To ensure your powers are ready."

Dread fills me. "What kind of test? What do you want to bring through?"

"Oh just...a few friends," she says with a smile. She waves to the three Brigade students and they rush across the warehouse, ready to appease. "Your services aren't required. Wait by the entrance." She points to the other side of the warehouse, where we entered through the library and began the long trek underground.

Shane takes issue with this seemingly careless order. "Mistress-Commander, you already refused help with the traitor's chains, I don't know if it's wise..."

"Are you implying I am incompetent?"

"No, no, Mistress-Commander."

"Good. The three of you, over there, now."

Shane shoots a suspicious glance at me but leads Emily and Laura away from the portal, back towards the entrance. Jadore watches them go, muttering under her breath, and walks to the set of consoles off to my left. To my surprise, she removes her sunglasses and hooks them on her blouse as she begins pressing inlayed buttons and reading screens.

My wrists begin to ache, as do my arms, from being forced in this position. I wonder if I can teleport out of here, even if I'm chained, or if I'd end up trapped in the infinite hallway with the amplifier. I test the chain's strength. Clearly she doesn't trust me—otherwise she'd just let me stand here. "So how does this thing work, anyway?"

Jadore doesn't look up from her work. "Do you know what Sh-wnilk'def Stones are?"

"No."

"Then there is no point in explaining the science to you."

Great. This relationship is off to an amazing start.

However, Jadore continues, "When I give the order, you will begin teleporting, as you normally do, but the amplifier will boost your power and focus. The portal is the gateway. Instead of you transporting to a location and physically retrieving someone, you will guide those on the other end to our side."

I frown. That is quite different than my particular power and operates on the assumption that me powering it is going to even work. "How will the people on the other side know to come through? Do I have to...tell them...somehow?"

"The portal's use is limited. There has to be a twin portal on the opposite side. They will know to step through when their corresponding portal powers on," Jadore replies condescendingly. She's extremely focussed on the console. It looks like she is doing math in her head and feeding the results, one symbol at a time, into the machine.

"I guess you probably build these on a lot of planets then," I say.

"Depends," Jadore says. "They are resource-heavy. Without a power source, useless."

"They must be part of a network," I say, half to myself now. "If you have people on the other side, waiting to travel, can they go anywhere, or does each portal only have one destination? They input their destination, and when the destination portal powers on, they know it's okay to step through? But that would mean that the receiving portals would have to be manned and constantly—"

"Ingrid!" Jadore cuts through my verbal train of thought. "Your fascination with the portal is not as interesting or as important as it is to activate the portal. Be quiet, or I will be forced to do something about your tongue, Campbell be damned."

The questions die in my mouth as I allow Jadore to complete her calculations. The console begins to hum gently, and in it, I can hear the undercurrent of a song. I close my eyes and think of Campbell, wondering if he would come now, if I called him. What would he say, seeing me chained here, helping Jadore?

"You haven't eaten recently, have you?" Jadore says, after several minutes.

"No."

"Hmm."

She offers me no food this time, for which I'm grateful. The last time she forced me to feast, I threw up and she was disgusted. Fortunately, it merely seems to be a factor in her calculations, as she makes no other attempt to interact with me.

At the end of the warehouse, the door squeaks open. I squint in the low light. Shane, Emily, and Laura are gathered there, speaking in low tones to someone on the other side. Jadore throws a glance their way, but returns to her work.

Then, Shane opens the door fully, and a parade of people march inside. As the green light bathes their faces, I struggle against my chains.

Oh no. They're here.

Four hafelglob security guards escort Misty, Jia, and Wil towards us. My friends' wrists are bound in thick handcuffs that obscure their wristbands. Wil and Jia have silently submitted to their captors, though Misty glares behind her, at Shane, Emily, and Laura, who give her a wide berth. My jaw drops. It looks like they put up a good fight. The hafelglobs' jackets are singed at the edges from Misty's fire.

Jadore's console lights up and hums louder. She circles around to meet my friends and the hafelglob who captured them, and smirks at me.

"Well. Intruders. I should have known," Jadore says lazily. "Oh yes. I *did* know." She addresses the Brigade. "Shane. You and the hafelglob will take Misty and Jia to Conrod Building for processing. Emily and Laura, I'll need your help with Wil."

My ears are burning, as though Emily had scorched me again. I rattle my chains. "Wait. What are you doing? Let them go! We had a deal!"

Jadore sneers at me. "Did you really think I would agree to some kind of bargain? Why would I do that when I can take what I want?"

I struggle against the chains and scream. "You won't get away with this!"

"Yes, I will," she says smugly. "Now bear witness."

Her hands cackle as lightning dances from one finger to another. With each spark, her skin morphs from its earthy brown tone to alien green. Shane, Emily, and Laura watch in amazement as Jadore's arm suddenly swirls with cackling blue lightning.

My heart pounds in my ears. It's happening. It's really happening.

I shout and scream, but my protests cannot be heard over the chaos that ensues.

Jadore thrusts her arm forward, punching the air, directing the lightning towards Misty. Misty raises her hands but she's too slow with her own powers. The lightning hits her in the chest and she slumps to the warehouse floor. Jia tries to run but hits a hafelglob, and turns to meet the lightning head on. She collapses next to Misty.

Wil, frightened, puts a hand to his temple and closes his eyes. Yet Jadore will take no chances. She throws her weaponized lightning at him too. It swirls around his body and he crumples, all of his mighty mind-controlling powers rendered useless.

Jadore's lightning fades into her skin once more, leaving her arm completely green. She grimaces at this and balls her hands into fists as she yells to the Brigade. "Well? Take them!"

My lips tremble. I can't believe what I just witnessed.

Whirling towards me, Jadore dusts off her hands. "Now that that's out of the way, Ingrid, we will continue our little test."

As Shane, Emily, and Laura stoop to retrieve the heavy, unconscious bodies of my friends, the hafelglob, dressed all in black move clumsily toward Jadore—and then stop. Jadore also halts mid-step on her way towards me and leans to the side, as if being tugged by an invisible force.

Jadore draws a deep, throaty gasp. She grips her throat. Her eyes widen in horror as she slowly turns to where she's leaning. The invisible horror doesn't reveal itself, but I hear a small gasp as Jadore slumps to the floor, unconscious.

Shane has Jia awkwardly slumped over his shoulders and nearly drops her in surprise. Emily lets out a surprised gasp and runs for Jadore. Laura frowns and pushes aside her ears. I notice, even at a distance, how overdeveloped they look.

"I *knew* there wasn't just—"

And then, the fabric of reality lifts a curtain, revealing the truth. From around the four hafelglob, Misty, Jia, Wil, Kimberly, Greg, Lynn, and Elisha—real this time—emerge.

Greg frowns at me as he quickly evaluates my tied-up form. "'You won't get away with this'? Can you be any more of a ham?"

I shrug. "It had to be convincing."

"You do know what it means to be a *ham*, right?"

Now Shane throws the fake Jia to the floor. He rubs his shoulder with relief, though his face tells a different story. "What is going on here?"

CHAPTER 13

"They killed the Mistress-Commander!" Emily shrieks.

"She's not dead!" Laura shouts, equally agitated.

"Hang on. If they're the real traitors..." Shane slowly puts the pieces together.

The four hafelglob in disguise roll up their sleeves and revert to their natural, tentacle form. My friends recoil from them as the four, fleshy masses sprawl out over the floor.

"Aww no," Shane says, backing away, waving his fingers skittishly, so afraid that he forgets the gun on his belt. "Not the tentacles."

The young women under his command are less cowed. Seeing their opening, they assume battle positions. Emily's gaze heats as she snarls with her sharp, pointed teeth. Laura removes her alien gun and points it with both hands at the hafelglob. "Shane?"

"Surrender, or you're going to burn," Emily says, too enthusiastically.

Reluctantly, Shane removes his weapon and points it, disgusted, at the hafelglob. "Yeah. What she said."

My friends meet their challenge. Misty's hands light up with fire and ice. Wil draws his machete. Elisha and Kimberly head for the console and with matching grins. Lynn holds out her palm and vines curl and twist upwards on their own accord. Greg rolls up his sleeves and raises his fists. Jia stands between them, poised, ready to snatch them out of sight.

I grin. It worked. And now we're here—ready to battle.

The hafelglob lead the charge, and without hesitation, Laura shoots one of them in the tentacle. It lets out an angry, gurgling scream. But that is the distraction Greg was looking for. He grabs Laura and spins her around. Her hair whips with the motion, revealing her overdeveloped ears.

"Oh. This is too easy." Greg unhooks his jaw and lets out a piercing scream.

Everyone except the hafelglob doubles over. Laura emits no sound as she slumps to her knees, hands over her head, face contorted in agony until she falls unconscious. A cacophony of colours streams before my eyes. A deafening ring settles in over the sound of the powered-up console.

I struggle against my chains in earnest his time. Okay. This wasn't exactly how I'd planned it. I can't complain; the hafelglob allies are keeping their end of the bargain. I'd hoped Shane and his Brigade friends would have dragged the fake versions of my friends out of the underground library before subduing Jadore. Mostly, I'd hoped that Shane and the Brigade would have minded their own business and not accompanied me and Jadore here. The hardest part was playing a convincing, snivelling traitor so that she would lead me here, and preparing for her inevitable double-cross, while my friends had to find Kimberly and free the non-powered students, and rally the three journalism students as well. Much easier, now that Wil has returned to us.

As we recover from Greg's sonic blast, the hafelglob surround Shane and Emily. Shane holds his gun and points it at one alien, and then the second, and then the third, unable to decide who to shoot. A fleshy tentacle wraps around Emily's arm, but not for long. It emits a disturbing gurgling whine and releases her. It begins to sweat and melt in place. The smell of unwashed bodies and garbage intensifies as the alien writhes frantically, until it suddenly becomes still. The other three hafelglob slither backwards, eager to find another target.

One hand over her ear, Kimberly leaves the console and hurriedly steps up onto the platform with me. Elisha seems to be fiddling with the controls. I notice both Elisha and Kimberly have wadded up toilet paper in their ears.

"Yeah. Greg is like, super loud. Get it? *Super* loud. Like it's his superpower? I guess that's not a joke. Anyway, here to rescue you!" Kimberly is yelling as she inspects the chains and then yells down to the battle. "It's not a key, just some kind of alien metal?"

Wil pops into reality from nothing, squints over at us, closes his eyes and concentrates, and I hear a click on both wrists.

"Can you do that with our regular wristbands too?" I ask him, holding up my arm.

But he isn't listening. He disappears into Jia's invisible world and rejoins the fight.

I step off the platform with Kimberly, surveying the fight, waiting for my moment to jump into the fray. Yet there's not a lot I can do with my superpower. Emily is the one to beat now. Jia, Wil, and Lynn are not in sight, yet every few moments, Emily spins around and dramatically flexes her hand, as if sensing their presence, while also dodging Misty's icy blasts. The hafelglob have slithered far away from her, unwilling to engage. They hurry past Kimberly and I, for the consoles. They gurgle something that sounds like an apology as they assess the portal consoles instead.

Misty has become enough of a nuisance that Emily calls out to Shane. "Use your strength on her!"

But Shane has barely engaged in this battle. He takes one last look at Misty's fire, and the loathsome hafelglob, and compulsively shakes his head. He turns tail and runs for the exit, gun in hand. "Not ready. Not ready!"

"You coward!" Emily puts her hands on her hips, and then realizing Misty is coming for her, snarls and hisses. She dramatically cups her hand, fingers widely splayed, as her eyes go red.

Misty folds her arms, watching Emily's attempts to boil her alive. "Nice trick, but here's mine." She grabs Emily's face with her icy hand. Misty puts all of her strength into forcing Emily to her knees as a thick layer of form-fitting ice slides from her palm and covers Emily's entire body. Emily struggles; her ability to run hot melts some of Misty's attempt, but Misty has had far longer to cope with her powers than Emily. When Misty stumbles back, pale and shocked, she takes in the icy statue.

"Whoa," Elisha says. "Cool."

Misty throws her an unimpressed look while Elisha beams at her pun.

Just as Shane reaches the door, he trips over something invisible. His gun slides across the floor. He rolls onto his back just as Wil materializes. I run towards them, Kimberly at my side.

You are a nuisance, Wil says telepathically to him.

Shane's eyes bug out of his skull as he scoots backwards,

trying to find his footing against the wall. "Aliens. You're all... aliens."

"We're just like you," I say. "Superpowered humans."

His nervous gaze darts from me to Wil. "Yeah. Right."

Wil rubs his bare head and when he sees Kimberly standing next to me, he seems resigned. "He isn't worth our time, but he is a risk."

Kimberly and I exchange glances. We get the message. She approaches him first and slaps him across the face, hard. "That's far less than you deserve for all the violence you've caused."

Shane winces. For a superpowered human, he is sure hesitant to use his powers. I am reminded of my own fears, and I wonder what holds him back.

As Kimberly goes to strike him again, Wil waves his hand, and Shane conks out on the floor in a loud snore. Surprised, Kimberly darts backward. "Oh."

Jia and Lynn come out of invisibility then, and for a heavy moment, the room is free of battle. Emily kneels, melting slowly in the middle of the warehouse. Shane is unconscious by the door. Jadore is near the console, passed out on her stomach. A squishy, icky hafelglob deflates near a corner. Laura has curled into the fetal position. The three hafelglob pretending to be Misty, Jia, and Wil breathe slowly and deeply where they landed.

"They are still alive...right?" Lynn asks.

Misty looks over at Emily's icy form. A small puddle forms around her feet. "Probably. Maybe?"

Will's gaze sweeps the room. "Save for the hafelglob, they're all alive. Even Shane. Though I should have killed him."

"Why?" Jia asks.

"Even without powers, he has influence," Wil replies, heading back towards the consoles.

Suddenly, it makes sense. "Shane really has no powers?" I ask, following. I remember his bragging, his lifting weights with ease and yet he had trouble lifting fake Jia—and his jealousy over Emily's augmentations.

"Hey! I got a good shot in. Didn't you notice? I don't need superpowers to do that." Kimberly rubs her hands as she follows Wil. "Though I think I've lost all feeling in my hand. Is that anything?"

"We should subdue everyone further, as much as we can, in case they come to," I suggest.

Lynn takes a sprig of grass from her pocket. She strokes it, concentrating, and within ten seconds, it twists tendrils around her finger. In under a minute, with some coaxing, the single strand of grass becomes a thick vine that twirls around Jadore's hands and feet.

"It'll hold her briefly," she says. "That's about as much as I've practiced so far. I'll see what I can do on the others."

"It's brilliant," I reply, as Lynn rushes off to our other unconscious foes. "Was it you who knocked her out, Wil?"

"Hmm? Yes." He looks up from the consoles. He's puzzling something out with Elisha, casting a hesitant gaze at the hafelglob. They have returned to human form and are still busying themselves at the other set of machines, in front of the portal.

I rub my wrists as I join him and Elisha. "How do the controls look?"

"Difficult, but manageable." He levels me with an intimate stare. He knows what is in my heart. "You're sure you want to try this? That this is what you want?"

I don't have to think. This is what I've been dreaming of. "We need to try. If I'm right, this will change everything. If I fail…"

Wil nods. "It'll work. You…have the ability."

"I couldn't do it without you," I reply with a smile.

"Thanks. But you can. And you will."

Jia, Misty, Kimberly, and Lynn drag the Brigade students' bodies into one of the offices at the other end of the warehouse. I return to the amplifier as the hafelglob patsies come to. Their forms jiggle and shake as they return to their male, middle-aged, clothed humanoid shapes. One of them is Hojshz, the hafelglob security guard. They lumber towards me awkwardly, sore from their run-in with Jadore's lightning.

"Thanks for your help," I say, pursing my lips.

Hojshz smiles and exchanges a knowing glance with his fellows. All of them wear the ally symbol on the collar of their jackets. "Crosskey will uphold her end of the bargain."

Nervously, I nod. It's a tall order. But I had given them my word. "I will find you and your loyal brethren a Collective-free place to settle."

Our terms solidified, Hojshz calls to the other four hafelglob in human form, and the seven of them head for the exit to keep watch outside. I take a deep breath, trying to rid my senses of their smell. I am still somewhat mystified by their devotion to me, and without Ohz around to explain it, I can only speculate. Perhaps someday, I will be powerful enough to rescue him in the infinite hallway, and I can take him to the rest of his brethren. For all the terribleness the hafelglob have caused during my time here at Sparkstone, they too are just subjects of a larger empire, and I have to take what allies I can get within the belly of the beast.

I step up onto the amplifier platform as everyone gathers around Wil and Elisha, who seem to have figured out the consoles.

"Which button blows this thing up?" Misty asks. "For after we're done with it."

Elisha monitors the alien symbols flashing intermittently across the screen. She looks to Misty. "Can you understand that?"

Misty concentrates. "I'd need about fifteen minutes."

"I don't know if we have that kind of time," Wil says, glancing at me. "I have modified the cameras here, though that may raise suspicion at headquarters. Likely they will detect our use of the portal, regardless of what authorizations Jadore may or may not have, and send a team to investigate."

He's offering me the chance to change my mind. I stare at the portal. This might be my only chance to stop the nightmares. To get real answers about Campbell, the journal, and the imminent invasion. I could eventually make the journey myself, over time, but at least this way, I won't wander the infinite hallways, lost. My friends don't raise last-minute objections or questions about why we're doing this. I just know in my heart, that this is what I need to do, that the last few months have been leading to this very moment.

"We will be quick," I say. "I'm ready if you are."

Wil blows out a sigh and claps his hands. "All right. I think I've calibrated this correctly. Let's begin."

I stand against the amplifier and take a deep breath. The chains hang loosely beside me, but I don't think I'll need them. I am doing this of my own free will.

The Collective is massive, and I am only one person. I need all of my friends, including my dead and unpowered ones, to fight with me to win this war.

Wil presses some buttons on the console, and my friends gather around him and the amplifier to watch. I shut my eyes and remember Jadore's instructions. Concentrate on the location I want, where the matching portal resides, send the signal, and guide them through.

Open the door. Open the door.

My body hums as the amplifier comes to life behind me and whirs. It's like standing in front of a blazing hot fan while wrapped in the softest down comforter. I could stay here forever. My mind drifts to the memory of my vivid dreams. The energy from the amplifier seems to extend my reach, and more than before I can see where I want to go and see it in real time, rather than just imaging it. My consciousness is fluid. I feel my feet firmly planted on the platform, and yet, I'm soaring above the quad, seemingly in a dream. Several spacecraft hover above the campus, and the half-destroyed dome protects no one.

On the ground, a portal roars to life. The cloud powering it stirs and circles hungrily. An army of fishmen waits on the other side, their catfish-like faces twitching and surveying the strange machine. They want in. They know there is another planet, ripe for the harvest, and they are waiting for the portal's twin to respond to their request for transport.

Not today. They will never set foot here.

Then, I see her. She's scraped and bruised and alone, but she's alive. She cannot see me, or feel me in the same way, yet her instinct tells her to run for it.

"She's...coming," I say, in my world, with corporeal lips.

I also become aware, in the warehouse, of a commotion by the door. Misty and Greg, yelling. Kimberly freaking out. I can't see them, though my other senses warn me that trouble is coming.

I can't concern myself with that now. I have to trust them to protect me while we complete the task.

The urge ebbs through me like a tidal wave; I sway with the undulating intensity. I am reaching out into the dream world, this other Earth so like our own, and plucking my friend from the nightmare, to save her from the impending darkness.

The portal hums and the horseshoe fills with blue-white light, swirling like a whirlpool. Just as I pulled Sunni's journal from what I'd thought was a dream, now, before me is a lake. In the real world, I stretch out an arm and extend my hand in invitation, and in the other world, the cloudy pool within the portal flares and cackles, catching unwanted attention from the waiting army.

Yet she sees it, and understands. She runs towards it. The aliens—fishmen and some humans in Brigade uniforms—notice her urgency, though they doubt that she would actually risk climbing through the Hunger and into the portal to who-knows-where.

But she knows exactly where it's going and she's ready to step through.

My vision goes dark, yet I feel the heaviness of someone holding my hand. The journey isn't long; there is no wandering within the infinite hallways, searching for the right door. There is only one straight path. Around me, I hear more commotion, arguing, screaming, weapons clanging, and I feel her hesitate— yet for her, this is a one-way trip. There is no turning back.

The portal in the real world flares as my real eyes open. A shadow of a person breaks through. Her blonde hair is a curly mess. Her face is scratched, nothing serious. She's out of breath and starved thin. Her white t-shirt is stained with dirt and blood, not hers. Her black sweat pants are too long. She steps on them with her sandals.

Sunniva Harris stumbles forward, out of the portal, and collapses on the floor, and huffs, "Took you long enough."

I gasp for air, fully returning to this world, as if my body has been released from weights anchoring me to the floor. Yet no one is paying attention to me, and that is to be expected, for I just pulled the spitting image of my dead friend—the young woman I've been dreaming of for months—from an identical world to ours.

Misty is the first to move. She rushes towards Sunni in near-disbelief. "Sunni. It's you. You're here."

Sunni's face reddens. "Misty..."

"I knew... I always knew..." Misty embraces Sunni, practically lifting her off the floor. Sunni is startled at first and pulls away to examine Misty's face, touching her nose and her eyebrow ring and her lips, as if she too cannot imagine that she is real.

"You know I'm not...your Sunni."

Misty's smile fades. She recoils from Sunni as embarrassment sets in. "Yeah. Ingrid said. But I'd hoped...I guess you're from another universe or dimension or whatever."

Sunni reaches for Misty's hand. "That doesn't mean I'm that different."

"No. No, I guess not." Misty brightens once more, cautiously, as her grip on Sunni's fingers tighten.

Their reunion has distracted me from the real problem. None other than Agailya, Mira—I mean, Gayarnu, but they are still in Mira's form—and three armed fishmen surround the group of consoles by the amplifier. They too have been distracted by

Sunni's arrival, though the fishmen point their sleek, rounded guns at Wil, who remains steadfast behind the console. Elisha frowns and ignores the potential threat as she continues to tap buttons and monitor the portal controls.

I step off the platform and address Gayarnu. "What are you doing here? I thought you didn't want to get involved." I desperately want to ask after Ethan—if they are not watching him, who is?—yet I resist the urge.

"I came to stop you," Agailya says.

"Why would you want to stop me?" I ask.

The fishmen train their guns on me. Misty is still preoccupied with Sunni, so it's Wil who unsheathes his machete from his belt and points the sharp blade at the nearest fishmen. Greg sighs and clears his throat, ready to scream. Jia, visible but ready to disappear, keeps her distance with Kimberly and Lynn by the portal.

Neither Agailya nor Gayarnu tell their lackeys to stand down. In the past, the fishmen have typically been under Jadore's command, and I'd even assumed they might be part of her original species, yet here they are, taking orders from Agailya, someone I considered to be sympathetic to my cause.

"It seems I can't," Agailya says bitterly, casting a glance at Gayarnu. "This project was not supposed to go forward. Not like this, and certainly not in Jadore's hands. We received a notification that it had been activated, but apparently we were too late." She narrows her gaze at Sunni. "You brought her through. A dangerous, foolish move. You reached into the multiverse— you might as well stick your hand into a muddy pond filled with flesh-eating monsters. What have you done?"

Sunni, seeing that her presence is under scrutiny, approaches us, hand-in-hand with Misty. "I asked her to bring me here. To defeat you and everyone like you." She addresses my friends with her heavy Texas twang. "Don't trust her, or any of her ilk. They pretend to help you. They pretend to only be here to cure their vitaphage. Yet it is the cure that was the death of my world. You saw what happened, Ingrid. The cure brought more soldiers into the Collective's army's fold and they devastated my Earth."

"We cannot be blamed for what any supposed counterparts in other worlds may have done," Agailya says calmly. Her voice has a soothing musical quality to it.

"I can and I will blame you," Sunni retorts. "I have seen your Sunni's mind. Our dreams were often one and the same, diverging only because of the differences..." She seems to notice I'm standing next to her, and she appraises my face, trying to place me. "Ingrid, is that right?"

"Yes," I say.

"Funny, we didn't have one of you," she says. "I only know you from my dreams."

Campbell had told me that there was only one of me, across the universes. That might explain my power and our involuntary tethering.

"Send her back through, to where she came from," Agailya continues sternly. "There may be consequences for her being in an alternate universe, where she doesn't belong."

"Who are you to say who belongs where?" I retort. "You collaborate with an enemy, you appear as my species, and you walk around doing terrible, inhumane experiments on my friends. How is disturbing our ecosystem for your planet's gain any different than me bringing Sunni here to help us defeat you?"

"Uh oh," Elisha says. "This doesn't look good."

Elisha isn't talking about my argument with Agailya. She's staring at a screen on the console. She looks to Wil. "The automatic shut-down you programmed didn't initiate. It's overheating instead."

"What does that mean?" I ask.

"If we don't shut the portal down, we're going to have more company," Sunni replies, worried.

She's right. The portal is still active, even though I'm not standing at the amplifier. The blue-white light has dimmed, yet the door is still open, so to speak.

"It's not the only army," I explain to my friends. "When I grabbed Sunni, I saw her universe's Collective with their army. A bunch of aliens, ready to go through a similar portal to this one. Imagine if they could harness my power and bring them through."

"They were waiting for troops too," Sunni says. "But if they knew there was an identical Collective here, they'd eagerly want to make that connection. If they're not already somehow finding their way through."

This only fuels Agailya. "I told you this was dangerous. I told you not to fight the Collective. They always win. It doesn't matter what you do. They will subdue your will until you are carrying out their desires."

"Yeah. Seems like you're doing a really good job of that," I reply.

Wil sheathes his machete and sighs. "Your petty arguing doesn't help. Elisha, are you reading this too? That seems to be a countdown."

"Can you stop it?" she asks.

Jia, Lynn, and Kimberly edge closer to us, giving the fishmen a wide berth. "What kind of countdown?" Jia asks. "A self-destruct?"

He frowns. "Looks that way. Although…"

"Self-destruct is what we want," Misty says. "So the Collective can't receive more forces."

"Yes, but if it overheats while we're still here, that's a problem," Elisha says.

The portal suddenly cracks, as if struck by lightning. The whirring sound from the consoles grows louder.

"If I'm understanding this correctly, it says we have five minutes to clear out," Elisha continues.

"That's doable," I say. "We find a quiet spot, and—"

"I can't let you leave," Agailya says. She nods at the fishmen. "If you destroy this portal, regardless of my feelings on the matter, Jadore will use it as leverage against the Council, and the project she stole from me will be discarded. My people will die. I have to protect their interests. If you care about Ethan, and his suffering, you will stop the portal from overheating."

This was only supposed to be a small strike. Get in, subdue Jadore, use the portal, and get out. Wil looks grim. "This is exactly…" He steps away from the console and casts a serious look at Agailya as he senses the truth from her. "You're not the only member of the Collective who knows we're here. You've got more troops on the way."

Agailya nods. Gayarnu stares at the floor, like an unwilling participant in the whole drama. I glance at the door. I sent Hojshz and the hafelglob out there, but they won't be any match for a whole army of hafelglob, fishmen, and possibly the Brigade— and whatever else the Collective has up their sleeve.

"Four minutes!" Elisha says. "We all need to leave. Now."

The fishmen turn their weapons on Wil. "Stop the countdown," Agailya says. "I know you know how."

Wil throws a glance at me, unconcerned with the three guns pointed in his face. He's calling her bluff. She wouldn't dare kill him. I don't know what Elisha's full range of abilities are, but Wil is the master of technology, and just as he can manipulate minds, he can bend technology to his will.

"Lynn. Check the entrance and see if you can clog it. We don't want the Collective barging in. Jia. Thoughts on the Brigade locked in here with us. When this portal blows, it will take out this entire warehouse."

Jia and I exchange glances. Her, with the sudden moral decision to save the Brigade. "You can't just put that on me."

"I'm delegating. You're the best person to decide. Their lives are in your hands," he says shortly. He looks to me. "There's only one way out of here."

My stomach drops. He's right. I need to teleport all of us here. "I haven't done this before, I don't know..."

His spoken voice resonates with far more authority than I've ever heard from him. Like he's had practice ordering a massive army. I'm about to comment on it when Sunni interrupts.

"Excuse me, who put you in charge?"

Wil stares at her blankly. "I've always been in charge. Your counterpart trusted my judgement."

"Well I'm not her. We had our own way of doing things in our war against the Collective."

From the sound of it, you couldn't stop them either, Wil replies telepathically.

"Hey, don't talk to her that way!" Misty says.

I come between the three of them. "Okay, okay, you can argue when we have escaped this mess."

The portal makes a terrible cracking sound as the blue-light swirling in the centre intensifies. Something is preparing through.

"Two minutes," Elisha says urgently.

It's not enough time. Couldn't we just use the portal? It gurgles again. No. I don't want to end up on the other side of...whatever is coming through.

We are all so preoccupied with the portal that I nearly fail to notice the sudden flash of green behind the fishmen.

Elisha is too concerned with the consoles and the countdown. Jia is on the other side of the warehouse with Greg, Lynn, and Kimberly, figuring out whether they are morally obligated to save the Brigade. Misty and Sunni, hands interlocked, only have eyes for each other.

Agailya and her people watch—and do nothing.

Jadore, her dark eyes filled with revenge, hooks Wil around the neck, and with surprising strength, shoves her broken cane-spear through his back.

Wil slumps to the floor, face-first, with a deafening thud.

A scream escapes me and my entire body stiffens. This is real. Sunni is beside me, but this isn't a dream.

Misty releases Sunni's hand and heaves a large fireball at Jadore. It flies past her as Jadore ducks, grinning. She slides her cane-spear from Wil's body and waves it at Misty. Jadore completely ignores Agailya, Gayarnu, and the fishmen. The dark look in her eyes says that this is personal.

"You are next, when I'm finished here," she says to Misty. "And then I'll kill Sunni again."

"I don't think so," Misty says.

Sunni and I hurriedly step out of the way as Jadore runs towards the portal consoles. The portal hums and snaps with such intensity that it is either going to explode or regurgitate an army at any moment. Misty is on her tail, throwing her fire and ice. Greg runs after her for support. Jadore calls her lightning and it nearly zaps Greg.

Agailya, Gayarnu, and the fishmen reverently step back from Wil. He grunts and I am outside my body as I kneel before him, turning him on his side. He's not just bleeding from his back. I tear away the front of his shirt and note the darkening of his chest. The blade in Jadore's cane is dosed in poison, produced by her own body. A scratch is fine—Misty survived that. But a strong stab wound through the back, near his heart...

Jia dashes towards us, hair askew, shocked beyond belief. Kimberly and Lynn are right behind her. Kimberly screams and cries—and Jia can only stand there, staring. She can't take her gaze from him, and neither can I. This can't be. Jia saved Wil. We've barely seen him for over a month—and he suddenly shows up here, at the beginning of the end, and now...

I look up at Agailya. "Well? Do you want the portal to be destroyed?"

Wil groans. He grabs my hand. He's trying to say something. He puts my hand on his chest and I see it. Green tendrils have surfaced from his internal bleeding and are making their way around his heart. He doesn't have long.

Agailya and Gayarnu bow their heads. "We honour you, Wil McBride, and your suffering."

I grit my teeth. To stop the suffering of another is a crime in their culture—that's what Gayarnu said. "Do you have nothing to ease his pain?"

Agailya says something in a singsong tone to Gayarnu, and they shake their head. The fishmen seem to understand this interaction and take off toward Jadore, Misty, and Greg, who are still hashing it out around the portal and its consoles. The two ahmei in human form begin a low song in C, which does nothing to soothe Wil's pain or nerves; it only agitates me, as they stand there singing, and Wil is bleeding to death, because none of us can help him.

"We are running out of time," Elisha says softly.

Wil squeezes his eyes shut, concentrating, and then groans and coughs up blood. It's dark and mucus-y. Elisha grips the console, unable to continue verbalizing the countdown.

Kimberly screams some more. She falls on her knees beside me, yelling nonsense at everyone, until she suddenly and serenely stops crying. Her gaze falls to him. He meets it and I know he's speaking to her privately, saying the kinds of things you do to someone you love when you're about to die. Then, noticing Jia standing over us, he invites her over, and she crouches at his head, bracing his back. Her fingernails dig into him as a silent sob escapes her, and tears soak into his jacket. Despite all the pain he put her through, the sacrifice she made for him, she couldn't stop loving him. It doesn't work like that.

My own face is wet and my hands shake. It's his time. Just as Campbell told me.

You don't have to forgive me, Wil says telepathically. He stares at Jia, speaking words only she can hear. She sobs and covers the lower half of her face, as she dares not take her eyes from him.

Wil's fading, unfocused gaze sharpens for just a moment as something behind me catches his attention. I strain to see, and I catch sight of something red dashing behind Elisha. I'm about to stand to confront it, or warn Elisha, but Wil's iron grip keeps me down.

"Wait...wait..." he says.

"It's all right, we're here," I say.

"No." His grip on me tightens, and with surprising strength, he pulls me closer to his face. Kimberly and Jia stiffen beside me, for these are his final moments, and he has chosen to give them to me. I turn my head, and in my ear, he whispers, "Wait for me in the music trailer."

My breath catches. I notice every detail. Jadore's scaled, yet human-like feet as she dances around the portal, trading lightning for Misty's fire and ice. Greg emitting a piercing noise, not quite a scream. Jia's awkward, sob-filled declaration of love and futility of her sacrifice. Elisha tapping on the console again. Lynn's nervous hand wringing. The swirling blue song of the ahmei that blends with the smell of ash and burning, the crackling blue and white of the portal, and the far-off sounds of the hafelglob rallying at the locked door. The Collective's forces must have arrived.

Above us, Sunni stands ceremoniously, and her face betrays nothing—because maybe she has seen this part already, although with a different Wil, on a different Earth.

In that perfect moment, Campbell's words begin to make sense to me. Not all of it, of course, but the very idea of him suddenly clicks. Past and present and future—they are all the same. We exist simultaneously in each. Trying to change the future is irrelevant, because it is already happening now. I feel our bond, as if he is touching my shoulder in reassurance, confirming this knowledge that seems so obvious, now that it lives within me.

What has happened has already happened, and it will happen again.

I stare down at him and shake my head. "How do I...?"

He chokes on a laugh and takes Kimberly's hand. I'm the one who can travel, not him.

The light fades from his eyes, and he's really gone.

Wil has died.

Just like Campbell said he would.

And yet—Wil *is* still alive. In the past.

I rise from his body, numb to Jadore's battle with Misty, Jia and Kimberly's tears, and the immediate threats of the portal and the Collective army. I run to the consoles. Something had been hiding there. Campbell? No, I would know if he were here. Nothing. No one. Elisha frowns and stares down at the console, unable to speak.

"My Wil died too," Sunni says absently, staring down in shock at Wil's corpse as I return to them.

"They'll harvest his DNA if we don't get rid of him," I say distantly.

The ahmei conclude their song with a low, extended note that echoes in the warehouse, and they say nothing more.

"His body will disintegrate when we destroy the portal," Sunni says. She glances over her shoulder at Misty, deeply worried. The fishmen are now guarding the portal and they have not joined in the fight between Misty, Greg, and Jadore.

For a split second, I agree. Then it hits me. Wil's body has already been spotted, before it disappeared unexpectantly from behind the music trailer.

Because I give it to Ohz, in the past, some time in *my* future.

My head spins. How can this even be possible?

"The countdown is still going. He must have added more time." Elisha tries not to look down at Wil's body. "But not much time. Maybe another five minutes at most."

Hiding beside one of the consoles so as not to get caught in the crossfire, Greg lets out another ear-splitting scream. Save for the ahmei and the fishmen, we double over. Jadore halts by the portal, her lightning sizzling around both arms now as more and more of her human beauty succumbs to her lust for power. She cups her ears and falls to her knees—and Misty slams her with ice.

"You deserve this," Misty hisses. Her ice isn't as fluid as it was when she was fighting Emily—she's spent a lot of her energy already. She's as pale as I've ever seen her and her lips are nearly blue. She's ready to collapse as Sunni and I run towards her.

Jadore huddles on the ground, gripping her head. No one moves to help her. She lets out a low hiss as she tries to rebut Misty's blows, but eventually, falls over.

Sunni catches Misty's arm. "It's all right. She's not goin' anywhere now."

"But...I can't let her..." Misty mumbles, and falls against Sunni. "She killed you. My Sunni."

"I know. I know." Sunni raises her eyebrows at me.

"Ugh. Had to wait to get that one right," Greg mutters as he emerges from his hiding spot.

Across the long warehouse, the door thumps wildly and suddenly bursts open. Whatever Lynn did to the lock is no more. Shouts and the sounds of lasers penetrate the warehouse. Our hafelglob allies spill into the warehouse, in alien form, and it's only their mass that's stopping the Collective's forces from physically entering the space.

By Elisha's count, we have four minutes, again.

"You get her out of there," I say to the fishmen, pointing at Jadore's once-more unconscious body. I hurry back to the ahmei, who haven't budged or said a thing since Wil left us. "Agailya, I know you're at odds with Jadore. So maybe now that you're about to save her life from the portal's imminent destruction, you can use that against her. Spin whatever tale you need to. But you have to hurry."

She considers this solemnly, and looks to Gayarnu. After conferring silently and considering the brewing storm behind them, they walk towards the portal. "We will deal with Jadore."

Misty balls her hands into fists. "You're not taking her from me. I'm not done."

"Shh," Sunni says fondly. "We have to get out of here."

Numbly, I nod. As the ahmei and the fishmen move Jadore's ice-covered body, I gather everyone around Elisha and the consoles. She plucks a USB drive from the console and shoves it in her pocket. Kimberly and Jia are still hovering over Wil. Two of the hafelglob at the door have succumbed to laser fire.

The portal is emitting a cracking sound every thirty seconds now. Beads of sweat pool on my forehead. We have three minutes remaining.

"You're going to try teleporting all of us?" Greg asks hesitantly. "Is that even a good idea?"

"Do you see another way out?" Misty groans as Sunni supports most of her weight.

Jia stands then from Wil's body. "Do you remember the place I told you? Where we'll be safe?"

I nod, feeling nothing but emptiness within as our backup plan returns to mind, the one we made before I faked my surrender. More fishmen are pouring in the door—ones not loyal to Agailya. They spot us and raise their weapons.

"Wait!" Agailya yells. Her three fishmen are carrying Jadore's unconscious form as they shuffle away from the portal. Agailya's cry is half-lost over the sudden rumbling beneath us. She catches up with the fishmen and exchanges curt words with them. The fishmen garbles at her, and then at more aliens pooling in at the door, and the gunfire ceases, at least for the moment.

"Two minutes," Elisha says. "Ingrid? Can you do this? Or are we in real trouble?"

I take a deep breath. Another, stronger rumble like an earthquake nearly knocks us all off our feet. If I can reach across the fabric of space-time and open the way for Sunni, I can get the nine of us out of here. Including Wil.

"Yeah," I say. "Everyone, grab on to me. I...I have never done this before." Not successfully, but only Misty really knows that.

"You're ready," Sunni says confidently.

Each of my friends places their hands on me: my arms, my legs, the back of my neck, my head. Greg and Kimberly drag Wil to my feet, and Kimberly hooks herself around him as she braces my leg for support. Another large earthquake nearly knocks us all over, yet our combined support keeps us upright.

I take one last look at the door to ensure the hafelglob have made it out, when I notice Shane, bruised and bloodied, with Emily and Laura. They slip out the door, but not before Shane catches my eye. He narrows his gaze and turns to leave.

But not before shoving past another human stumbling into the underground warehouse: Ethan.

No. No he can't be here. We have mere minutes before this place blows. I can't have his life on my consequence. I almost start towards him, but Gayarnu notices him as well, and their speed is uncanny. My friends have me locked in place, and if I let go of them now, I risk leaving them behind.

"Ingrid? We need to go. Now," Misty urges.

Sunni takes one look at Ethan, pales, and then takes Misty by the hand. "I'm not going with *him*."

Gayarnu reaches him and says something soothing, because to him, they're still Mira, yet he recoils from her, disgusted.

He only has eyes for me as he points. His hair and clothing are drenched with sweat. He's as pale as the newly embalmed dead.

CRACK. ROOMPH. THWMP. The noises of the portal overheating are becoming more powerful. Ethan nearly trips as he runs towards me.

"I remember everything," Ethan whispers. Blood drips from his nose as he falls to his knees, his hand outstretched to me. "Ingrid…"

"Ingrid. No, we have to go," Sunni urges.

Ethan's whole body shakes as beads of sweat pool on his forehead. He gasps for air. His lips are already blue. Just a few more inches, and he'll be touching me.

He remembers me. My heart pounds with joy and relief—until I remember the consequences of him remembering *everything*.

Whatever trauma he experienced, superpowered or not, it is killing him. I am filling with the sorrowful knowledge that not one, but two of my friends have died, and although I can travel to save Wil, how can I travel to save a man who won't remember me?

"What is happening to him?" I shout at Gayarnu. "Help him!"

Worried, they hurry again to Ethan's side. But Sunni grabs my face and swivels it. "Don't. You can't. You lose your nerve now, and we all de."

Gayarnu keeps Ethan upright and he struggles to get away, but he's too weak. If I can't take him, Gayarnu will have to, and they have less than a minute to clear the warehouse. Tears roll down his face. In his eyes, I see his feelings for me, laid bare.

"Come with me," I say, wrenching from Sunni's grasp and extending my hand.

I see Gayarnu hesitate. They glance at the door. Only hafelglob and fishmen bodies remain. Everyone else has gone. They know they won't make it.

CRACK. ROOMPH. THWMP. CRAACK.

The portal whirs and I hear garbling from within. The unseen enemy is nearly through.

I take a deep breath and keep my gaze locked on his. I take in every detail, even the gross ones. His sweaty, floppy hair. His pouting lips, bluer than blue. His pale blue eyes. They were not always blue. Once, they were a sparkling green. The dark circles of sleepless nights due to his obsession with painting his lost memories.

My body feels light. It's working. Thinking of Ethan carries me away, because even if he is dying, he is still here, with me.

"I love you," he whispers, and stretches out his hand. "But I'm—"

Our fingers touch...and then I slip away.

CHAPTER 15

We materialize in the middle of a snow-covered field beneath a big, sunny sky.

I fall into the snow. Every part of me has been bruised, lightly burnt, or scraped. I can't feel my arms. Wil's body lays beside me. The blood from his wound still looks fresh. However long we were in the infinite hallway, it seems to have preserved him. Around me, the voices of my friends, one by one, sound off, as they too evaluate their wounds or vomit, as is custom for one's first time teleporting.

We all made it.

And then my heart sinks, because I know even before it's confirmed.

Everyone made it, except Ethan and Gayarnu. *But I'm...*had been his last words. *But I'm dead.*

"Where are we?" Sunni asks. She and Misty hug each other for warmth. It's not as cold as Christmas, yet it's still nippy.

Jia cracks a genuine smile, the first I've seen from her in a long time. "We're on my property. You did it, Ingrid. You remembered my description."

Although all I want is to flop down in the snow and sleep, I force myself to sit up. I blink against the blinding sunlight. In the distance, I spot a farmhouse and a couple of barns. One in particular looks worse for wear. They're connected by a dirt road that eventually meets up with a paved road that stretches far into the horizon. The snow is clean here, marred only by our presence. We're definitely in rural Alberta, where the plains are flat, the sky is big, and the farms are massive.

"Why here?" Elisha asks. "You couldn't have chosen something...further?"

"You'd like to go back to Sparkstone, would you?" Greg demands.

"Now what are we going to do? It's freezing. Where's the closest restaurant?" Lynn asks.

"We can hide out in that grey barn. Mum and Dad never go in there," Jia says. She starts towards the dilapidated building and then looks back at me, kneeling before Wil's body. This sobers her enthusiasm.

"I'll help," Misty says, and with Sunni, we manage to pick up Wil. He leaves a trail of dripping blood in the snow as we trudge after Jia.

"If we don't do something about him," Misty continues in a lower voice, "he's gonna start to smell. Not to be crass or anythin'. How long can we stay here without Jia's folks getting suspicious? I assume they've been subjected to the same treatment as your parents?"

She's right. But I am weak and tired, and a million miles away. Ethan had been right there. If only I'd tried harder. Wanted him more.

But I'm...gone.

It's too painful to think about him dying. I focus on my body instead. I have more pressing matters involving our immediate survival. I've been walking for days. I recall a long, solemn march up and down endless corridors, bitter complaining, and the weight of knowing if we are chased, we would not escape easily. "Does anyone know the time and the date?" My voice is hoarse with the effort of keeping my true emotions buried deep.

Behind me, Greg pulls out his phone and answers, "Eleven in the morning. January fifteenth. Oh my god. January? Is this right?"

Weeks. We've been gone for *weeks*.

Ethan is surely dead by now, if not by the explosion, then because of Agailya's experiment and how it exasperated his trauma. That's how I'm thinking of it, because there is no way that regular trauma could physically kill you like that.

Jia leads us to the grey, dilapidated barn and everyone, except Wil, who we bury temporarily in the snow outside, files inside. It smells like old hay, but no animals have lived in here for a long time. Many windows line the first floor and the loft above, yet most are broken. The barn door doesn't shut all the way. The Fields seem to use it for spare parts storage. Bits of machinery line the back wall, completely disorganized. A bail of forgotten hay sits in the loft.

"It's not much. It'll do," Jia says, determined.

The afternoon stretches on as everyone seems to pair off and carry out tasks that leave my lips, but I don't specifically remember: gather logs for burning and sitting. Scavenge for food and use the bathroom in the house before the Fields' return from their grocery shopping. Raid Jia's closet for unused mittens and winter wear. Steal all the linens and blankets you can without looking suspicious. All of this, done under Jia's cover of invisibility.

I participated. Or rather, my body participated, while I distantly piloted. My body is free and my mind is not.

Ethan is dead. *But I'm* alive.

And yet, I'm a time traveller. I have been to the past before, and I probably will travel there again, to dispose of Wil's body.

Somehow, I can save him. I have to.

I'm sitting around a makeshift fire pit someone has crafted. It's dark now, though we haven't lit a fire yet, as we're waiting for lights out in the main farmhouse. My friends are chattering away.

Jia stands at one of the broken windows, watching her former home. She gives Misty the signal. "Okay. Main floor lights are off. Just looks like a lamp in my parents' bedroom, and Paige's light is still on, though she won't leave her room now. She's probably on her phone or talking to her friends...anyway, she won't leave her room."

"It's only eight," Greg says, in disbelief.

"They're farmers. They always go to bed at this time," Jia replies.

"Good enough." Misty scoots over to our neatly arranged fire pit, complete with dry hay and twigs we'd scavenged throughout the barn, and with a single finger, lights it up. Beside her, we'd managed to lug a couple of pieces of real firewood from Jia's parents' stash in the other barn. Another pile is the food she scavenged: some chips, hummus, frozen vegetables grown on their farm, and the end of a loaf of bread. She also dug up a glass pitcher that we filled with fresh water.

We ration and divide the food, and as my friends devise a

plan to raid the nearest grocery store nearly twenty kilometres away, I'm vaguely aware of Sunni beside me, holding my hand, anchoring me to the present. As if my anxiety doesn't do that for me. She gives me a wide grin.

"Hey. Feelin' okay?"

I shake my head. "I saw your Ethan kill your Misty," I say quietly, so as not to disturb my other friends. "That's why you hate him?"

She squeezes my hand harder. "Yes. Though he is a collaborator. In my universe. You cannot trust him."

"He doesn't know," I mutter. "He's a victim, in an experiment."

"He's a collaborator, Ingrid," Sunni warns me. "The ahmei have him, and they will always have him."

I can't believe her. But he was trying to tell me something before I disappeared. Could that have been it? I shake my head. My Sunni would not speak like this—but what do I know? I only knew this universe's Sunni for twenty-four hours. Ethan, I have studied for days and days. I have laughed with him, and kissed him, and even when his memory was spotty, I loved him anyway, because we can create beautiful music together. My Ethan does not wear a Brigade uniform, and he would never kill one of my friends.

Eventually, the fire burns as bright as we can allow, and the night carries on. Sleep hugs me, and I'm tempted to give in, yet my mind won't stop turning. One by one, my friends settle down around the fire. To sleep anywhere else would mean freezing to death, or at the very least, hypothermia.

After a time, Jia slips out, and I don't have to ask where. If I had the power of invisibility and a blissfully ignorant sibling I missed dearly, I'd spy on them too, so long as they weren't up to anything indecent.

Soon it's only me, pretending to sleep, and Sunni and Misty, who are still awake. Misty is wide-eyed now, seemingly recovered from her many battles, no doubt helped by Sunni's presence. She's volunteered to keep the fire going for as long as she's able.

"So all this time...you've been sending Ingrid the dreams?" Misty asks.

"You sound disappointed," Sunni says, not unkindly.

"I guess I thought...it was my Sunni. In heaven, or you know, whatever."

"She knew it was her time," Sunni replies softly. "I can't pretend I know her, even though we are almost the same, but, she thought of you fondly."

Misty thinks about this for a time. "Did you have a Misty too?"

Sunni takes Misty's hand and squeezes it, and Sunni lowers her voice to whisper her story. I wait until they decide to move away from the fire and settle down before I get up, not that they might notice me at this point anyway.

Outside, it's bitter cold, and I miss the dying fire. Still, I look up at the sky, and feel some measure of relief. I am no longer at Sparkstone. I saved my friends. I opened the door, and I saved Sunni.

Could that be the *her* Campbell wants me to save? Or is there a different woman out there, in those multitude of Earths like ours, that is far more important than me and Sunni?

I don't want to think about it. I pull my jacket tighter around me and walk around the side, keeping one hand on the barn. It's dark: no city lights, no campus cameras, no exterior lights. Just the stars and the moon, and the extremely faint light of the fire within. Even the Fields farmhouse has no outside light. This suits me fine.

I lean against the splintery barn and hum something sad in E minor, because that's how I feel. It doesn't take long. I need him now, more than ever, and he seems to know it. I keep my eyes closed as the snow crunches and he crouches beside me, shoulder to shoulder.

"Where am I?" he asks.

I press a warmed hand against my cool forehead. "The beginning of the end."

"So dramatic. Though if I had to guess, we're still in Alberta, no? How about your friends?"

"Wil is dead. Just like you said. But I also understand now, how to get him back. How I can fix everything." I am light already. I can see the path before me, winding in and out of the past several months. "You told me I was special. Chosen."

"You are," he says, in a sultry way.

I shake my head. I keep turning Agailya's and Gayarnu's words over in my mind. I am nothing but circumstance and DNA to him. I know I am powerful, that I can make a difference...but by myself I am just a speck of dust next to the power of the Collective.

However...

"I can fix everything," I say. "I know how. Or, I think I know. Right?"

Because we are tethered, he knows my thoughts. "Time travel isn't a bandage," he warns. "Do you really want to end up like me, tethered to a human being, forced to wind around her life like ribbon on a May Pole, never knowing when you will finally arrive at the day with the right tools to achieve what you have been made to do?"

"I have teleported to the right locations before. I even rescued my friends from Sparkstone. I can teleport again—to specific times and spaces. I could prevent the Collective from even forming."

I hear the smile in his voice. "I cannot stop you from achieving your true destiny."

No, he can't. Although we have escaped and destroyed their precious portal, the Collective is plotting a devastating invasion. Jadore is probably still alive.

He gets up and strides by me. I note his shoes: tall boots, made of fine leather. He stops in front of a cloudy window. "That's quite the crowd in there. I don't see your friend, Ethan."

I rest my chin on my knees. "I don't want to talk about him."

"Ah. Very well." I hear that he wants to say more, so I don't stop him. "The Alt-Sunni believes he is a collaborator. She told you this, didn't she?"

"Were you listening?"

"In a manner of speaking."

I hesitate. "Is he?"

He doesn't reply, and when I look over, I no longer see his shape, or feel his presence. He's gone. Again.

Resolved, and despite my lack of sleep, I stand and prepare myself. We covered Wil's body in the snow, because it was the only way we could think to keep him from decomposing. I try not to think of that as I uncover him unceremoniously, saying a little prayer to whatever god that exists, and reach under his shoulder. Rigor mortis has already set in. I'm going to have to drag him through the infinite hallway, aren't I. He deserves a far better grave. I just have to figure out where—and when—is best.

What will happen, has already happened. It had sounded so

grim when Campbell first said this to me, months ago, and yet now, the possibilities swim in my mind.

I have the power to influence the past.

I have escaped Sparkstone, but so many, including Ethan, didn't. Regardless of his true trauma, and where his loyalties lie, I owe it to my memory of him to discover the truth. And I refuse to let our world become as ravaged as Sunni's.

I touch Wil's chest, and holding my hopeful desires close, I reach into the darkness once more.

The Sparks return to stop the Collective once and for all in the
final installment:

BOOK FIVE
THE SPARKSTONE SAGA

About the Author

Photo Credit:
Terence Yung

CLARE C. MARSHALL grew up in rural Nova Scotia with very little television and dial-up internet, and yet she turned out okay. She is the founder and author-publisher behind Faery Ink Press, where she publishes young adult science fiction, fantasy, and horror novels. Her YA sci-fi novel *Dreams In Her Head* was nominated for the 2014 Creation of Stories award. Her fantasy novel, *The Violet Fox* was given an honorable mention in the 2016 Whistler Independent Book Awards. She is also a freelance editor, book designer, and web manager. When she's not writing or fiddling up a storm, she enjoys computer games and making silly noises at her two cats, Pinecone and Pavlova.

Acknowledgements

Desperate to please book publishers everywhere—and the Acknowledgements Faery herself—Sir Copy Right created a website where authors could go to write their heartfelt acknowledgements. If they ran long, or became too mushy, the publishers could include a link to the acknowledgements within the book so the reader could view the text in its entirety. He also created an identical site for the copyright page, as he was desperate to appease the publishers and make up for the Acknowledgements Faery's actions.

Sir Copy Right thought this was the best solution.

But he was wrong.

The Acknowledgement Faery couldn't believe what he had done. The publishers, angry at them both for interfering with "their" domain, had used Sir Copy Right's websites...and removed all copyright and acknowledgement pages from all books!

Now both Sir Copy Right and the Acknowledgement Faery were furious. It just wasn't fair!

So, they thought and thought, and finally, a solution dawned on them...

How will the story end? Tune into the final Sparkstone Saga book to find out!

Acknowledgements

Champions of the Acknowledgements Page

Thank you to my family—Mum, Dad, Jessie, Marie, Joe, and Kerry for all your support over the years. And of course, many thanks to Pinecone and Pavlova, who are good companionship, even if you want to hunt moths or cuddle on my desk while I'm trying to put together a book.

Thank you to Samantha Beiko, aka Sam—you constantly inspire me with your tenacity and creativity.

And of course, many thanks to Dave, for his continued support, constructive criticism and taste, and (hopefully) undying love. This is a good place to write the rough draft of my wedding vows, right?

Website: FaeryInkPress.com
Facebook: Facebook.com/faeryinkpress

If you enjoyed this book, please consider writing a review on Amazon or on Goodreads. Thank you!